NIGHTCRAWLERS

KAYLEE MCHUGH

ISBN: 0615916465
ISBN-13: 978-0615916460

DEDICATION

A BOOK IS NOT WRITTEN BY A SINGLE PERSON BUT BY THE EXPERIENCES AND PEOPLE IN THEIR LIFE THAT INSPIRE THE STORY.

"THE BLOOD-DIMMED TIDE IS LOOSED, AND
EVERYWHERE

THE CEREMONY OF INNOCENCE IS
DROWNED;

THE BEST LACK ALL CONVICTION,

WHILE THE WORST ARE FULL OF PASSIONATE
INTENSITY."

- THE SECOND COMING, W. B. YEATS

TABLE OF CONTENTS

PART I

PART 2

PART 3

PART I

1

When Micah opened her eyes at exactly 6:42, three minutes before her wrist began to ring, she could see the sunrise as it sliced through her closed bedroom blinds. She tipped her ebony head a little off her soft pink pillowcase to check the clock on her arm. Realizing that, yet again, she had deprived herself of an extra 13 minutes of sleep (counting the two snoozes she usually pressed), she plopped her head right back onto the pillow and let herself sink into it. Once her brain was up it was up, but her body was a different story. She lay in bed soaking up the few last minutes of relaxation before yet another day, yet another static 12 hour routine.

"GOOOOOOODDDDD MORNING SECTOR 15! It is a GLORIOUS 80 degrees outside, a perfect start to a perfect morning! I hope you had a restful night in preparation for a restless day!"

The loud, boisterous voice erupted from the small metal circle embedded into her wrist and turned into daggers that pierced straight through her ears.

"Oh god," Micah thought as she threw her attention hogging right limb over the side of her bed and with the other arm bundled her blanket a little closer to her body. *"Why couldn't they have found a man with a less annoying voice for the morning announcements?"*

"AAANNNDDDDD now for last night's report. A startling *seven men* were arrested last night from the underground! Three for trying to break into a Dayman's grocery store, and four more for sneaking into the Dayman's hospital! What a *shame*. All seven are now awaiting trial at the government house and can be visited at any time. If you have a free moment, stop by and show them what you think! This is yet another reminder to *be careful* folks! These hooligans can be vicous! And remember, if you EVER see one, report it! YOU are the reason these streets are safe today and will stay safe until tomorrow. 'Til then!"

The radio went silent except for a soft buzzing. It told Micah to turn it off now, or that man and his unnatural early morning cheer would be back in less than five minutes.

Micah took a deep breath and then, in one swift motion, twisted her body, tore off her covers, and slammed her left palm onto the top of her arm. The silent buzzing was replaced by the faint sound of her mother preparing breakfast a few rooms away. She could hear the slight sizzle of bacon and sudden clink of glasses and plates from the table. Her mother always woke up before dawn.

Nuzzling her toes into the soft carpet, she stretched her arms toward the ceiling and barely touched the popcorn finish with the tips of her polished fingernails. She was a little over 5'6" but the ceilings were so low that even she sometimes felt cramped. She could only imagine how her father and older brother must have felt. But, the government had to cut spending somehow, and vaulted ceilings were just not in the budget.

While stretching her body, she let out a soft groan and slowly brought her arms back to her sides. Placing her hands onto her slender hips, she sauntered over to the full-length mirror on the opposite side of the room and grabbed the school uniform that delicately balanced on its top left corner.

Her uniform was simple- white blouse, high waisted red slacks, a dark brown leather belt, and brown, strapped one-inch heels. It took her no more, and no less, than three minutes to completely assemble onto her 150-pound light brown body, aided by years upon years of practice.

Every morning.

Every year.

Six days a week.

No covering of the feet, and no exposure of the ankles. On the shirt? All buttons closed to the top, and sleeves pushed up to the base of her INSAV at all times.

It took an extra minute to pin her dark hair back into a tight ponytail and to curve that ponytail into a loose bun secured by a few shoddily placed bobby pins. Makeup wasn't allowed, but Micah always gave her eyes one swift go with her eyeliner just enough to emphasize, but not exaggerate, her piercing blue eyes before plopping in a set of light brown contacts to cover them.

She didn't even bother to give herself one last look before heading out of the bedroom door. She had looked the same almost every day for the past 15 years and knew her reflection in this uniform like a spider knows its own web. And, if something did look a little different, maybe it would help her catch a few more flies.

Micah's tweed bag was already slung over her chair at the breakfast table when she entered the room where the rest of her family had already started their morning. Her mother sat in an outfit much like her daughter's, red slacks replaced by a tight, dark red skirt that ran to the top of her knees. She had one hand laced around a large cup of steaming coffee and the other projecting a stack of paperwork that she was quickly flipping through by pushing her finger across the grain of the wooden table. Her father sat across from her, already in his long white medical coat and wearing a demeanor of controlled chaos. To his right was her brother, Gabe, only three years older but already neck deep in one of the most dangerous and esteemed careers in the city. He had been awake for at least two hours and was inhaling a ham and egg bagel sandwich, only giving himself enough time to take a breath and sip of his cranberry juice.

Micah plopped herself down across from Gabe and reached towards the center of the table to grab a pile of scrambled eggs. She looked around for a piece of toast, but only saw a mound taking up half her brother's plate. She gave him a menacing glance before standing up and swiping a piece for herself.

"Good morning to you too," Gabe said in between a powerful swallow of his sandwich and giant gulp of juice.

"I would have said hello if you hadn't taken all the food," Micah replied, shoveling eggs on top of her toast.

"You try spending all of dawn with those... *Nightcrawlers*," Gabe said, sandwich swinging in his left hand for emphasis, "doing as meticulous of a job as mine, and *then* sitting down for breakfast. You'd be fucking starving!"

He paused for a second, a smirk slowly building on his bagel crumbed lips.

"Oh wait, you never will."

"Gabriel that's enough," their mother immediately interjected, translucent screen still displayed and blocking the line of sight to her son. "She didn't choose her job, just as you didn't choose yours and I didn't choose mine. If you're bitter about the amount of work you have to do, bring it up with the government. I'm sure they'll understand."

"She may not have chosen it, but it sure did choose her correctly. Cushy little life where she'll sit at a desk all day, sorting segregation papers, while I'm out there making sure those papers actually exist. Protecting everyone! Protecting *your* life, and *your* life, and *yours*," he said, pointing to each of his family members with his sandwich hand.

"Dad does a lot more protecting than you do." Micah retorted. "He's a *doctor*, for Christ's sake. You're a trashman."

"He does the protecting from within, and I do it from within *and* without. The only reason *we*, as a community, can continue to exist, is because of me."

"Yes, Gabe. You're very special," their mother completed with a sigh as her papers disappeared into a wispy blob that floated above her right shoulder. "Use your special mouth to finish your special breakfast so you can run with your special legs down to the store for me."

She reached across the table to hand him a short list.

"And don't forget the soap like last time, I hear there won't be another handover for at least two weeks."

Gabe finished the last bite of his sandwich and, with greasy fingers outstretched, gathered the information by pressing his INSAV against his mom's. They both blinked light blue before becoming blank again.

"Anything you say mom," he said, glaring straight into her eyes with a playfully menacing look. "But then I'm taking a nap."

Micah got up from the table with her glass and walked across the kitchen to the sink. Their kitchen was large compared to everyone in the rest of the sector-- the fact that they could fit a table large enough to seat all of them, plus a few guests, was representative of that. Most everyone else she knew could barely sit together as a family in their living room. For those families a communal dinner was out of the question unless it included the wall projection. But, that was one of the perks of having a mother high up in the government. Her family was treated much better than most of the aboveground, and definitely better than everyone underneath it.

She filled her glass up with tap water and stared out the window overlooking the sink. She had read in her historytexts that a long time ago in other cities from a window like hers people used to peer onto trees, or benches, or parks. When Micah looked out the window all she saw was the brick that embraced yet another residential skyscraper.

The knob to the sink gave out a small squeak as she turned it tightly off and headed back towards the table, taking quick sips while she walked.

"Honey, we're going to leave in about five. Are you all done eating?" Her father asked, rising from his seat to gather his medical supplies.

Exactly 7:06. Right on schedule.

"Yeah, let me just wash off my plate and I'll meet you at the door."

Micah and her father traveled together every morning. They would glide down the hallway of their apartment building, making sure to say hello to old man Davidson as he opened his door, always turning his head back to tell his wife he was leaving for work without her. Even though they were both higher-level government employees, they had chosen to leave ten minutes early for as long as Micah could remember.

"Give me a minute, would ya?! It's hard to get these tights on!" or "There's just *one* curl that isn't right!" she would scream. There was always something.

All members of the same profession were instructed to leave at exactly the same time to prevent overcrowding in the streets. Shopkeepers and agricultural workers went first, followed by teachers and lower government employees, then medical workers and students, and finally the higher government employees. All ten minutes apart. Exactly enough time, the government argued, to walk to work. The sector wasn't very big, after all.

Each profession's morning timing was also tied to apartment size. Those that went to work first were considered less costly to manage and given small, one-bedroom apartments on the higher floors. They left for work first in case there were any straggling Nightcrawlers.

"Better they be contaminated than me," her mother always said.

The Davis' apartment was at the very end of the hallway on the first floor. As Micah and her father traveled down the dimly lit beige hallway, doors opened and closed behind them with other doctors and students traveling to work and school. She could hear their heavy footsteps on the worn carpet and feel their solemn faces behind her.

Micah always wished the government would spend a few bucks painting the hallway a brighter color than the dull, oppressive, sorry excuse for brown she was forced to face every day. But, as her mother reminded her, that took time and money. Neither of which were apparently available.

Micah and her father opened their INSAVs to scan out of the

building. They pushed their respected devices across the black recorder and shoved the heavy door open. She followed her father's gleaming white coat out the thick metal barrier and was immediately greeted with the powerful glimmering of the sun.

Her filled, but silent, apartment building was replaced with the quick bustle of every doctor and student in the sector, plus a few straggling lower government employees scurrying to their occupations. The school and hospital were on the same side at the northern edge of the sector, so each individual was traveling in the exact same direction. Thousands of people communicated through quick steps of short heels and long strides in flat loafers down the smooth, black tar that made up the sidewalks of Sector 15.

Micah caught up to her father, who was walking three paces in front of her, and grabbed his right arm.

"Dad, I'm really sorry I forgot to ask you this earlier, but is it ok if I stay out a little later tonight? I promise I'll be in before dusk," she loudly whispered into his body since she was too short to reach his ear.

"You know, you really should have asked your mother. I might be staying overnight at the hospital."

"I know, but I promised Sasha I would help her write that paper on the values of segregation." She's just training to be a shopkeeper like her mom and could really use the help."

Her father smirked and quickly glanced down at his daughter.

"Well, your mother would approve of that. I'll stop by her office later to let her know."

They walked the rest of their half-mile journey together in silence. Mr. Davis gave his daughter a quick peck on the cheek before turning left towards the hospital.

Relieved to have some time to herself before seven hours of

regulation, Micah took a deep breath and slowed down her pace. She looked up and saw a sea of white blouses and colored pants overwhelm the narrow sidewalk in front of her. The loose fabric waved on each body as legs bounced their way towards the school. The sidewalks were just large enough to fit about ten bodies across, or the width of a single trash truck.

The 30 and 45 story brick, metal, and glass buildings that surrounded her always made her feel as if she and the other students were just ants walking across the bottom of a metropolitan canyon. She had seen pictures of real canyons in historytexts, but since travel across sectors had been banned since she was little it was impossible to see one in real life. She always thought it was funny that, in the past, people from all over the world would travel to places like Utah and Arizona just to walk in them and, intentionally, feel as small as she did every day. She also thought it was funny that in the past there were places colorfully named Utah and Arizona, not just blandly assigned areas like Sector 10 and Sector 103.

She tried to understand the beauty of these canyons-- to appreciate their ribbons of burgundy and tan sandstone as reminders of the past. But, when she looked around, the only ribbons she saw overhead were of brick, steel, glass, and pixels. She would always try to look up and past the buildings that surrounded her, attempting to see a glimpse of the skyline that was rumored to, at one time, make her sector famous. But, only if she looked close enough, could she make out the slight dissipating zigzag of buildings following the alleyways and sidewalks of the city. She was in a canyon, all right. She wondered, though, if those families of the past were never allowed to leave the canyon they traveled long and far to see, would they still find it beautiful?

All she knew was that never leaving this sector made her completely dismiss any beauty an outsider may have been able to find. She hated its height, its order, and especially the large screens wrapped around the first fives stories of every building updating the citizens with the daily news and current trends. Each screen, and each building, conveyed the exact same message. While the citizens of the city were hushed as they scurried to their destinations, the faces on the screens and voices preaching from them made up for the silence.

The man from the morning announcements once more interrupted Micah's contemplation and popped onto the streets, his thick face smiling down on every doctor and student in the sector.

"Goooood morning academics and medics! We hope you're having a wonderful walk this morning. In case you missed it in the wakeup call, a startling *seven men* were arrested last night from the underground! Three for trying to break into a Dayman's grocery store, and four more for sneaking into the Dayman's hospital. And, breaking news! Their hangings are scheduled for the hour before dusk today. They can be viewed at any time in the government house before then. And remember, if you see anything, report it! Have a wonderfully *safe* day."

He ended with one last grin, superficially white teeth overtaking the side of every building. She was staring into it trying to guess how many whitening procedures he had most likely completed when a hand suddenly grasped her right shoulder and the body of a dark skinned, dark eyed girl swung beside her. It was Renee, a girl who trained in the same department as Micah and whose parents both worked higher-level jobs for the government.

"Mornings are always such a drag," Renee murmured, staring

straight in front of her. "Even though we're not allowed out at night, some days I would give anything for just one more hour of darkness."

"I know exactly what you mean. I'm definitely not looking forward to Mrs. Domney's lectures."

"Oh, God. I can't wait until we're done studying the 'lifestyles' of the Nightcrawlers and can move on to more important things, like what we get to do to them if they're ever found during the day. That's what really keeps me going," Renee said, smiling. "We really lucked out with our jobs, didn't we?"

"Yeah, I guess we did. Can't wait until I get that extra ten minutes of sleep, too. I bet my mom is still sitting at our kitchen table smoking one of those cigarettes she thinks I don't know about."

Renee let out a large laugh.

"Your family, I'll tell ya! Your mom can get away with practically anything, your dad can save practically anything, and your brother can find out practically anything. And you, well… you know what you're good at," Renee smirked, winking at her friend.

"Can I still count on you for after school?"

The school building was quickly approaching and, although Micah enjoyed Renee's presence, she was ready to break from the conversation. She changed her pace so that the *plop, plop, plop* of her pumps against the pavement sang a slightly quicker tune than those around her.

"Have I ever let you down?" she whispered behind as Renee fell in with the rest of the crowd, an ad for a new INSAV game surrounding them in the background.

Never.

THE LIFESTYLE OF A NIGHTCRAWLER

By: Ian Dale

As you already know, a **Nightcrawler** is a citizen that lives underneath a sector. Their origins can be traced back to a time in our history when overpopulation and many types of cancer, the most common being skin cancer, were rampant. Disease rates were rising 5 percent each year, and over 65 percent of the Caucasian population was diagnosed with malignant skin cancer growths. This was due to the amount of sun exposure their fair skin was given. Due to increasing UV rays, those with pale skin were no match for the sun, despite many advances in skin care.

The environment was also quickly depleting. Throughout the world, there were no more than ten trees per square mile, on average. What were once sprawling parks and fields were converted into residential and industrial areas to support the earth's overwhelmingly increasing population. If nothing had been done to either separate or reduce the world population by 50 percent over 13 years, it was projected that disease and malnutrition would shrink the earth's population to 10 percent its original 20 billion. In order to save the lighter races and the cities that both the fair and dark skinned lived in, President James Lithgow, along with leaders of the most prominent countries around the world, determined that billions of dollars would be dedicated to creating a safe haven for the lighter races underneath the earth. Old sewer and subway lines were extended and transformed into streets connecting expansive underground apartment buildings, stores, and factories. These advances were considered international marvels. Oxygen systems were created to provide clean, fresh air to these underground cities and underground lighting mimicked that of the sun without the consequences of its harsh rays. The project took over ten years to complete. By this time, the rates of skin cancer in the lighter races had risen over 70 percent and the rates of urban disease were detrimental. Unfortunately, those already affected by the disease could not be saved. On October 30th, the lighter populations were relocated to new underground homes and the cities that once had names such as New York, Philadelphia, and Washington DC were renamed and redistributed into smaller, numbered sectors. The city of Washington, DC, for example, was split into 50 sectors. Those of darker descent were permitted to continue living above ground, as their skin was able to absorb the UV rays of the sun with much lower rates of cancer.

With the creation of these underground sectors, jobs worldwide were redistributed. The lighter races were, at first, given jobs to perform at the underground factories and within the underground sectors. Those of darker complexion living above ground were placed in charge of farming, government, and business administration for both the above and below ground sectors. Reserved in each sector was a plot of land large enough to support the 60,000 or so members of each area above and below ground. However, when the management of these plots proved to be too large of a task for one population to manage, many of the agricultural jobs were redistributed. A select number of the lighter skinned population was permitted to emerge above ground at night to tend to agricultural work that did not require direct sunlight. Below is a chart of the modern day agricultural job distribution.

DAYMEN	NIGHTCRAWLERS
Water crops	Bake goods such as bread
Tend to animals	Butcher animals, prepare and can meat
Harvest, vegetables, wheat, other grains	Prepare and can vegetables and fruits
Manage wages and order supplies	Restock food supplies
Manage and operate stores and other businesses	Clean stores and businesses

Although some Nightcrawlers are given the opportunity to arise from the underground at night, if seen above ground during the day they are subject to arrest, punishment, and possible death. This is for many reasons.

• We are no longer sure of which diseases may still be carried by the Nightcrawlers and inspect the food they handle very carefully. There have already been outbreaks of at least five lethal diseases since their relocation.

• It is our duty to protect them from the harmful rays of the sun and to ensure that they live as long and healthy a life as their darker skinned counterparts.

• Since the segregation, there have been many reports of murder and rape by the Nightcrawlers to members of the Daymen. Although violence is not characteristic of every Nightcrawler, we find these instances have decreased substantially since the enactment of the Law of Segregation and Punishment. We will talk of this further in the next section of this series.

Because of the extremely high risk associated with the interaction between the underground and the above sector, the only profession within the Daymen allowed to have contact with Nightcrawlers are the **trashmen**. Trashmen, sometimes called trash collectors, are responsible for making sure, every day before dawn, there is no trace of the emergence of the Nightcrawlers in the above ground sector. They ensure that none of your useable goods are taken to the underground by clearing the streets in the hour before nightfall. They also act as a police force in the later portion of the night, monitoring the restocking of food and goods to the shelves of our stores and afterwards wiping the areas clean of contamination from the Nightcrawlers. Although these trashmen take the largest risk, they also receive the largest reward. If you see or know of one, as they are hard to come by, make sure to thank them today for keeping your city safe.

Here is a quote from an esteemed trashman's biography, *A Life of Treasure.*

> "The hardest part of my job was, by far, listening to them [the Nightcrawlers] speak as they butchered the meat that was to be canned. They speak with an accent that pierces the ears, even if you don't hear the words they say it is easy to assume that they are speaking of something crude and vulgar. From what I gather, their lifestyles are riddled with misogyny, crime, and many other unspeakables. One man talked of his wife as if she were an animal to be slaughtered, all the while an axe in his hand and decapitating a chicken. Although I know some must have good in them, I cannot seem to find it. Who knows if this mindset were ever to affect our beautiful sector full of kind, intelligent people. It gives me great honor to be chosen as a buffer between these unrefined people and my own."

Micah closed her INSAV and lifted her eyes to the board in front of her classroom. Her instructor, who was now sitting at the front of the room on a tall, four legged stool grading papers, had projected on the board in swirling letters,

Explain, in two paragraphs, why the passage you just read proves your importance as a segregation specialist. Are there any new precautions you would put into place?

Micah opened the writing wrist section of her INSAV and let the overwhelming white screen of an electronic document sit in front of her. She tried to begin.

Segregation specialists make sure that the laws which separate us from the Nightcrawlers are up to date. Without these laws, our city would be in complete havoc. The possible diseases of their kind could infect each and every one of us. Interaction with them could lead to interaction with something that will never leave us. They are tainted.

She stopped. Her historytext told her all this was true. It had to be true. Still, she couldn't stop thinking of that day when she was about 12 years old and a Nightcrawler had been found in the street outside her apartment building.

She and her father had just left for the morning when a sudden swarm of trashmen came barreling forth, pulling what looked like a white animal behind them. They had tied his hands together with a thick, tough rope and covered his mouth with a large piece of tape. His clothing barely covered his frail body, exposing something Micah had never seen before. It was a boy about her age, maybe a little younger. The boy's fraying, white shirt and light brown pants seemed to blend in with his skin. Micah was terrified to look at him but couldn't turn away. He looked like a ghost. Like something that would haunt your dreams every night and return for more. As the men walked him forward towards the government center where he would undoubtedly await trial for whatever crime he committed, he seemed to be fighting back with everything he had left. He swung his hands back and forth against the rope and many times stopped in his tracks until the force of the twisted cloth chains brought him forward again in a giant leap. His skin was so light that Micah was convinced he would just disappear into the sunlight. Take one giant swoop with his hands and then suddenly be gone into the shining rays. As he walked within a few feet of Micah and her father she sometimes lost the outline of his arms or the top of his ears in the light.

There was one thing she could never forget. After trying once more to stop dead in his tracks and falling onto his knees with a forceful pull by the trashmen, the boy suddenly seemed to give up. He shrunk in size as the muscles of his shoulders and arms relaxed in defeat. He sat, for just a few seconds, staring at the pavement as it began to pool with blood from his knees. Everyone surrounding Micah continued to walk past, around, through him, but she couldn't move. Everything else disappeared as she looked at him. Slowly, he began rubbing his hands together above bent legs. She watched them, watched how the dark red stains of blistering cracks stood out against white knuckles. She wondered how he got these blisters but knew there would never be an answer.

This boy, who just a few seconds ago was fighting for his life, seemed to have lost all the life in his fight. He slowly released his hands from one another and pushed them down onto the ground. There, he stayed. Head bent, it was as if he was saying goodbye to the ground beneath his feet. Slowly he rose and, with knees still slightly bent, turned his head towards Micah. His blood encrusted ears and shaggy brown hair gave way to eyes she would never forget. He stared straight at her. Micah braced herself for a paralyzing fear, but what arose instead was completely unexplainable. As she gazed into his crystalline blue eyes, she became lost in comfort. It was as if, with this glance, he was trying to unlock a box within her that she didn't know existed. Inside that box was everything he had but could no longer hold on to.

She stared at him until his watering eyes blinked, producing a single tear that fell onto his blood stained cheek. He smiled quickly and, without wiping the tear from his face, turned away and continued walking.

When she returned home from school, her mother told her that the young boy had been caught stealing food from the Daymen's grocery. He arrived at the store during the night but became locked in until the owner came in right after dawn. She immediately alerted the trashmen, who brought him to the government house to be hanged. Micah's mother then asked if she would like to attend the hanging which would take place the next afternoon. Micah politely declined and said she would rather just do her homework. She didn't dare tell her mother, but she knew she had already seen the boy die.

Micah looked back down at her paper.

Interaction with them could lead to interaction with something that will never leave us. They are tainted.

3

SSchool lasted for exactly seven hours Monday through Saturday. It didn't have a definitive start or end time, as the hours were adjusted daily to the rising and setting of the sun. Today, Micah exited the thick windowless door of her classroom at 2:19 and, after packing her bag and putting to sleep the school section of her INSAV, left the foreboding double doors of the school at 2:23. On the second to bottom step leading up to the entrance she met Renee, who had already taken her hair out of its restricting bun and let her dark locks fall onto her shoulders. She was turned towards the school entrance waiting for her friend.

"What a day," Renee said as Micah plopped onto the step next to her. "All we did was read that fucking text! I don't even think I need to see a Nightcrawler anymore, I already know too much about them! What they eat, how they dress, what position they like to fuck in and how they snuggle afterwards. I swear, if we don't start doing something else soon I'm just going to dye my skin and sink down there with them."

"Stop being dramatic!" Micah quietly laughed, tapping the corner of Renee's arm in a hushing motion.

"You need to be quieter! Someone might hear you. Plus, I didn't think the passages we read were that bad."

"You're right," Renee scolded, twisting her collar up. "They're not worth getting that worked up about, anyways."

Micah laughed, undoing the top button of her own. "You ready to go? I told my dad that I was helping Sasha Dolton with an essay."

"Good cover, I hear she might be there today, too."

"I love it when these things work out," Micah stretched, pushing her arms towards the sky. "Let's head out."

Side by side, the two girls stood up off the steps and headed down the street.

"I don't know why you keep lying to your parents about where you go after school. I told my mother a long time ago and she's *proud* of me for it." Renee said as they walked past a small grocery store that loudly displayed a glowing ad for potatoes from the wide, smiling, soft faces of Sector 31.

"Your mother is a lot different than mine. Mine... I don't know," Micah said, squinting her eyes against the harsh sun. "She still places me in a certain light, and I guess I'm afraid of what she'll do if I fall out of it."

"You'll never know unless you try."

"Yeah. But if I try, and I fail, I'll wish I never did."

"But really, I mean... what's the worst than can happen? At least half the girls at our school do this, it really helps them later on. Tell your mom it provides connections, or security, or some shit. Does she want you to be a 40 year old bore who sits in her apartment, *alone*, until her final days?"

Of course that wasn't how Micah wanted to be, but her current after school activities weren't the only way to eliminate that from her future.

"Again, you're being dramatic."

"No, dramatic would be saying this is between life and death. Which is how I explained it to my father."

"Who responded with…"

"My baby. My baby!" Renee exclaimed in a deep voice, waiving her hands in large circles to complete the impression of her father. "'She's just growin' up so fast!' and then he gave me a hug and a kiss and we haven't talked about it since."

Micah laughed at Renee's spot on representation of her father. He was one of the only men in the sector to be originally from a different one. In his mid twenties he was transferred to Sector 15 from an area on the upper east coast to monitor trash clean up. He was from a sector that used to be a borough of New York City. Whenever Micah went over to Renee's, her father would always sit her down on their green loveseat and, with a beer in hand, give her an earful from the "old days" and the "old country" in a sector that had "really always been a sector." He was proud of his roots and always told Micah "New York City had an underground city before people were ever told to live underground!" He would then go on to talk of his adventures "underneath," and of when he would have to travel below to seek out a Nightcrawler who had broken a law.

"There was this scrawny, nasty boy who got caught above ground during the day one time. He had found, or stolen, a shopkeeper's uniform and was roaming our streets like he owned them. He must have been mixed breed or something, because he was wearing a hat and for some reason no one seemed to realize who he was! Well, I took one look at him and

I knew. He had a long nose and I could see little strands of blonde hair tucked underneath his hat. Almost got away with it, that sneaky bastard!"

At this point Renee's father would always scoot a little closer to Micah on the couch and point his middle and index fingers straight at her eyes.

"I looked him straight in the eyes and he knew. I was comin' after him. He darted across the street! Ran into an alley! Jumped a fence! But I was right after him the whole time. Gaining on him little by little. Suddenly, though, like magic, he jumped into a street drain and seemed to vanish. I paused for a second, *just...* for a second. Why the hell would a kid jump into a drain! He would've been stuck right there! But, I peered my head in between the grates, and do you know what I saw?" He would always ask, never actually waiting for an answer.

"There was a human sized tunnel where the water one should have been. A motherfucking tunnel! I mean, I *could* not believe my eyes. There was a gateway to the underground right underneath my feet, the whole city's feet! the whole time and no one knew it. It looked like there was a hatch that those Nightcrawlers would put back into place whenever they needed it. Unbelievable! Well, I knew what I had to do. I had to follow him down there. So, I undid the hatch, hopped into that drain, and went down. And what I saw there.... Phew. Let me tell you. You don't *want* me to tell you. But, I chased him, and grabbed him, and brought him back up- none of the others down there dared to mess with me- and brought him to our government building.

"They were astounded. Little old me, I was only fifteen at the time, who was destined to be a farmer, caught a Nightcrawler. They promoted me to trashman right then and there. And I've been chasing those dirty sons of bitches ever since. Following that kid down that shoot was the best decision I ever made."

He told this story everywhere. To his friends, to his family, at almost every government event, all but the last line. That he seemed to reserve especially for Micah. He was, after all, a hero. She was sure this was where Renee got her passion for punishment.

"We're here," Renee said, veering towards a large, red brick building promoting the segregation department on their right. The ad showed four employees, wearing the typical segregation red and white, with their backs against one another. "Protect from Within." the screen said in black lettering above their heads.

With Renee in the lead the two girls scanned their wrists and entered a small glass door on the side. In front of them lay a narrow, dark wooden staircase accompanied by small spotlights that illuminated every three or four steps. The staircase led up three stories at a sharp angle and ended at a black door with a red knob.

Renee began walking up the stairs, expecting as always for Micah to follow close behind. The short heels of their leather shoes reverberated off the deeply glazed wood. Neither girl held on to the railing on their left and chose to tilt their bodies slightly forward to stabilize themselves instead. It was at the top of the landing that Micah now took the lead, undoing her hair as she stepped in front of Renee.

Micah took one final calming breath, like she always did, before turning the red knob and emerging into the dimly lit room that she knew all too well.

The room was hazy from the smell of cigars and stench of adolescent curiosity. It wasn't a large room, wide enough to fit fifteen groupings of tables and chairs. It wasn't busy that day, only about four of the arrangements were occupied. In the background a faint sultry tune enhanced the rich carpeting and large, sweeping chairs and couches that Micah would stiffly sink into after grabbing a drink.

"I'll get them today," Renee said from behind her. "You grab our spot before it starts filling up."

Micah nodded and veered towards the back left corner. She, Renee, and sometimes others sat in the same place every time they came. Towards the back, but not completely in the shadows, with a circular table large enough to invite more if they felt so inclined.

She placed her bag to the right of the couch and plopped into the same corner, resting her arm on the sloping leather armrest. She looked around at the heads floating above the black and dark brown leather couches, every once in a while coming across a thick arm draped across a pair of slim shoulders supporting a thin white blouse. Bouts of hushed laughter would occasionally accompany the low, surrounding music that seemed to become more distant with every moment. Micah reached into her bag and took out a small mirror from the side pocket and thin, deep lipstick the color of an overripe apple from a secret pocket in the front. She placed the mirror right in front of her face, staring deeply into her own light brown eyes, for just a second, before taking out her contacts and placing them into their solvent case. She could only expose them in this environment. The men inside The Red Knob loved them, but in the outside world the attention they would have brought her would be too much. They made her look too much like... them. But, in a place like where she was, their true color made her unique and desirable.

It was because of her eyes that she had built a reputation for herself within that place. There was only one other girl whose irises broke from the normal pallet of hazels and dark browns. She, as Micah knew without looking, was already sitting at the bar with a regular. Micah had never spoken to her, but they had made eye contact many times. There seemed to be an unspoken bond to never speak to, but always respect, one another.

Renee weaved around the grouping of chairs and sat down next to Micah, handing her a tall, thin glass.

"I was going to get you a Blue Tingler, you know that drink that makes your tongue practically vibrate? But the bartender says that there wasn't a handover this week. I guess they ran out at Sector 5. All they had was warm whiskey left over from last week. I had absolutely no idea what to order, but remembered a guy last week bought me something he called a Baby Blanket. Here's to our childhood, I guess."

Renee handed her the drink. The light brown liquid was in a tall, ice filled glass and topped with a plump apple slice and thin, white straw.

"Isn't this the drink that you blame made you go back with that tall, skinny guy with the funny accent?" Micah asked, popping open the cap of her black market beautifier and rubbing the crisp gel over her tightened lips.

"Ha! Accent? You can say speech impediment, it's ok. I know what I did. But yeah, it was. I mean, it does make you feel like you're wrapped in your own little sexy cocoon. But, that was after a few of them. One should make us just warm enough to get this afternoon started."

"I don't think we need the drinks to get noticed," Micah responded, peering over the rim of her glass at the two men who had just entered through the black door and handing her friend the stick of red gloss. "I haven't seen them here before."

"Maybe they were just transferred to the sector. I heard from my father that they're trying to completely revamp the trash cleanup program. I guess there've been a few too many instances of Nightcrawlers coming up at night who shouldn't be there at all. My dad's been pissed about it for weeks."

"But trashmen aren't allowed here."

"Yeah, I know. But maybe they're the Gov employees in charge of redoing the program. You never know until you find out," Renee said with a wink while taking a large gulp from the side of her drink, ignoring the straw touching her cheek. She pursed her lips at the end and released them with a loud smack!

"Phew! These are *strong*."

"Strong enough to make a difference," Micah said, almost to herself.

"Exactly," Renee responded, standing up and handing the lipstick back to her friend before heading towards the two men.

"I'm going to solve this little mystery."

Micah stayed behind, moving only to adjust her body so that her red pants would no longer stick to her against the hot leather of the couch. She knew her role. She would sit, cross-legged, pretending to stare at Renee and the men longingly until Renee would point at her. At this she would wave to the men by slightly lifting a few fingers from her glass and then look away. This, of course, would make them want to come over, as Micah was now as much of a mystery to them as she many times wished to remain. But, without fail, Renee would lead the pack to the dark couch across the room and there they would sit, for about an hour as the alcohol took its toll, until the girls were ready to initiate the second part of their journey.

This was a common practice for the girls in Micah's grade.

They were in their final year at school before starting their life careers. Although it was never discussed, Micah saw many of her classmates here. One by one, her peers would disappear behind the back curtains only to emerge shortly after with an accomplished air and newly applied coat of lipstick.

Where the men came from Micah never knew. It was a requirement, on their part, to be a government employee, but why this was or how it came to be she never discovered.

Today, after Renee pointed, Micah waved, and the men were brought over with two fresh drinks for the two girls. Micah accepted and motioned for one to sit next to her. The men looked to be eight to ten years older than the confident schoolgirls. The first, who stood a little behind Renee, was about 5' 10" and was wearing the regular government uniform. She noticed, however, that the normally floppy white shirt that was required by all stretched across his flat chest and fit him snuggly. The second man was a little heavier, but also a little taller. His skin appeared to be slightly darker than the first man, but Micah couldn't tell if this was just because of the lighting. He, as well, was wearing the same uniform as the first, but with a slightly charismatic touch. Across his collar, where there was normally just a hint of an undershirt peaking through, this man wore a small striped bow tie. It was he who sat down next to Micah when she motioned forward, pushing past his friend to take a place next to what she was sure he considered to be an overtly seductive bombshell.

Although the couch was large enough for five, he slid across it so that the red of his pants barely touched the fabric of hers. He smiled as he placed another Baby Blanket in front of her.

"I hear you're fond of these," he said, swinging his arm across the couch behind her.

Micah smiled, large enough to show that she was interested but not large enough to show that the battle was won even though they both knew that there was only one possible outcome. She placed her empty drink on the side table and picked up the one he had placed in front of her.

"Today I am."

"What's your name."

"Janet, and yours?"

"James."

Both knew what had just happened, but both knew the rules. You don't give away any true information until afterwards, and that's only on special occasions. Micah had only done this once in the past year.

*   *   *   *   *   *   *   *   *

It had been a strange afternoon. She had decided to come by herself. Renee's father was the keynote speaker at an educational meeting on the safety of the sector and was being presented an award for outstanding patriotism. Renee wouldn't have missed seeing her father speak to hundreds about his regulation of the Nightcrawlers for the world. Micah, however, didn't have much interest.

"But don't you want to hear him talk about jailing them, and hanging them, and making them go back to where the belong?!" she begged her after school.

"I can go to your apartment to hear about that."

She was sitting at the bar because she felt strange being at a large couch by herself. It was as if by sitting in her usual spot she would have been showing the rest of the room how completely alone she was. Which, undoubtedly, was probably what the men wanted. But, her pride got in the way and placed her, cross-legged, on a tall stool in the middle of the bar. She had just ordered a vodka cranberry when she felt a body slip into the seat next to her. She looked to her left and saw a man with crystal brown skin and a pair of hazel eyes staring into hers.

As she looked back at him, she realized that she desperately wanted to encourage him, impress him, but couldn't seem to find a single word to say. She was completely lost. She opened her mouth, expecting her usually quick mind to fill the gap between her throat and the air, but nothing followed. She took another sip of her drink to mask her nerve.

"I've seen you here before," he said, lifting his gaze.

"Oh," Micah responded. Nothing else seemed to fit.

"You come with another girl usually. I recognized you by your eyes," he said, lifting his hand and brushing her cheek with the side of his finger.

Her nerves were starting to die down, but she took another large sip of her drink just in case they disobeyed her.

"And why, sir, would you remember my eyes?"

"They remind me of somebody I used to know. You seem to have every hue of blue resting in small pools above your cheeks."

He didn't say it in an overly endearing tone. He was matter of fact, as if her eyes were something he had spent hours analyzing and these two sentences were his only conclusion.

"Well, that's amazingly kind. But, I'm sorry it's just, I don't remember ever seeing you here before."

"That would make sense, I'm usually pretty quiet. Sometimes I come and I don't even take anyone to the back. Every once in a while it's nice to just sit and watch. That's how I noticed you."

She placed both arms solidly onto the bar and leaned in towards him.

"Now that you've noticed me, what else can you see?"

"I can see," he began, inching his body closer to hers, "that you want to do something you've never done before. You're angry. You want to scream, jump, run. Anything. I've noticed you sit in the back with your friend, but you never pursue. You wait. At first, I thought this was how you hooked your bait. But then I started watching you as you walked behind the curtain. You would walk towards it with confidence, always in front of them. And they would always, *always*, follow you. But, I caught you once. When you were leaving. I expected to see the look of a satisfied seductress. Someone who had gotten what they came for. But that always seemed to be the look the men would leave with. You would walk in front of them, but you never looked satisfied. You looked as if you expected to find something behind that curtain, but always left empty handed."

Micah just sat, listening. She couldn't believe that someone she didn't even know existed before a few minutes ago was analyzing how she lived her life. She suddenly became angry and twisted her legs away from him in preparation to leave.

"You don't know anything about me. You don't even know my name. I wouldn't keep coming back unless I was satisfied."

She pushed her feet against the lower peg of the stool to rise, but the man lightly grabbed her arm.

"Or maybe it's the opposite," he smirked, leaning even closer to her.

He could tell she was offended, she was sure of it, but he wasn't giving up.

"If you're satisfied I'm sure you wouldn't mind sharing some of that satisfaction with me."

Micah paused. She already hated this man, despised every fiber of his being, but she couldn't bring herself to walk away. Everything he had said was too true, too stupidly, amazingly true. She had slept with dozens of men within these walls, all of them the same. She knew what they all wanted, she knew what pleased them. This man seemed... different. A challenge. He seemed like the mystery she knew she was to the men who pursued her. She relaxed her body and placed her legs back under the bar.

"Buy me one more drink first."

Behind the curtain, her physical interaction with him was initially not out of the ordinary. They stood in front of one another and undressed, taking off first their pants and letting them drop to the floor at their feet. Then, almost synchronized, they worked their fingers through the buttons on their white shirts, starting at the bottom. It was then, when they stood facing one another, that things became different. Instead of stripping further, the man stepped closer to Micah so that she was at eye level with his chest. She didn't look up, but breathed into his soft skin and dark whisping hairs. Everything calmed within her as she breathed in and out, in and out, becoming engulfed in his scent of lemon, perspiration, and cigarettes. She relaxed, and let her head fall forward as she glided her hand down his chest and onto his hip. He gently tilted her head up with his fingertips until they were once more looking into each other's eyes. But, she couldn't look at him. There was something strange, something she couldn't describe but couldn't resist. She closed hers as he pulled her face towards his.

He didn't even know her name.

She clenched his hip harder and pressed her other hand against the small of his back as his hands became wrapped around her ears. They rolled their foreheads together and she listened to his breathing before hearing one giant gasp and feeling warmth against her lips.

Suddenly they were against a wall, fallen onto the bed and fallen onto the floor all the while embraced within one another. She continued to run her hands across his back, racing her nails in zigzags when she felt things a little more powerfully.

She didn't even know his name.

When she had, at one point, fallen underneath him on the floor, she let her fingertips slide down his sides, grasping when they felt the elastic fabric brush against them. She pulled them off as far as she could reach and then pulled her foot up to hook the end around her toes and slide them off without having to adjust her body below him.

She didn't know what overcame her. She had sex with many men, many times, many men many times even in this room, but it had never been like this. She wasn't trying any harder than normal, that wasn't the point. Somehow it was as if everything she did over the hour in that room was no effort at all. Every new experience brought forth a burst of energy. She didn't like him more than others, that couldn't be the case. After all, she had hated him within minutes of knowing him. But, there was something he had that she wanted. She just didn't know what it was yet.

When they were finished she simply got off the bed and began getting redressed. He lay still on top of it, arms behind his head, staring straight at the ceiling. Nothing was covered as the blankets and pillows had all fallen to the floor.

She grabbed her shirt from the corner of the room and looked over at him.

"What's your name?"

He paused. She could tell he was contemplating whether or not to give her his real one.

"Tyrone. And yours?"

She didn't care whether or not his was true.

"Micah."

"Micah," he repeated, flexing his toes. "Micah. You know you kind of look like them," he said, staring straight at the ceiling.

She was rebuttoning her blouse, legs still bare.

"Who?"

"The Nightcrawlers."

She laughed, fastening the last button at the top of her shirt. "And how would you know that?"

"I've been there."

"To prison?"

"No. Down there."

She stopped, pants at her hips but completely undone.

"Why the hell would you do something like that?"

"They brought me there. I used to sneak down to the lower floors in the hospital and talk with them. After I got out they invited me down."

"But, how did you even get down there?"

"There are ways. Or, were ways. But you, you look like them."

"Shut up. I have dark skin and dark hair, and everything about me looks like I belong here."

"Except for your eyes.

They're beautiful.

They really are."

He lifted his head towards her as she glared back. How dare he, after the way she just was with him, accuse her of being something she knew she wasn't.

"Haven't you ever noticed why barely anyone up here has blue eyes? Don't you ever wonder where they all went? It's not natural for there to be a world full of just one color."

"Evolution, mutation, that's what I learned in school. Stop accusing me." She wasn't screaming, but could feel her muscles clench and face begin to warm.

He shrugged and looked down, pushing the thumb of one hand into his other palm.

"I'm just saying I've been there, and I know what they look like."

She wanted to run away. To whip open the black curtain and storm out. She didn't know what he could have contracted down there and just given to her. She kept hearing the voice of Renee's dad in the back of her head,

And what I saw there.... Phew. Let me tell you. You don't want me to tell you.

She finished buttoning her pants and threw on her shoes. Grabbing her bag from the side table she had delicately placed it on hours before, she turned to leave. But, something stopped her. Suddenly her mind was filled with unanswerable questions. She looked back over at Tyrone. He seemed completely normal. More than normal. Kind, intelligent, and extremely observant. How could someone like that go down there and not make it their life goal to destroy them? She walked towards him and stood at the foot of the disheveled bed.

"What were they like?"

He looked back up.

"Something tells me you already know the answer to that question."

"I don't. I mean… I have an idea. But I don't *really* know."

He reached under the bed for his shirt and sat up, bare back against the white wall.

"The only difference between us and them is that they live in a darker world. Don't let anyone tell you differently."

"Were you ever… with… any of them…."

"Even they wouldn't have allowed that," he replied comfortingly. "I just went down a few times. When I was younger I used to get sick a lot. My parents would leave me in the hospital all by myself for days, so I would wander. Head out at night when most of the nurses were off duty and travel up and down the halls, searching for something. Anything. In the very back of the hospital on the first floor there was a janitor's closet that I knew was usually left locked. I had never seen anyone go in or out of it. I would always start my night there, hoping that one day it would magically be left open for me. I went years doing this. Every time I was readmitted I would always check, each time imagining something more and more extravagant behind it. I remember I used to lie in bed and think to myself, 'I bet there are dinosaurs back there" or 'maybe it's the hospital's secret swimming pool.' It's funny what kind of stuff kids can make up when they're sick and bored. For some reason, four years after I first started checking, I was sick that often, the door was left open. The closet had no lights except for two small circles against the back wall. It was an elevator, and it had a down button. I had never been more excited for anything in my life. This had to be the access to the underground floors of the hospital. I took the elevator down one level. On my way down, I was so nervous. I had never met anyone who had traveled to the underground before, and the rumors I used to hear at school were awful. That it was full of fire. That is was full of ice. That everyone had knives for fingers. That they had red eyes and boils all over their skin. Do people still say things like that?"

She nodded, still clutching her bag and standing statuesque at the foot of the bed.

"Then you must know how terrified I was. When the elevator door opened I expected a ball of fire to whirl towards me. But, there was nothing. It opened, and I thought for a second the elevator hadn't moved at all. Everything felt the same. The room was still dark. I exited the elevator and headed out of the closet. When I opened the door..."

The curtain swung open. The woman working as the bartender that night was standing behind it.

"Sorry guys, but we're closed for the night. You have to get dressed and leave," she said in a very unapologetic tone.

"Ok, give us one more minute?" Tyrone asked, standing up to look for his pants.

"We have to clear everything now. It's almost sunset. I'll stand here until you're ready. Sorry." Again, not seeming to be apologetic.

Tyrone finished dressing himself, every once in a while looking up at Micah with a smile.

"Alright, I'm done. I think we can walk ourselves out."

The bartender gave him a deadpan stare.

"You know the rules. You walk out at least five minutes before she does. Wouldn't want anyone to suspect anything."

"Right," he responded with a sigh and turned to Micah. "Maybe you'll get to see it for yourself one day."

He gave her a kiss on the cheek and walked past the curtain. Micah sat on the bed and waited for her turn. After the bartender gave her permission, she practically ran out of the club and down the stairs. When she exited the building, she walked in a brisk circle around it looking for Tyrone, but couldn't find him. She never saw him at the club again.

On the brick of the building projected a new ad, this time for the trashmen. They stood in the exact same positions as the segregationalists, same exaggerated grins, but in the prestigious uniform of a blue jumper and black hardhat. Above their heads read a slightly altered black lettered slogan.

"Protecting from Without."

4

"How was he?"

Micah and Renee were sitting across from each other on the curved couch. The men had just left and they were sipping on one more drink before heading home.

"Good," Micah responded. "And yours?"

"Oh, he was phenomenal! Did this thing with his tongue, wow. You should have been there."

"If they come in again we can switch."

"I don't know if I'd want to give this one up. Even told him my real name," Renee said with a wink.

"You say that like it's unusual for you."

"Hey! I only give it out, like, once every two weeks. I doubt it'll ever get back to me. *You* need to stop being so picky about giving away yours. The sex is wayyy better when you tell them the truth about who you are."

"I just don't want my family to find out."

"Micah, I've told you before. It's bound to happen. Better

they hear it from you than through the grapevine."

"Maybe I should stop watering my grapevine."

"Nonsense. You love this! And what would I do without you? Come on, let's go. I think the bartender is about to give us the get the fuck out look."

The girls left their drinks on the table, pinned back their hair, wiped off their makeup, and left the club. When they got outside, the sun had begun its descent towards the ground.

"Ah, I've gotta run home. Tell your mom I said hi! Or, no. Tell her Sasha said hi."

When Micah unlocked and opened the door to her family's apartment the sweet smell of apple wood bacon crawled into her nose as the sound of crackling grease dripped into her ears. She dropped her bag to the right of the door and walked past her brother, who was draped across the couch watching the news, and towards the kitchen in the back.

Her mother, still in her work uniform, was huddled over the stove in between a large bowl of lettuce and a cutting board full of tomatoes, blue cheese, and a long loaf of bread. She had a recipe brought up on her INSAV and was squinting at it and pulling her wrist closer to her head, trying to decipher its directions. Micah brought her palm her mouth and breathed out one last time to make sure she no longer smelled of her earlier activities. After passing her own test, she went up next to her mother and picked up the serrated knife accompanying the cutting board.

"Hi mom, how was work today?"

Her mother was tossing the bacon with a spatula.

"Fine, absolutely fine. And school?" She asked, not looking up from the pink and white sizzling strips.

"Same old same old. We're still reading about the lifestyle of the Nightcrawlers."

"Ah, I remember reading about that. Do you have that historytext by, oh god, what was his name. Davis? Dallis? Oh wow, my memory's really hurting, huh?"

"Yeah, I think his name's Ian Dale."

Micah had begun cutting the bread into thick slices.

"Oh, yes! I really should have remembered that. He came to speak at my office a few years ago. Smart guy. In case you can't already tell we're having salad for dinner. Your brother actually went to the store like I asked and picked up a head of lettuce for me. Would you mind setting the table?"

Micah put the knife down and reached above her to open the cabinet that held the plates and bowls.

"Gabe! Get off your ass and grab the cups for me!"

Her mother whipped around, spatula in hand, and glared at her daughter.

"Micah! How many times do I have to ask you and your brother to speak nicely to one another! You're 18! I really shouldn't have to be telling you this."

"Dearest Gabriel," Micah mockingly screamed. "Can I please be honored by your presence whilst setting the kitchen table this fine night?"

"Well since you asked so nicely," Micah heard in a singsong voice from the other room.

Their mother simply rolled her eyes and turned back towards the skillet. With a stack of plates, forks, and knives across her forearms, Micah headed towards the other room and began setting up everything for dinner. Her brother was soon behind and with every plate she set down he followed with a cup and napkin.

"I know where you've been."

"Mom told you I went to Sasha's? I'm glad Dad was able to visit her at work."

"Don't play dumb. The club on Eighteenth isn't as big of a secret as you'd like it to be."

Micah could feel the blood drain from her face as the tips of her fingers began to shake. She was on the second plate at the table and continued looking down.

"Club? What club? As far as I know Eighteenth Street is all residential."

"Yeah, if residential means drinking and fucking. Which I guess people do sometimes in their homes."

Micah could suddenly feel every gland in her throat. She swallowed as they tightened. Third plate down. Fork on the left. Knife on the right.

"That's disgusting, Gabe."

"Not really. I know lots of girls that do it. But I never thought one of those girls would be you."

Cup and napkin to follow.

"I'm not." Fourth plate down.

"But you are." Knife and fork. Micah swiped the last cup out of her brother's hands.

"Prove it."

"Oh, Dad's already taken care of that. Mom doesn't know yet." He slid a folded napkin underneath the last fork. "But she will." Gabe went back to his position on the couch. A woman's stern voice rang from the wall projection.

This afternoon three Nightcrawlers were hung in the government center for theft and four more have been jailed for emerging during the day.

Micah stood, paralyzed, clutching the back of one of the chairs surrounding her family's dinner table. How did he find out? She had been so careful. Never giving away her name.

Always sitting in the back. Only going with Renee.

Renee.

Someone must have recognized Renee or had been talking about her in public. Goddamnit. Why didn't she listen? Everything would have been fine if only Renee had been more careful and less of a..."

Micah heard a door open from the left side of the apartment and all her thoughts froze. From where she was standing she had a direct view to the hallway that led to the bedrooms. The sun was setting, creating slanted streams of light across the carpeted cream floor. Slowly her father emerged and turned towards his daughter. The glare of diminishing light against his glasses masked his eyes from her, but it didn't matter. Micah could tell he was looking directly at her. Stern, tense lips supported by a tightly clenched jaw replaced the smile that usually greeted her every dusk. He sauntered towards her, with slow powerful steps, and stood across from his daughter at the table. Without saying a word he pulled his chair out and sat down, making sure to tuck himself entirely under the table. He looked back up at his daughter. Micah braced herself.

"Sweetheart, could you grab me a glass of water?"

This was more terrifying than anything else he could have said. Mr. Davis's temper wasn't explosive, but built steadily upon itself. She remembered, from when she was younger, how she would know whether or not he was angry simply by the way he gripped his fork or forcefully moved his fingers against a wall or table to scribble notes onto a medical document. He would never scream, but because of that Micah was always extra sensitive to the tone and inflections of his voice. When he asked her to get him a glass of water it was in a sharp, almost mocking voice. It was as if instead of asking to quench his thirst, he had told her "you know that I know, and I'm going to wait until it drives you insane before I say anything."

She already knew that they would play their game throughout dinner. He would sit, calm and collected, while he waited for her to crack and she would sit nervously, fidgeting, hoping whatever it was he was angry about would blow over. But, it never did. He would win. He always won. Still, as if from habit, Micah would silently fight against him even when she knew she was wrong.

"Sure, Dad."

She took his cup and raced into the kitchen.

"Oh honey, I'm glad you're here. Take everything to the table, will ya?" Her mother instructed, placing the large bowl of lettuce into Micah's left hand. Micah balanced it in between her arm and chest and, without responding, filled her father's glass and went back out to the table. Her brother was sitting at the far end, napkin in his lap, grinning. She placed the bowl in the center of the table and handed her father a glass of water.

"I didn't have enough hands to get you any ice."

"No problem. Would you like to be served first?" His voice was dry, seemingly emotionless, but Micah knew this to be the same as dripping with parental menace. Guilt was always his first tactic.

"Why don't I serve mom first since she made everything?"

"That's what a good daughter would do. Looks like we raised you well."

Micah felt the pit of her stomach turning as she placed salad onto each of the plates around the table. She couldn't crack. He might not know as much as she thought.

"And the bread?" Her father asked after she had rested the salad tongs inside the edge of the bowl. Her mother emerged from the kitchen with a plate of crumbled bacon in one hand and a butter dish in the other.

"Denzel, don't make her do everything! The bread's in front of Gabe. Honey, give everyone a piece."

"But Micah told us she *really* wanted to."

"What's with your attitude today? Just do it Gabe," her mother smiled at her. "And here, pass around the butter."

The family prepared their meals in silence. Micah piled a large mound of bacon on top of an equally large mound of lettuce. She knew she wouldn't eat all of it but couldn't stop her hands as they flew across the table, grabbing everything in front of her. The longer she took preparing her dish the longer it would be until her father and brother began talking. Gabe, however, knew this and reduced his normal preparation time in half. When Micah looked up he was already drizzling the dark purple balsamic dressing on top of his plate. He looked straight up at Micah, smiled, and began.

"So, everyone, how was your day?"

This was Gabe's method. Suspense.

"Mine was actually pretty good, but stressful," their mother responded, taking the dressing from her son. "The entire office was in shambles this morning trying to reorganize the trash program. Although you guys do the actual clean up," her mother pointed towards Gabe, "we have to modify some of the rules, talk about your schedules, discuss some new reprimands for the Nightcrawlers. It's going to be great for the city, but is a night*mare* for us."

Jane Davis laughed a little at her own joke. The rest of the table was silent.

"Great. Am I going to have to work longer hours?" Gabe asked, shoving a large forkful of salad into his mouth.

"No, dear. It'll actually be better for you. As of right now you only work the dawn shift, but at multiple locations. They have you monitor up and down the southeast side, right? In a few months you'll be working the dusk and dawn shifts, but monitoring only one or two locations right next to each other. That way you won't be running all over the sector. Your shifts will be shorter, but you'll have two of them each day. At least, that's what it looks like right now."

"It seems pretty stupid to make me go to sleep late and wake up early."

"Yeah, it might be hard to adjust to, but you'll have your whole day free and will only have to work two or three hour shifts. There'll be someone else, a night guard, to take your place after the transition between night and day is through."

"And what new laws are going to be put into place about the Nightcrawlers?" Micah's father asked.

"Ah, well we've had a lot of trouble with them lately. No matter what we do it seems like they just keep popping up. The Prime Minister of the sector is worried about a possible revolt against their own leader, which is really the last thing we want. He thinks they're coming to the surface because conditions are getting worse down there, but he also thinks it's their own fault. Our laws are going to become a little more strict."

"Which means…"

"It's tough, because it's not like we can monitor each and every one of them. It's too expensive to record each of them in our database so we can't really give them INSAVSs or track their whereabouts, even though I've told him I think that's the only solution. He wants to decrease the requirements for jailing and for the death penalty. He thinks that any one of them caught above ground during the day should be automatically hung. They're voting on it next week, and if it passes you're looking at the lady who'll be writing the first draft."

"So you agree with it?" Micah watched her father's hand as it gripped his fork a little tighter.

"It pays the bills. And really whatever keeps them off the streets. I think a group of intellectuals, like the officials in our government, know better how to do that than anyone else."

"I see. Has this been tried in any other sector?"

"Oh yes. And it's been very effective. They've even brought in two men from Sector 40 to headline the project. They got here a few days ago."

Micah's father looked up, just for a second, at his daughter before returning his gaze to his wife.

"I think I may have met them. They dropped by the hospital right before we closed for the day. One man wears this crazy bowtie, right?"

He knew so much more than Micah previously thought.

"Yes! Shawn Drextel is the one with the bowtie, and the other must have been Travis Drem. That's right, they told me they were going to head over to the hospital after they left the office."

"They came by right when we were closing, but I told them to come over for an early dinner one of these days."

"That's a shame. They must have gotten distracted with something. They told me they were heading straight there after work. But yes, dinner will be lovely. I'll make sure to mention it to them tomorrow."

He was a master of guilt and Micah hated him more at that moment than ever before. She took a deep breath to prepare for her imminent exposure. She waited for her father to respond with,

"I know exactly what they got distracted with. Our daughter. And do you know where she was? That club we told her for years to never step foot in. That cesspool of vulgar bodily interactions."

"Let me know when they're coming and I'll ask Mrs. Dern to save us a chicken."

Micah looked up. She peered to her brother, who sat with his mouth wide open.

"But Dad, don't you wanna tell Mom…"

"That her co-workers are welcome here anytime? Yes Gabe, I had hoped she already knew that."

"And yours as well, dear. Micah honey, you haven't said much today. How was your day? I know you had to do that awful reading, but I hope the rest of it was much better. Did Sasha finish her essay?"

Micah looked at first her brother and then her father. She wanted to jump up to them, to hug her father with everything she had. While her father dealt with anger through passive aggression, her mother responded with detachment. If he had bombarded her with Micah's secret at the dinner table, they all knew her mother wouldn't speak to her daughter for weeks. At the news, Mrs. Davis would have sat, dumbfounded, and asked to be excused before locking herself in her room for the rest of the night. She wouldn't have commented, or accused, but her silence would have been more hurtful than any words that could have emerged from her mouth.

"Yes, I don't think I'll need to be helping her after school for a while."

The rest of dinner was quiet. Micah could tell her brother was angry with their father for not exposing her and that her father was angry for the position she had placed him in. She offered to clear the table so her mother could finish reading the leisuretext she went on and on about during the second half of the meal. Her father's guilt had worked in a mysterious way. While Micah washed each dish and bagged the leftover food the men in her family sat at the projection and watched a re-run of a once popular comedy about a shop owner in Sector 11. When she finished she tiptoed into the living room and sat down next to them.

"Why didn't you say anything."

Mr. Davis used his INSAV to turn up the projection so his wife, down the hall, wouldn't hear the conversation he was about to have.

"You don't sit here and ask me the questions. You lost your right to ask questions the second you entered that club. But god Micah, do I have some questions for you. First of all, what were you *thinking*? Did you really think you could continue doing this without us finding out? Did you forget who's in your family? If this were to ever get back to us, both your mother and I would be beyond embarrassed. Do you understand that? You aren't like Sasha Daniels, you can't tramp around and do whatever you want."

"I wasn't with Sasha."

"I don't care who you were with. I don't care if you were by yourself or with your entire grade. Other parents might approve of it, but we both know that you knew that your mother and I wouldn't. Why did you lie to us? If you had just told the truth things might have been different but, god Micah, this is the worst lie you could have told. Not only did you lie about where you were and who you were with, but where you were doing it..."

"What? Just because I'm your daughter I'm not allowed to do what everyone else does? I lied to you because I had to. Because you wouldn't understand otherwise. Because it was the only way I could do behind your back what everyone else does without remorse. You make me feel so awful sometimes for trying to be like everybody else."

"That's because you're better than everybody else. Or at least I thought you were. If your mother had found out about this before I did, especially by the people I found out from, she would have never forgiven you."

"Well Jesus, Dad, maybe if you weren't talking about promiscuity at work we wouldn't be having this conversation! You walk around this town like you're all high and mighty but where are *your* morals? Why were you talking to him about that in the first place?"

She was beginning to raise her voice. She could feel the anger building in her lungs, in her throat, in her mouth, but she couldn't stop it. She knew she was wrong, she knew she shouldn't have lied. But she wasn't going to apologize. She was tired of trying to live up to his standards and would find a way of hurting him in any way she could. She opened her own wrist remote and turned the projection up four more notches. Looking back on these fights with her father she would always regret the way she said these things to him, but never what she said.

"Don't you *dare* speak to me of morals. You want to know how I found out about this? In the break room. Over a cup of coffee. These men were at the table next to me, talking about a girl they had just slept with..." His voice cracked at the words. "...with beautiful blue eyes. They said she had shoulder length black hair and deep dimples. The guy with the bowtie started talking about her red painted fingernails and I knew. It was you. Congratulations, Micah. Your after school activities have been reduced to a half a shitty cup of coffee. They didn't even talk about you for the whole cup. The man got halfway through his before switching to the girl he's planning on getting with tomorrow. Is that what you want? Is that what I'm supposed to be proud of?"

Micah could feel tears welling up in her eyes. She tried to hold them back but one dripped down her cheek as she blinked.

"At least people talk about me. At least I'm not some mundane doctor who disappears into a building every morning to see 50 patients he can't remember the names of and comes out eight hours later exactly on schedule. You may not be proud of me, but I'm proud of the fact that I'm not you. And that I'll never be you."

She muted the projection and walked back to her room.

"Thanks for turning it down, sweetie. I couldn't concentrate on my leisuretext," her mother yelled from her bed.

Micah closed her door and lay flat on the ground, supporting her head with folded arms as she let tears fall down her face. She wasn't crying because of what her father had said. Everything he had accused her of was true. She had known it all along. But it wasn't until she was confronted with it, until someone else proclaimed everything she had thought about herself but was too afraid to admit, that she realized what she had done. She had dug herself into a swirling inescapable hole. Her image to her father, and to her brother, was ruined. It was only by the good graces of the two people she had hurt that she had anyone left at all. When she should have talked to her father about her loneliness, and her insecurities, she chose instead to yell and accuse him of being everything she knew herself to be.

She flipped her body and lay on her back with her face towards the ceiling. How did she get this way? She told herself she would go there once, just once, and one year and 42 men later there she was, lying on the floor, telling herself like she did every night that she would stop. Did her family's intervention change anything? Would she stop now that they asked her to, now that it was no longer a secret? She couldn't stand the thought of waking up every morning, going to school every day, listening to the same lectures and passing the same notes between classes to the same people. And after that? Spend every day of her life sitting at the same desk, working on the same proposals, living in the same apartment. She cried not just out of pain and guilt towards her family, but pain and guilt because she suddenly felt that the hole wasn't just where she had dug herself that night, but that she had been digging it every day since she was born.

Little by little she had played into their system, doing as she was told, picking up handfuls of sand and throwing them to the side. Now, she was looking up from the bottom of the hole. She could see the top, see the surface, but knew there was no way to get there. No stairs. No ladder. No rope. She would try to climb, but the red polish of her fingernails would be replaced with red drippings of blood and she would have to give up. She cried because that was it. Like her mother, and her mother's mother, and her grandmother's mother she would be born, live, and die between the four square miles of Sector 15. Anything else was out of the question. Anything else would turn her fingers into the dirt she had been pushing aside for so many years.

She closed her eyes and felt the hard ground beneath her. It gripped her body. It didn't mold to her, she molded to it. She found solace in its harshness. She imagined she was on the bottom of this hole, back against the cold dirt. She breathed, in and out, in and out, feeling the back of her diaphragm press against the ground with each expansion. She would lie there forever listening to her own body. There was nothing else left to do. The world as she wanted it was so far away, so high above her, and there was no way of getting there.

She turned her head and pressed her ear against the ground. Everything became hollow. She felt trapped inside of it.

It was then that she opened her eyes and saw a thin yellow something peaking between the wooden floorboard and the wall. It took her a moment to realize what exactly it was. It was something she hadn't seen for a very, very long time. But, suddenly, a memory from her childhood brought everything together. Micah couldn't imagine how, or why, but knew it was a piece of paper.

5

Hello,

I don't know who I'm writing to, and there's no way you know who this is from, but please PLEASE promise yourself right now that you'll read this entire letter. It's not long. I just want to tell you a little about myself.

I have lived under your building for my entire life. Before I can tell you more about me, I need to tell what I know of you. I can hear your footsteps when you wake up in the morning and smell your dinner at night. I don't know how old you are, or what gender you are, but I know you like to blast music in your room on Saturday afternoons and that you wake up in the middle of your sleep at least once a week. The smells that come through my vents are much sweeter than anything I have eaten and the voices that I can sometimes hear, if I listen very closely as I'm going to sleep, are much smoother. Other than this, though, I don't know anything about your world. I don't know what makes this sweet smell, and I don't know what these voices talk about. I don't know the songs you blast on Saturdays, and I'm sure I don't know the dances you do to them. But, I want to.

With these letters I am offering an exchange. For every detail of your life that you give me, I will give you some of mine back. I am curious, more than curious-- longing-- for anything about the aboveground. But, I also know these letters are more dangerous for me than they are for you. If anyone finds these I will be hung. Part of me thinks this is a better alternative to living in ignorance of what is right above my head. I have to take this chance, and I hope you will too. So here are some things about me.

I am a 39-year-old male with three children. My wife is the mother of the younger two and we have lived under your building as a family for about 15 years. Before that I lived here with my parents, siblings, and eldest son. They now live next door, probably still under your property.

My father was a distributor and my mother was a teacher. My father would wake up every night and help to transport the goods prepared aboveground around our city. He was never allowed above, although he sat 10 feet away from the entrance every day of his life. My mother taught elementary math, I even had her as a teacher. Once I reached the age of 16 I left school and helped my father with distribution, taking over his spot after he reached a certain age. It wasn't common for students to leave school as early as I did, but my parents were very old when they had me and my father needed a replacement. I now sit in his spot, every night, 10 feet away from the exit. When I was 18 my first son was born, and so started the rest of my life.

Now please, if you are at all as curious as I am, tell me about your family. Tell me about your childhood. Tell me anything you'd like. To send a letter back, you need to only drop it down the vent.

Good luck and god bless,

P.

Micah couldn't sleep. Every time she closed her eyes her mind was filled with visions of who this man was and what his life was like. Did he look like Tyrone had told her? Did they all look like the boy she had seen on the street before? Did he secretly know about her eyes, and that's the reason he contacted her? What do they do down there? What does it look like at night, and during their day? She closed her eyes and saw a pale man with dark brown hair, she closed her eyes and saw a pale man with curly blonde hair, she closed her eyes and saw the wrinkles of his hands, the curves of his lips. She closed her eyes and smelled his perspiration, smelled his breakfast, smelled his desire for something more. When she opened them, surrounded by the darkness of the night, she could almost feel him moving underneath her. She imagined him going through his day, doing everything in his life while she was asleep. She had to figure out a way to write back.

The first, and most difficult, hurdle to jump would be to find something to write with. Most of those supplies had been banned since she was little. She could use the back of P's letter to respond but had no idea how she was going to get a pen. The last time she had ever seen either was in their neighbor's, the Davidsons, apartment, and that must have been at least ten years ago. The only reason they even had either, and really the only reason Micah even knew what a pen was and what it did, was because before the complete insertion of the INSAVs Mrs. Davidson used to be a pen artist as well as a digital one. She designed almost all the advertisements for the trash collector's guild and was able to keep a few pens and a pad of paper as memorabilia to be displayed in her home. Micah had a vivid recollection of going over for dinner when she was about ten and stumbling upon the collection. As she fell asleep, she fell back into the memory.

Her family didn't visit other's apartments very often. It was hard finding time to socialize when both parents had demanding careers and both children were training for two of the most prestigious professions in the sector, not to mention that nobody could leave the apartment complex after dusk. But, every once in a while they would find a few hours here and there to share with others in their building. It was the first time they had gone over to the Davidsons', as neither parents shared any strong professional connection to them and Micah wasn't particularly fond of their daughter, Raziela. She was a strange girl, who lived up to neither of her parents' expectations and tested to become a simple secretary for one of the smallest bureaus, the lowest level of government employees. Micah would sometimes pass her in school, but they never said hello to one another. At lunch, as Micah was sitting with a gaggle of training segregationalists she would spot Raziela in the corner by herself, INSAV always open to her wrist drawer. At least she seemed to have gotten some talent from her mother.

That night the Davises had brought over a large pork roast to share. The two families had sat snuggly in the living room with one another, squished into two sloping black couches and a purple loveseat. They made casual small talk, nothing that particularly stood out. Micah did, however, remember Raziela's glares of hate that escaped through the black strands of hair that constantly blocked her eyes and corners of her mouth.

"Why don't you girls go and play?" she remembered Mrs. Davidson asking them as Gabe sat fiddling with a game on his INSAV made strictly for training trash collectors. "Raz, I bet she'd like to see your room."

"Can't," the girl immediately fired back. "You told me to clean it, but I didn't."

Mrs. Davidson forced a crooked smile onto her face.

"Oh, I see. Well, we can talk about that later. You two can play in our room until the living room is cleaned up."

Without waiting for Micah Raziela quickly slid out of her seat and scurried down the hall.

When Micah arrived at the frame of the door, Raziela had already set up shop on her parents' bed playing with two dolls by herself. Micah walked to the foot of it and stared at the strange girl, wondering why one doll appeared to be hanging in the air and the other strangled by her own hair.

"Is it ok if I play?" she asked, placing her hands on the bed to lift her body onto it.

"No," Raziela retorted, still looking at her dolls. "You wouldn't understand the story."

"Well, can I try? Tell me about it," Micah tried.

"I said no," Raziela glared again, moving further back on the bed. "Go play over there, near mommy and daddy's work stuff." She pointed to a small desk in the corner of the room that was underneath a tall, glass case.

Micah didn't fight the demand. She didn't want to be there anyways.

What she found against that wall was more interesting than any deranged tale that Raziela could have been concocting in the other corner. Micah stood on the chair underneath the desk to see everything in the glass case above it. On the left she saw a row of long, shiny black and silver sticks and on the right a pile of a thin, white frail something or other that had black lettering all over it in neat rows.

"What are these?" Micah asked Raziela, who was busy squeaking the climax of her story to herself and dropping one doll to the floor in a giant crash. She didn't seem to hear her.

"Raziela, I asked what are these?" Micah said louder, almost falling off the chair as she leaned forward to emphasize her speech.

Raziela looked up for just a second to see what her neighbor was talking about.

"Oh, those things? They're my mom's old pens. You never seen one before?"

Micah shook her head no and Raziela rolled her eyes in discontent.

"Well that's stupid. They're pretty important. It's how old people used to record stuff, before we had this thing," she said, throwing her INSAV up in the air.

Realizing that she had something over her neighbor, Raziela dropped her dolls and proudly stood up on the bed.

"You wanna touch one?"

Micah's eyes widened.

"Won't we get in trouble?"

"Trouble shmoble, they'll never know. And what are you, a scaredy cat?"

Micah was, but would never admit that to this girl. She again shook her head no.

"Good," Raziela said as she hopped off the bed, ran across the room, and burrowed under the desk below the chair Micah still stood on. "Mommy doesn't know that I know where the key to the case is."

Micah heard a pop and Raz re-emerged with a stout golden object. "They're too scared to put the code into the INSAVs so they use this old thing. It's called a key."

"Woah," Micah responded, leaning closer to look at it. "What does it do?"

Raz hopped onto the desk and gave Micah a deadpan stare.

"It opens things, duh. Geez, you'd think you live underground or something."

She reached up and pushed the object into the side of the case. It turned and Micah heard another small pop. Raz looked around before sliding the case slightly open.

"There," she proudly stated. "Reach in and touch it."

"I don't know... will it hurt?"

"Will it hurt? Are you stupid? It's a pen. You use it to make shapes on that thing over there," she said, pointing to the white pile on the other side of the case. "I think it's called baper. No, no. Paper."

Micah couldn't believe her eyes, but was too scared to ask questions. She simply reached in, poked at the smooth, cool object in front of her, and then immediately retracted her hand. They heard a voice from the other room.

"Micah, honey, I think we're going to head out."

Micah jumped from the desk and onto the bed while Raziela twisted back the lock and hid the key. When Micah's parents came in to get her they were both quietly playing with the dolls on the bed.

"What fun you guys are having! We'll have to come back again soon so you two can play."

WWhen Micah's alarm went off at exactly 6:44 she was wide-awake but unwilling to get up. Slivers of a rising sun began to illuminate the room, gluing her eyes to the section of the wall where she had found the note the night before. But, there was nothing. She lay there until she heard footsteps outside. To avoid suspicion from her mother, she slowly rose and placed her blanket back onto her bed. But, instead of continuing her normal morning process, she sat on its edge waiting for something to emerge from the cracks. She sat until her mother called her for breakfast, telling her she'd be late if she waited any longer. She quickly placed her uniform onto her body, looking at the space between the wall and the floor as often as she could. When she left her room, though, there was nothing.

Breakfast was quiet. Nothing said between Gabe, Micah, and their father could be said in front of their mother, creating a noticeable tension around the table. Their mother didn't seem to notice and sat, as she always did, with a cup of coffee in one hand and INSAV projecting from the other. Micah and Gabe didn't bicker. After everything was eaten, Micah and her father rose to leave. After closing the door to the apartment, Mr. Davis walked three feet in front of his daughter. When they passed the Davidsons on their way out, Micah quickly stopped and said hello. The couple was immediately taken aback. Although the families had been associated for decades, neither had officially acknowledged the other's existence for quite some time.

"Good morning to you too," Mrs. Davidson practically exclaimed, buttoning the last button on her shirt as she walked out the door. "I hope you all are doing very well."

Micah nodded, smiled, and continued following her father, who had failed to stop and greet his neighbors.

He looked back at her only when they parted in the street next to a talk show advertisement.

"I'm sorry," Micah tried to say as her turned away from her.

Renee tapped Micah on the shoulder a few hundred yards away from the school.

"You'll never guess what I found out about those guys last night," her friend squealed with twinkling eyes.

Micah tried to smile, but couldn't seem to part her lips.

"What?"

"They're the new segregationalists of the trash program! I told you going to the club would pay off. I hear they'll be there tonight, too. My guy from last night told me to come, asked me to wear a little more makeup this time. You should really consider telling your parents now, how can they be mad about you landing an official like that! And an immigrant, too! When I told my mother she nearly fainted."

"Renee, my parents already know."

Renee grabbed Micah's arm and slowed their walk to a halt.

"What! You finally told them! Thank *God,* sneaking you around was getting really annoying. I told you everything would be fine. It *was* fine, right?"

"I didn't tell them. They found out. I guess your *guy* was talking about us in my dad's break room at the hospital. They didn't appreciate me lying to them," Micah glared at her friend.

"Hold on, you aren't blaming me for this. Are you? I told you to tell them ages ago! This is in not my fault. Jesus, take credit for your own actions for once."

"I would if they were my actions, but you practically begged me to go with you every week!" Although Micah was just loudly whispering to her friend, the silence around them created the illusion of a scream. "Good friends don't make people do shitty things! I hope you have a great time with your 'guy', but I'm done."

At this, Micah's legs carried her in a run into the thick double doors of the school. She burst into her classroom and threw her bag onto the desk. She didn't cry, there had been enough of that the night before. Where there should have been sobs she released burning breaths of frustration. She could feel the eyes of the other students in the classroom piercing her neck, but she refused to look around. She buried her head into her bag.

It was all Renee's fault. She would have never done any of this unless Renee had forced her to. Yes, she enjoyed it at times. She had to admit that. But she never needed it, never found purpose in it. She made a mental note to tell this to her father after school and looked up to the board where the morning assignment was artfully scribbled across the electronic surface.

Regular text, pages 123-30

THE SEXUALITY AND FAMILY REARING OF A
NIGHTCRAWLER

By: Ian Dale

As one may have guessed, the sexual habits of the Nightcrawlers are much different than our own. The male Nightcrawler has been known to be completely promiscuous, it is not uncommon for a man to have many children with many different women. The women, however, are not much different.

The underground lifestyle is not one that promotes a nuclear family. Children are many times not raised with their parents, but form living groups without any adult supervision. Whether this is due to inadequate parenting or rebellious personalities has not been determined, but it is safe to assume that both traits are at least somewhat factors. These "child gangs" can range from just a few children (3-5) to hundreds in number. These children have children of their own when they are very young. Births have been known to occur as early as the age of eleven. Because of this, the underground is slowly becoming a land reminiscent of old-time slums. Hundreds of thousands of people linger around their streets and decrepit buildings, living there without paying rent or taxes. The underground government is not strong enough to fight this and unfortunately must succumb to the pressures of their sheer numbers. Very often there are reports of deadly turf wars between these child gangs, but there is currently no way to stop or even reduce them. Fortunately, these groups have not begun breaking in to other's homes or attempting to take them over, but such acts as these would not be surprising.

Those that are lucky enough to remain a nuclear family do so in the loosest definition of the word. To my knowledge, there are very few families that remain as a "one man, one woman with children" unit. As said before, many of the men have children with many women. Therefore, these families may consist of children living together with many different maternities, or children living in a house with many different wives. Their marriages are not identified under the court of law. Since one man is not legally bound to one woman, it is common for him to practice what we may consider infidelity or polygamy.

Micah looked up from her pages. None of this matched what the man below her floor had written. Although he said to have had one son with another woman, he was married to the one that birthed the other two. They have lived together for years, and all their family, even grandparents, live together. She flipped through the historytext to see if there was any author information on the back.

Ian Dale has written over 20 educational historytexts on cultures and above/below ground relations. He resides in Sector 26 with his wife and two children.

Well, that told her absolutely nothing. What credibility did he have for this information, anyways? His biography didn't say at all how he acquired the facts that were supposed to make up her education.

She raised her hand and stared the professor straight in the face.

"Professor Domney, who's Ian Dale?"

Without diverting her glance from the projection in front of her, the professor slowly raised her head.

"He wrote our historytext, Micah. You can see that on the cover."

"Well, yeah. Of course. I know that. But, where did he come from and how does he know so much? It seems like it's pretty classified information."

"That doesn't matter. What matters is that you get this reading done in the next five minutes."

It was at that moment she fully realized there was no choice. If they were still there, propped in a neat line inside a glass case, she was going to steal one of those pens.

It was the first day in almost a year that Micah had walked home by herself straight after school. Even if it was a day where she was not expected at The Red Knob, Renee would accompany and drop her off before continuing to her own building. After class had finished, she quickly deactivated the school function of her INSAV, grabbed her bag, and bolted from the classroom. She didn't want to give Renee an opportunity to confront her about the harsh words they had exchanged. Or, rather, the harsh words that Micah had thrown at her without opportunity for rebuttal.

It was strange, being encompassed by advertisements and nothing else. Every building was lit up on every corner and every wall, displaying everything from tips to be safe in the streets to a quick recipe for bread. When she had walked for about a minute the announcer's chipper face took over all the screens.

"Gooooood afternoon students! We hope you had a wonderful day today, and that you learned something that you can share with your entire family at dinner tonight! Remember to be careful walking home, sightings of Nightcrawlers are becoming more and more frequent. We wouldn't want you to get caught near one of them and pulled down into the underground. Remember, we're doing all we can to protect you, but you have to help us out. If you see anything, report it! Let's keep Sector 15 safe. Have a wonderful night!"

His smile took over the sector once more before the screens were again replaced with advertisements.

"I don't know if getting pulled underground would really be the worst thing anymore," Micah thought to herself as she envisioned the world P had described to her in his letters.

She had to get that pen.

Her hand, curled into a tight fist, floated in front of the Davidson's front door. There was no way Mr. and Mrs. Davidson would be back from work yet, if anyone was about to answer it would be Raziela. All Micah knew of her now was what she saw in the hallway. Although Raziela got taller, the rest of her body had gotten disproportionately larger. While she now sat with a few other girls at lunch instead of by herself, her hair still constantly hung loosely over her face and her clothing was never quite properly tucked in. Micah knew absolutely nothing about her other than what she could deduce from across the hallway. She just knew what she needed from her.

In a gust of confidence she strongly knocked on the door and waited, slightly untucking her own shirt and loosening some strands of hair from her bun. After about 20 seconds she knocked again quietly, positive that no one was home and she would have to try again tomorrow.

"What are you doing at my door?" She heard a voice from behind her ask. She turned and saw Raziela standing behind her, looking more disheveled than she did in the school hallway. Her yellow shirt was completely untucked from her forest green pants, which Micah noticed had a small red stain right above the knee.

"Oh, hi Raziela. I was just checking if you were home."

Raziela looked confused.

"Uhuh," she responded in disbelief. "What do you need? Flour? Milk? No one else down the hall had any of those?"

"No, I... I was just wondering what you were up to. I realized we hadn't seen each other in a while."

Raziela looked even more confused than before. She shoved past Micah and placed her INSAV in front of the scanner to her apartment.

"We see each other every day. We just don't talk to each other."

"I know, I realized that. I don't know, we're about to graduate and I thought it might be nice to hang out before we do."

Raziela's expression changed from confusion to disbelief. She looked Micah up and down, sizing up the white shirt and red pants that contrasted so harshly to her own uniform, and let out a laugh.

"Ok, whatever. Come inside and you can chill for a few minutes. I'll make you tea or something." She pushed open her door and stepped inside, carelessly throwing her bag to the right and tossing her shoes in front of her. Micah quietly followed.

Their apartment looked exactly as it had ten years earlier. Same worn carpet, same black and purple couches in the exact same place, and same daughter who had already sat down at the same coffee table. The only difference was that this daughter was now reaching into her pocket to grab a pack of cigarettes and fiddling with a matchbook that had been left on the table.

"I didn't think you could smoke in these buildings," Micah started, walking towards her and sitting down on the opposite end of the same couch.

"You can't," she said, placing a stick to her lips and a long, thin flame to the other end. "But I do."

Micah nervously laughed.

"Ha, yeah. I think my mom does too."

Raziela peered up at her and took the cigarette from her lips, releasing a long gust of smoke that quickly hit the top of the table and danced away.

"You want one?" She asked, extending the pack towards her neighbor.

"Oh, no. No, I'm fine."

"Take one," Raziela demanded, refusing to retreat her offer. "Everyone knows you do worse things with your days than smoke a cigarette."

"Like what?" Micah questioned, pulling the stick from its case and grabbing the matches. She knew what Raziela was alluding to, but had to remain friendly if she was going to get what she wanted.

Raziela rolled her eyes and lit the match for Micah, who was fumbling to push the red tip against the rough brown side.

"You higher govs think The Red Knob is such a secret, don't you? Can't believe they didn't teach you how to use a match there."

Micah couldn't tell if Raziela's reaction was out of anger or jealously. The Red Knob was an exclusive club for only the highest esteemed workers. Raziela would never have been able to go there even if she wanted to. She knew that it wasn't really that big of a secret, but didn't realize that even people she hadn't talked to in ten years knew about her activities within it. Maybe she had kept it a secret from her family for a lot longer than from the rest of her school.

"Yeah," Micah laughed, trying to control her budding anger. "Guys love that, you think they would have."

Raziela laughed, actually laughed without a twinge of judgment or bigotry.

"What's it like in there, anyways? I've always wondered how the inside of a whorehouse would look."

"It's not..." Micah began, the rising anger raising her voice. She stopped, though, and remembered why she was there.

"...it's not really that special. Probably exactly what you'd imagine."

"Good to know, because what I imagine is pretty fucked up."

Micah was becoming frustrated. She knew what she did inside its walls weren't moral, but it had been her only true form of joy for over a year. She didn't like that Raziela was placing judgment onto a place she had never been to and probably would never go.

"It's not just about sex, you know," Micah reasoned. "It's about finding people to spend time with and sharing something personal with them."

Raziela stood up and chuckled.

"Is that what the bartenders tell you when you're ordering those nice cocktails?"

Micah blushed. It was.

"It's true though."

"Uhuh. What kind of tea do you want? Black or green?"

"It doesn't matter."

"Black it is," Raziela decided as she headed into the kitchen. Through the swinging door Micah heard Raziela fill the pot up with water, set it on the stove, and light the burner.

As Micah sat by herself she panicked. It didn't seem like Raziela was enjoying her presence and would probably kick her out soon. She had limited time to get what she needed and limited ways to do it. She thought of how she could get away from the living room and into Raziela's parents' room.

Half of Raziela's body popped out from behind the door and Micah quickly glanced up to her with a forced smile.

"Speaking of sex," Raziela began, still halfway in the door. "My boyfriend's going to come over soon, before my parents get home in about an hour. I promised him I'd make him some food, so I'm just going to be in here cooking for a while. I'll bring you your tea in a few minutes. After you're done, though, would you be alright leaving me to finish? I don't know if he'd be ok with you being here."

"Oh," Micah said, unaware that Raziela even knew exactly what sex was, not to mention that someone like her had a boyfriend. "Do you want me to help you cook?"

"No, no. You can just stay there. I'll be out in a few. You can watch the wall projection, if you want. Come here so I can give you the code."

This was going to be her chance.

Micah walked up to Raziela and pushed her INSAV against her own so that the projection controls could be transferred.

"Let me know if you smell anything burning," she said as the door closed behind her.

There was no time to think about what this meant. There was no time to reconsider. This was it.

Micah quickly turned on the projection, checked the kitchen door once more to make sure it was closed, and tip toed to the end of the hallway. As quietly as could be, she slid open the door to Raziela's parents' room and bolted to the far corner. It was the moment of truth. She looked up at the glass case.

Ten years later, in the exact same spot, the pens were still there. Still in a neat little row, black and silver metal staring up at her. Asking her to take one. Now she just had to check for the key.

She bent onto her knees, grasping underneath the desk for the false bottom. She found the grooves, popped it open, and felt the thick metal against her fingers. She had done it.

She pushed the key into the metal hole, turned it, slid the glass open, and pulled out a pen.

It was so light. Lighter than Micah had ever imagined. She dropped it into her bra and closed its container.

She put everything back into its place and ran back down the hall. When she reached the living room Raziela was reemerging from the kitchen, two steaming mugs in her hands.

"Where'd you go?" She inquired.

Bathroom," Micah immediately replied. Her father was right about something-- once a liar, always a liar.

Raziela shrugged, and the two girls sat in the living room smoking cigarettes and drinking their tea.

SShe didn't know how to place the pen in between her fingers, didn't know which end made the marks and which would just make indents on the page. She tried placing it in a fisted hand and pressing down as hard as she could, but the page ripped under the pressure of her failing efforts and she gasped in frustration and horror. How was she going to communicate with the underground if she couldn't even use the one device that would make it possible? She smoothed the rip and tried holding the pen, other side down, with fewer fingers. This time she balanced it between her thumb, index, and middle fingers. Finally, small black lines began to appear on the yellowing sheet. She moved the pen up to the corner of the letter and made short lines, checking to see if she could even hold the pen steady at all. She was impressed with herself, the lines she made travelled parallel to the top of the page and only had slight bumps. She brought the utensil back down to where the writing of P's letter stopped and gingerly, hesitantly, began her own.

P.,

I have been sitting in my room on the floor for the past hour trying to decide what to say to you, or if I should say anything at all. But, like you, I don't think I can go on not knowing what makes up the ground beneath my feet. So, here's a little bit about me.

I am an 18-year-old girl who has lived in this apartment my whole life. I live here with my parents and older brother. My father is a doctor and my mother works for the government. I like to listen to Rodriguez in my room on Saturdays and dance by flailing my arms around while I move my feet. I don't know if there is any way for you to listen to my music, but maybe someday I'll try to play it extra loudly so you can dance, too. What do you listen to music on, anyways? We have small devices attached to our wrists that can store millions of songs. They're called INSAVs. Have you ever seen one of these?

The sweetness you smell is probably from my mother's fruit pies and tarts. She loves to cook them as often as she can, but there aren't as many handovers as there used to be. As you probably know, apples are grown on our land, but that's the only fruit. Does your family not get to eat fruit, then, is it a smell you don't recognize? What do you eat? And when?

Are most people in the underground raised their whole life to be one career? Or, do most people get to pick? Can you tell me more about your childhood? What do your schools look like, and what do they teach there?

Thanks,

M.

Micah's hand was shaking as she put down the pen. She folded her note six times, making sure to press the creases with the back of her thumbs on each fold. She stared at the square of paper resting in the palm of her hand. It looked like a miniature present, but a present for her or P. she didn't know. She took a deep breath, scooted her body towards the wall, and stared at the vent below her window. For 18 years she had felt alone, isolated in this room, but for 18 years there had been someone just a few feet below. Hands still shaking, she pushed the frail pile into the top slot and watched as it fell down the aluminum frame. Even after it disappeared she kept looking, expecting a pair of eyes to emerge from the depths. After five minutes, nothing happened. Micah stood up, took the comforter from her bed, and laid it on the ground. She undressed and slipped her naked body between the sheet and the wooden boards. There she laid, ear to the floor, and listened for a sign from below.

M.,

Yes, please play your music very loudly one night. I will try to wake up early and hear it. Hopefully you can play it loud enough, as I do not have anything underground that could do the same. I don't know of these music players that hold many songs. All of the technology we have originally came from your people and, frankly, many times it does not work as it should. We buy all our goods at what we call "Second Light" stores. After most purchases I have to give whatever I have acquired to my oldest son, who is training to become a technology repairman. He is absolutely wonderful with tools and I am thankful every day to have him. Last week I brought home a television that not only would not turn on, but also had a large crack in the screen. He fixed everything in two days and now my family can watch all of the movies your people don't need anymore. Which reminds me, do you know if the actor Daniel Dranov is as funny in real life as he is on screen?

Fruit pies, you say? I cannot say I have heard of them. The only pies we make are called "root pies" and have beets, sweet potatoes, onions, and sun chokes with spices like cinnamon, graham masala, and a little bit of brown sugar that we must conserve. I will place my wife's recipe at the end of this letter in case you would like to attempt to make one.

Yes, most people have a single profession for most of their lives. However, most can choose. I was not one of those, but only because of a family obligation. It is common for the oldest son to take over the position of his father, but not a requirement. I am in no way offended that my oldest, Silas, does not want to follow in my footsteps. If I was in his position I would not want to either. I have always wondered what it would be like to act in a movie.

This fascination probably began in my childhood. Although my father worked an awful job and did not make much money, so did the fathers of many of my classmates. My mother loved my sisters and I more than anything, and continues to do so to this day.

I am the youngest of 5, but the only son. All my sisters were born much before me, at least 7 years. My parents just kept trying until they had me and consequentially were given a few too many mouths to feed. Because of this, my mother became a great cook. The recipe I have given you is one she has passed down to my wife and was always one of my favorites.

As I have said before, we lived, and continue to live, in a small apartment on the top floor of our building. We are one of the lucky ones. A small part of our sector looks like what I would imagine your own to look like, there are streets surrounded by buildings that all rise five stories. Where I have been told is your sky for us there are instead long sheets of metal and concrete that make a net around the buildings which disappear above. We cannot see the roofs of any of our buildings, they instead just seem to continue to your world. I wonder if we are living in identical cities, just one on top of the other. If this is true, I hope yours is much more beautiful than mine.

Although our buildings extend five stories above our streets, they continue to grow up to 30 stories underneath them. I say I am lucky because I live on the fifth floor and our apartment has one small window that looks onto another building. Many do not have even this. How tall are your buildings?

My school was in the 10-15 sublevels of a building a short walking distance from my own. Depending on what grade I was in I would slowly sink deeper and deeper into the earth until given a degree at the age of 18. I think we learn subjects similar to yours-- math, science, reading, and history. Do you learn about us like we learn about you? I doubt it. In school I was taught by my teachers that your people are kind hearted and sacrificial, yet by my peers I was taught that you are more evil than the devil himself. Many down here are not fond of your people, and the opinions are becoming more and more negative every year as less and less of our people come back at night.

We do not understand this and are extremely saddened by it. I have friends who secured passes for their sons and daughters to gather food from the aboveground because they are desperate for anything, but many times these children are never seen again. Do you know what happens to them?

Anyways, here is what was once my mother's, and now my wife's, recipe.

Root Pie

1 Sweet Potato

1 onion

1 beet

a small handful of sun chokes

1 tbs cinnamon

1 tbs graham masala

1 tbs sugar

oil

Crust

2 cups of flour

1 stick of butter, room temperature

1 egg

Egg white (optional)

Sprinkling of cinnamon sugar (optional)

Preheat oven to 350 degrees F

Dice sweet potato, onion, beet, and sun chokes into medium sized pieces. Set aside.

Place spices in oil and heat on a skillet until oil begins to pop. At this point, place diced vegetables into hot pan and toss in oil. Allow to sauté for 10-12 minutes.

While vegetables are sautéing, prepare crust. Beat butter and flour together until a semi-smooth consistency is formed. Beat in the egg. On well-floured surface, smooth dough until it forms two flat spheres, equal size. Place one sphere in a pie tin.

Take sautéed vegetables, which should be semi soft without completely losing their crunch, into the pie tin. Place second sphere over vegetables and pinch around the edges.

If desired, brush with an egg white and sprinkle with cinnamon sugar. Place in oven for 30-45 minutes.

Enjoy!

P.

P.,

I would love to make your mother's recipe, but do not know where I would get many of these ingredients. Just as you have not heard of fruit (which is amazing to me!) I have not heard of beets and sun chokes, but maybe our grocer is hiding them somewhere in her store. Next time I am asked to get the food for my family I will make sure to search for these items. Based on what you have told me about the pie, though, I will have to make sure to try it someday. Although this may be no use to you, I will write up one of my mother's recipe at the end of this letter so that one day maybe you, too, will be able to taste what I taste.

It is absolutely amazing to me that we can live so close to each other yet not even share something as simple as food. I will have to try and ask my family or a teacher when exactly this started.

Speaking of which, it sounds like our school systems have some similarities but, when it comes down to it, show that we come from different worlds. Each sector (the 1/2 mile long block where we live) has a single school that holds all students. Our school is on the first 10 floors of a 45-story building, but as you get older your classes are on higher and higher floors. From a very early age we are given a profession and are trained until we reach the age of 18. I can't even imagine being able to decide for myself. If I could, I don't know what I would choose to be. I guess I have never thought about it before. I have always imagined escaping, but never knew what I would escape to.

Because of this law, I am training to be a doctor and following after my father.

She couldn't tell him the truth. She couldn't stand the truth.

After this year is over I will begin shadowing him and performing minor things, like bandaging and stitches. In a few years they will determine what section of medicine I am fit for. My father is a surgeon and maybe someday I will be, too. Who are the doctors in your sector? I wonder if we have the same medical practices, it doesn't really seem like we share much else.

But, I do wonder if our buildings share the same structure. Is there any way you could send me a diagram of your sector? I wonder if our schools, hospitals, and stores are in the same places.

Or, here is an easier way. When you walk out of your building, is there a bank directly across the street like there is for me? Everything my family ever buys is recorded on a small device attached to our arm that we also use for identification. In order to enter or exit any building we have to swipe it and all of the data is sent over to the bank across the street. Actually, all the data from the entire sector goes to this building. But, our INSAV also acts as a bankcard, among countless other things. I have a few friends who are studying to be bankers and are constantly telling me of all the information they can find out once they graduate. Of course, they technically aren't allowed to use any if it, but every once in a while I guess it doesn't hurt to break the rules.

The bank takes up 13 floors of a 43-story building. In my sector the buildings are not extremely tall, but continue to grow each year to fit our growing population. When I was younger the tallest building around me was about 35 stories, while today it is 50. Any windows above the 30th floor are darkened so we can't see what goes on in other sectors. Our government argues this is to improve work ethic and productivity on these floors, but no one's really sure.

You may think that my section of the sector we both live in is more beautiful than yours, but I doubt it. Although there are a few days each year where the sky is extremely blue and has beautiful fluffy clouds, most of the time it is probably as grey as the concrete above your head.

My grandmother told me back in her day this was not the case. She says when she was younger there was still one small park left in the sector and she and her parents would often have picnics on it. She has explained picnics to me as something families did when they wanted to eat and spend time outside. Why anyone would want to do this is beyond me, ever since I can remember the air outside has been grimy and almost as grey as the sky. But, she promised me things were not always this way. She said she was about 15 when the last park was finally converted into a skyscraper. Do you have any open areas underground? The closest we can come to this now is with our rooftop gardens. Because there isn't really enough room on the ground, most buildings under 30 stories try to grow vegetables on their roofs and a few have benches were you can sit and relax. Sometimes I will go to the top of my building and read, but this is only on those few days when the sky is actually blue. Well… I try to read but usually get distracted by the shapes above my head. If I'm lucky enough to be the only one on my roof I'll lay down on the bench and stare up at the sky, trying to make shapes out of the clouds above me.

Oh! I just realized you probably don't know what clouds are!

I don't really either. They are just white blobs in the sky that are constantly moving. I've always wondered where they go. I always imagine being able to miraculously create a ladder tall enough to reach them and riding one out of the sector. I wonder what the world would look like from way up there. I'm sure some day soon, when the population of the world is too big for both our grounds, they'll figure out how people can live in the sky. I hope I can be one of them.

Here is my mother's recipe for an apple pie. I wish there was a way to send you ingredients along with this letter! If only my vent was bigger.

Apple Pie
1 ½ pounds apples
½ cup of cinnamon sugar
2 cups of flour
1 egg
¾ cup of oil
pinch of salt

Mix flour, egg, and oil together to make the crust. Roll flat between two sheets of plastic and drape over pie tin. Repeat to make a second crust that will go over the apples.
Slice apples in wedges, then cut the wedges in half. Mix with cinnamon sugar and place the combination into the piecrust. Place second crust over the mixture and press the edges of the top crust into the bottom crust with a fork.
Sprinkle remaining cinnamon sugar over the top of the pie. Cut three small slits in the top for air to escape while baking.
Preheat oven to 350 degrees. Place pie into oven and bake for approximately 30-40 minutes.

THE LAYOUT OF THE UNDERGROUND

By: Ian Dale

The architectural layout of the world beneath us is extremely different from the one we live in above ground. There is no rhyme or reason to the layout of their land. When the underground was first created, the architects and engineers of the area spent many years trying to determine the most effective placement for many of their buildings. Everything was taken into consideration, from predicted population growth to airflow. As it is said in the beginning of this text, when this underground was formed it was considered an engineering masterpiece.

When the designers of the underground, Karen Daniels and Keith Loveland, began their blueprints, they first planned to create something that looked much like our own community. Each sector had a planned "city block" in which all government and financial buildings were erected and surrounded by residences, department stores, grocers, and other locations necessary for a successful community. Daniels and Loveland are quoted with feeling initially "ecstatic about the program. It was their chance to create something that is as lasting as time itself." They felt they were creating a "Rome that would never fall, a Cairo that would never disintegrate, and a New York that could never crumble. " This project was intended by both to be the capstones of their careers and place them eternally in high esteem.

When the underground was finally completed, after ten years, it was exactly this. The first step these revolutionary minds enacted when beginning the project was to extend and strengthen the foundations of all existing buildings. Since the ground around them was to be excavated to create street like tunnels for the new tenants, each foundation had to be strengthened and many times completely remolded, replacing fraying concrete with thick bands of steel. After this point the foundations were extended up to five stories further. After each building was extended, creation of the tunnels commenced. A large, circular machine slowly cut through the hard rock that makes up the upper layers of our earth. A skilled team of workers followed this machine, chipping away at the excess rock with anything from a chisel to dynamite until it exposed the newly constructed extended foundations of each building. This was a very delicate process and took the most time out of all steps, approximately six years. Once the tunnels were created they, too, were strengthened with bands of steel. The roofs of the walkways were meticulously painted to look like the most vivid of skies. These paintings still exist today and are considered by many to be more beautiful than the real sky we lay our eyes on every day.

After the tunnels were completed and perfected the lighter races were slowly repositioned into the underground. They were, of course, allowed to bring all their belongings and many were given similar jobs to what they held above ground. Each family was given their own spacious apartment and offered such amenities as free public schooling, fresh foods, and free, secure banking.

Here is a statement from one of the first residents of the underground, Sandra O'Connell. She was a 35-year-old Asian female with three children when relocated.

"My family and I absolutely love it here. Not only are we now completely protected from the harmful rays of the sun, but we are given more opportunity to thrive here in many other ways that I would have never thought possible. We were given an extremely beautiful, completely furnished apartment that is a mere 7 minutes walk from the school! I was able to re-open my women's clothing store in virtually the same place as it was above ground, just a few feet below! My kids are doing wonderfully in school and my youngest son has even joined the soccer team. Moving to the underground was the best thing that ever happened to us."

This was, as well, the response from many other families that were relocated. After relocation had been completed, a survey was administered to the UG residents and the new community received a 95% satisfaction rating in almost all categories. This is most likely due to the pristine layout and design of the area, as well as the exceptional programs that were put into place. Approximately 65 years after its creation, the Aboveground board decided that the UG could handle everything on their own and released all control of the community by selecting certain members of the UG to take their place.

This, however, is where the underground started to go awry. The new board, which was now made entirely of UG community members, almost immediately lost control. Within weeks of their election there was a violent uprising in which many were killed, including women and children. The violence was completely inescapable. We now consider this to be the UG Civil War. A revolutionary leader was put into place and it is currently his successors that control the ground beneath us. Under their rule unemployment has increased twofold. There is virtually no police force and I have been told that many community members live every day in fear of their life. No new building has taken place and the community that was so meticulously created by Daniels and Loveland is now overcrowded, dirty, and dilapidating. Residents have been forced to begin digging primitive tunnels underneath their buildings to find places to stay.

We are doing them a great favor by continuing to employ their people on our own lands. Without us, their economy would completely collapse. It is quite devastating that a community with such potential now relies so heavily on their creators.

When Micah finished reading the passage, she looked up at her teacher's directions on the board.

When finished reading, please come and see me so I can give you a number. This number will correspond with your assigned group. Once everyone is done reading, you will split up into these groups and complete an activity with one another.

Micah quietly closed her text and burrowed her head into her folded arms. Since she began writing letters to P. nothing she was taught in school seemed to make any sense. Her historytext was leading her in one direction and the letters were pushing her in another. It was as if they each had a grip on one arm and kept pulling her back and forth. One day she would be pulled to the right, the next a little to the left. She no longer had a center, or if she did it was continually shifting. Nothing that she learned in school matched up with what she was told in her letters. But, before a few weeks ago, school had been her life. The texts and movies she was assigned to read and watch were her only connection to a world bigger than her own. Through Ian Dale, as dry as he may be, she was able to, maybe just for a second, escape the borders of Sector 15 and travel to a place she could only imagine.

But now the world she had created within her head was

changing. She had always envisioned the UG to be exactly what her text told her. It was cold, dark, damp. Downtrodden. Dangerous. Deadly. And, according to Dale, it as all their own fault. But now, her visions of anarchy were being transformed into dreams of democracy. The world of ignorance and danger she had spent years piecing together in her head was being bombarded with new information that didn't match up. Her historytext told her that the underground had no order, yet P stated that their structure was as solid as the ground itself. Ian Dale wrote that the underground didn't know what family was, yet the mysterious man beneath her feet seemed to care more about her family than anyone else she knew. Who was she to believe?

Everyone in her 20-person class quickly finished. She was brought to a table with three other classmates-- a short, stout girl with braided ponytails whose red pants bunched a little too tightly around her waist, a tall, skinny boy with thick glasses and a voice that neither raised nor lowered, and another boy, slightly taller than the girl but much shorter than the first classmate, who could never seem to keep his shirt tucked and moved as if he was always about to get up and jump around. His legs constantly shook as his feet tapped the floor in a perpetually unmelodic rhythm. He always looked as if he was somewhere else, playing a song in his head that was more important than anything that could possibly be found in front of him. Jane, Cedric, and Tom.

All the students in the class knew each other very well but would never address each other comfortably. Something about the building they were in and the uniform they were forced to wear made even the most casual chats a little bit formal. There was always the worry that someone might pop up behind you after lurking in the back of the classroom searching for disobedience during a conversation. A girl that was in Micah's class, as well as everyone else's, was once joking with another student while completing an assignment about how she wouldn't mind being a Nightcrawler for a few days. She could take a little break from school, sleep all day, and not have her parents nagging her about taking out the trash because she would constantly be surrounded by it. Micah was leaving the classroom right behind them, they mustn't have been speaking much louder than to be able to hear one another, yet the girl was gone the next day and didn't come back for two weeks. When she re-emerged into the classroom she barely spoke at all and continues not to. Micah scanned the room to find her. She was in a group near the far left corner, siting with wide eyes and pursed lips. She always looked like she was waiting for someone to come back and take her away.

Tom flung his chair back before thrusting his bottom down into it and jamming his feet against the rim of the table. His hands took over the movement that his feet could no longer accomplish and he alternately tapped his fingers against the top of his cloth pants. Everyone else was already sitting down with historytexts projected and flipped open to the reading.

"Alright everyone, please settle down," their teacher demanded to the already silent classroom. "On your table you'll find some questions that may stimulate conversation. The point of this exercise is to practice how you may one day conduct a meeting with other members of your segregation departments. There are many issues that we need to confront and a lot that needs to be changed, as many of you may already know from your parents. Many of these issues are written down on the piece of paper in front of you. By the end of this exercise I expect your group to write down two possible solutions to each problem. Don't worry, they don't have to be perfect, but do know I may be sending a few of your suggestions down to the government house," she said with a smile. "Ok everyone, you have 45 minutes. I'll be walking around and listening in on some of your discussions. Begin."

With this, Tom pushed his feet to the ground and swiped the instructional sheet from the center of the table. He looked at each of his group members with a sly smile and began reading.

"Number one. As you have read, the UG is currently falling apart. Their self-elected leader is destroying any infrastructure we've put into place. Is it worth the risk to go back under and help them, or should we let it disintegrate? Why or why not."

He put the paper down. "Anyone have any ideas?"

Jane, who always had a suggestion for everything, immediately sat up a little taller in her seat and folded her hands over one another.

"We should absolutely not waste our resources, which are already scarce enough. They are the reason they're going hungry, they're the reason they have no government. If the UG community had just abided by the laws we put into place they would be a thriving society right now that could contribute to the good of us all. I think we should let them be until they're desperate enough to come to us."

"What about when they do beg?" Cedric asked without inflection. He always spoke as if emotion was something that made his already frail demeanor weaker.

"Give them minimal supplies. Make them sign a treaty that states our elected leaders will always be in power. We tried giving them responsibility, but they couldn't handle anything on their own. There are consequences to that."

She seemed very proud of her response. Micah had planned to sit in silence and observe during the meeting, but suddenly her mouth opened without any control of her mind.

"What would you say about minimal supplies, like food and water? Shouldn't everyone have a right to that?"

Jane twisted her head towards Micah and slightly rolled her eyes.

"There are consequences."

"So, our answer is no," Tom repeated from behind his screen. "And our reasons are…"

"It's a waste of resources," Jane replied.

"Ok. And…"

"…and they won't appreciate anything we do for them unless they are absolutely desperate for help. In order to retain their loyalty, and help them where they can't help themselves, we must wait."

"So ultimately our answer is yes, but not right now?"

"Yes, not for a while. Not until they beg for help."

Micah's hands formed into tight fists under the table.

"Why are we assuming they'll beg for help? You really don't think they might figure something out on their own, or be so proud that millions will die before we can give them enough for just a few to survive?"

"If they wait until almost everyone is dead before they ask for help, that's not our fault. And, really, it's economically better for us. It's less mouths to feed and less people to regulate once we get down there."

"Good point, Jane" Tom said, typing frantically. "Cedric, you agree?"

Cedric, arms crossed loosely on his chest, nodded his head yes.

"Alright, perfect. One down, four to go. Question number two- As you read a few days ago, the family structure of the underground is extremely skewed. Families, in their totality, no longer exist and have been replaced with complicated networks of large communities that don't have the capabilities to support one another. Work ethic, consequentially, has been drastically reduced. How should we fix this structure?"

"Now, this just completely amazes me." Jane proclaimed. "If they don't have a family, then what do they have? I mean, honestly. I think that is the definition of barbaric."

No, you're the definition of barbaric," Micah thought. She could feel her face flushing with anger but did everything she could to hold it back. P, whoever he is, not only had a family but seemed to care more about them than anything else. She wanted to jump across the table and throw her hands around Jane's throat.

Everything her classmate said now sounded so ignorant, even though Micah knew she was just repeating what she had been taught in her text. Jane had no idea she may be getting lied to about the underground, she didn't understand that she was creating solutions to "problems" that probably didn't exist. Jane was just acting like Micah had her entire life before a few weeks ago, yet even though she had no right to Micah still hated her for it. Jane was just being a good student who one day hoped to be a great Segregationalist. Every voice in Micah's head was telling her to challenge Jane, to take her down in one fatal swoop, but the even smaller voices that controlled those reminded her of the inevitable consequences. Micah would be barely through her first criticism of the text before their teacher, or an official hidden in the hallway, would grab her and whisk her away. At this point she was sure they would search her room and find the letters. In order to possibly change the thinking of another one of her classmates, Micah would ultimately be risking her life, her family's life, and the lives beneath her. She took a large breath and slowly unclenched her fists. For the rest of the activity she simply observed.

Question #1

As you have read, the UG is currently falling apart. Their self-elected leader is destroying any infrastructure we have put in place. Is it worth the risk to go back under and help them, or should we let it fall apart? Why or why not.

No, it is not worth the risk. By placing our citizens in their jurisdiction, we are exposing them to possibly lethal dangers. To protect their health, and to keep the streets above untainted, we should allow the underground society to digress until they ask for our help.

Question #2

As you read a few days ago, the family structure of the underground is extremely skewed. Families, in their totality, no longer exist and have been replaced with complicated networks of large communities that do not have the capabilities to support one another. Work ethic, consequentially, has been drastically reduced. How should we fix this structure?

Once the underground has almost completely destroyed itself and they have finally asked for our help to place themselves back together again, we will restructure the people and assigning "new families". These new families will be comprised of a man and woman over the age of 22 with 2-3 children assigned to them. We will assign these new families new homes.

Question #3
About three weeks ago, it was voted that requirements for the death penalty are to be lowered. Now, if a Nightcrawler is caught above ground without a pass during any time of the day or night, they are automatically sent to the courthouse and tried. Do you agree with this change in law? Why or why not?
Absolutely. The safety of our people is our first priority.

Question #4
Suggest two new laws that could be put into place to reduce Nightcrawling crime. These suggestions can be improvements on current laws or completely new ideas.
Law #1 Increase work hours of both men and women to reduce idle time. With less opportunity to come above, it will reduce the amount of Nightcrawling crime we are exposed to and provide extra income for the Nightcrawler's families.
Law #2 When one Nightcrawler is found above ground, we must punish not just them but other members of their family. Many times one family member is sent up by others, and when one member does not return they simply send up another the next day. To reduce this cycle we must give harsher punishments to not just what we find above ground, but the people who sent them up in the first place.

8

FFor weeks Micah was emotionless. Every time she began to think, really think, of everything she was told in school, by her friends, and by her family she was filled with a fit of rage. She began to notice a single trait that all of them seemed to possess without effort or remorse. Hate. They all hated every piece of the underground as if they had been there, as if they themselves had been below and witnessed the atrocities they all seemed to believe. Her eyes and ears were constantly filled with descriptions of how the underground was a society tearing itself apart, but the letters she received from P were tearing her heart and moral compass apart. She couldn't participate in class anymore; she no longer believed anything she was taught. But, she also couldn't stop doing her work. From an early age her path had been set in stone and, even though she hated it, unless a better plan was miraculously put into place it was the only path she would ever have. Unless she thought of an alternative she was going to be a segregationalist. There was no second option.

There was no changing her mind. Plan B only existed as a pill to take after a mistake at The Red Knob.

In order to get through her day she began to sit through class with her head in her palms, elbows dug into her desk. With her eyes she would trace her teacher's steps as she paced across the room, watching her mouth speak but not listening to a word that came out of it. She learned how to hear a word without actually picking up on its meaning. That way, when her teacher asked her what she had just said, Micah could respond with "raise their taxes" or "10,000 hangings a year" without having to accept what the words meant. She couldn't accept what the words meant. She refused.

When Micah got home from school, she would make herself a snack, do the minimal amount of work possible, and go straight to bed. There she would lay, covers up to her chin, until another family member got home. If it was Gabe, she would stay tucked in her room and tell him she was reading for class. He, especially, was becoming harder to face. She used to imagine what his day was like. She used to be proud of his job, his title, the stories he would share at the dinner table of sending yet another Nightcrawler to the government house. Now every time she imagined what he did she imagined him doing it to P and his family. She imagined P being captured by Gabe and forced to leave his loved ones with nothing. She imagined his friends. She imagined the children they would probably never see again, all because they dared to venture where she walks every day. She even stopped responding to Gabe's quips and insults. He would make fun of her and she would just give him a small, tight smile before bowing her head again. She no longer felt the burn of his words. She could see the fire they came from, and see it as it engulfed her body, but she would walk through uncharred. The fire was there, but it no longer possessed any heat.

Her mother didn't seem to notice this change in her daughter, as she was a woman who spent more time inside her own head than trying to communicate with anyone else's. As long as her daughter would respond with a quick "yes" or "it'll be done in five minutes" their relationship remained stable and content. Micah's father, however, was becoming increasingly concerned with his daughter's demeanor. When he arrived home from the hospital every day, most of the time after the rest of his family, he would immediately walk and find her, whether she was laying in bed, helping to make dinner, or quietly sitting in front of the television, and ask her how her day was. She would always initially respond with "fine" and he would always push further and ask for details. These details, however, usually remained about the same. "Had a tough quiz today", or "they ran out of juice during lunch" were common responses no matter what actually happened. Micah had learned the truth didn't matter as long as your lies were consistent and told the story everyone wanted to hear.

After a particularly quiet dinner Micah overheard a conversation between her parents as she washed dishes and bagged leftover pasta.

"I'm just starting to worry. It seems like she's shut herself off. I don't understand what happened- less than a month ago she was excelling at school and constantly moving around this house. Now it seems like she's just blank."

"Denzel, she's probably just going through a hard time. I remember when I was her age I was the same way. Hated everything, just wanted to leave it all behind. She's starting to realize what the rest of her life is going to be like. She's almost done with school. It's scary. I think she's just having a hard time dealing with reality."

"I think it's more than that. I mean.... She really seems... disconnected. And not just from us. Her teacher came into the hospital a few days ago and told me that Micah's been acting differently."

"Has she not been turning in assignments? Should we be checking to make sure she does all her work? It seems a little excessive to be hounding an 18 year old like that."

"No, no. That's not it at all. She does all her work. And, according to her teacher, she's actually doing it pretty well. All her essays are completely based on her readings. But, that's the thing. Remember when she was a little girl, and we couldn't get her to stop asking us 'why?'. Why this, why that, that girl took everything with a grain of salt. She's always been that way. She's always challenged us on everything. Remember when she was thirteen and I told her she couldn't have a boyfriend yet?"

"Ha, of course I remember. She wrote you a five-page letter on adolescent psychology, and how girls her age need the support of someone outside their family. She found facts to back up everything that she argued with you."

"Exactly, and after that letter, when I still disagreed with her and told her the answer was "still no because I said so", she ran away for three hours in the middle of the day. Do you remember where we found her?"

"In the back of Mrs. Dern's store. She said she was going to live in the fruit aisle for the rest of her life."

"It was then that I realized I could never tell her "because I said so" ever again. She never let anyone tell her because I said so. But it seems like, all of a sudden, she is. Haven't you noticed that?"

"I've noticed she's been quieter."

"But that's not the daughter we know. The daughter we know wouldn't do absolutely everything she's asked without question. I don't know what happened."

"Maybe it's about her friendship with Sasha. Ever since they had that falling out about, I can't quite remember what, she's been coming home straight after school every day. Gabe says when he gets home she's always in her room. Should we invite Sasha over, do you think, so they can talk out whatever it is they're angry at each other about?"

There was a long pause.

"No, no. I don't think that's it. You and I both know that Sasha wasn't the best influence. Rekindling that friendship would only make things worse."

"Well, then, we have to find her something to do. Maybe she feels like she isn't being challenged enough."

"You're right. Could she maybe start coming with you to work? Maybe seeing her future job will inspire her again."

"I would, but everything's really tight right now. They're not even letting anyone into my department who doesn't work there. We're in a major planning stage and... well... my department isn't letting anyone know about the plan until it's finished. But, how about yours? Can she come to the hospital after work?"

Suddenly her father's voice became very tense and, even though Micah couldn't see him through the wooden door, she could imagine him taking off his glasses to clean them and straightening his shirt as he spoke. "What? That's ridiculous. What use does she have for medical knowledge? You really can't get her into your building at all? It doesn't have to be your department."

"Not right now. Maybe in a few months but really Denzel, not right now. I can't exactly tell you why. But, what are you talking about! She doesn't have to be on the medical track to use medical knowledge. It's really useful for everyone to have. Are there any openings for volunteer nurses or secretaries?"

"I... well... you know the building could always use help."

"Perfect. Let me go get her."

"No, wait. I'll need to ask."

"Ask who? You're the head surgeon. If you say your daughter is going to come in as a volunteer nurse she's going to come in as a volunteer nurse."

"Fine. You can tell her to stop by after class tomorrow."

P.,
I haven't heard from you in a few days and am getting worried. Is everything ok? Send me anything you can so that I know the answer is yes.
M.
P.S.- starting work at my father's hospital tomorrow.

When Micah arrived at the Sector 15 hospital after school her father was waiting for her at the front door. He looked nervous for reasons Micah couldn't explain. Many of her classmates had shadowed their parents at work, some at this very hospital. She was sure her experience wouldn't be very different from theirs. Once through the doors Micah walked three paces behind her father as he led her around the building.

"The first floor is just for check in, as you can see behind these windows there are secretaries that take the name and number of each patient who comes in."

"Yes, Dad. I've been here before."

He stopped to face her and the pair stood still against the fluttering crowd.

"I know, but now you're going to work here. It's much different. I want to make sure you know absolutely everything."

He continued walking, this time at a faster pace.

"When someone walks in they're directed to a section of the waiting room based on their injury or ailment. Broken bones go to Section 1, coughs and flus to Section 2, stomach-based issues to Section 3, etc. This helps us to place the more serious cases first. Each patient is given a number within their waiting section and called accordingly. Once called up they are directed to a floor where a nurse is waiting for them. This will be your job. All you have to do is take the patient to their room number. Do you think you can do that?"

"Yeah, Dad. Somehow I think I'll be able to manage."

"This is serious, Micah. Not at all a joking matter. You'll most likely be assigned to a different floor every day. We try to mix things up as much as we can for certain staff members."

"How kind."

Mr. Davis acted as if he didn't hear her and walked to the window of Section 5, for sprains and minor stitching. "Let's run through this. When a patient gets their number called from Cindy... Hi Cindy how are you doing today? Oh, this is my daughter Micah."

"What a darling! I remember when you were as tall as this counter!"

"I know, I know, she's grown up so fast. But, she'll be working here now."

"How fantastic! Well, looking forward to seeing you Micah."

"You too, Miss Cindy."

"Like I was saying, when their number is called by Cindy

they'll be given a new room and floor number and sent up to you. They'll go up this elevator," her father said, pointing to the metal doors on his left and reaching to push the arrow, "and meet you on their floor."

The doors opened to reveal a small boy with a thin line of stitches above his left temple. He was holding his mother's hand and had a long white stick poking out of the side of his mouth. His mother looked tired, yet the boy skipped down the hall until they were out the door. You would have thought she was the one who just received medical treatment.

Micah and her father replaced the mother and son and rode to the 7th floor.

"When the doors open, you must be waiting for them. You'll immediately ask for their identity and gather the information on your INSAV. Once everything is registered on your screen a room number will pop up and all you have to do is walk them down the hall."

"How many rooms are there in each hall?"

"30, give or take."

"And do I stay with them in the room?"

"No, you shouldn't. A doctor will be with them shortly and you'll have more people to seat. Alright, let's get your uniform."

The uniform wasn't much of a stretch from either of the outfits she had worn for the majority of her life. Instead of a white blouse she was given a blue one, and instead of red pants she was given a red jumper that had straps to go over her shoulders. The shirt was a little too tight and the jumper just plain uncomfortable and ugly, but her father reassured her that this was how everyone felt when they first put on the uniform. She would get used to it eventually.

The hospital quickly became a place of solace for Micah. It

seemed to be the only building where people cared more about what was in front of them than what lay unseen underneath. When someone entered the double doors of the structure they were no longer concerned about the increase of Nightcrawlers surfacing within the district, or whether or not the request to fix a leak in their apartment would actually be fulfilled by the government. The second someone walked in all other concerns became trivial to their health. All that mattered was what could be done for their bodies. Micah enjoyed being cut off from the world in this way. Her three hour shifts, six days a week, at the hospital allowed her to escape from the hate she had been trying to run away from. She knew, of course, that this hate still existed within everyone at the hospital at some level, but luckily that level was hidden during most of their treatments.

Most, but not all. She had been working at the hospital for about three weeks when a particularly odd case came in. At this point she had still been communicating with P, but sparsely. Their letters had grown further apart and were filled with less detail about their lives. Micah couldn't quite figure out why, although she noticed that P had begun sending her shorter letters she still replied with the vivacity of their first few encounters. She was always thirsty for more information about where he was from and how he lived, but it seemed to have gotten to the point where he no longer cared about her. He stopped asking for details of her own life and would respond to her questions, when he did respond, with short, one lined answers. One morning, after writing P a long letter earlier the night before, she found a small note that she took as his response. She had filled her letter with question upon question.

Does your family have enough food? Are your children still able to attend school? What did your son fix for you this week?

Did your wife get over her illness?

But, all that lay in the letter's place the next morning was a crumpled, yellow piece of paper.

All is well.

P.

Before this point she had kept his letters in a neat pile between her mattress and bed frame until she decided to write back, but this time she tore the small note into pieces and let the remnants sprinkle across her floor. She couldn't believe that this was now all he was giving her. She hadn't written to him since, and he hadn't sent her a note asking why.

When the doors of the elevator opened on the sixth floor and Micah's eyes met those of her new patient, it took her a second longer to produce the cheeky smile she gave to each man and woman that she encountered within the building. The thick, metal doors revealed something she had never actually seen. Behind them lay a woman with short, fluffy white hair being held in place by skin, wrinkled as deep as a canyon, that made waves across her forehead and underneath her eyes. The eyes themselves were sunken deeply into her skull and seemed to have lost the small shimmer of life that before this moment Micah didn't realize every person possessed. Her body was hunched and frail, the woman couldn't have been more than 80 pounds and taller than 5 feet. She was wearing a long, loose floral dress and large clunky shoes that appeared to stabilize her wobbly body, which was supported even further by a curved black cane. This was, by far, the oldest person Micah had ever seen. No one she had ever met had lived past the age of 60. The poor air quality and necessity to expand food with artificial byproducts had been reducing lifespans exponentially for the past 50 years. Micah couldn't even begin to guess how old this woman was. 80? 90? 110? As far as she knew the old woman could be 160, it would have made as much sense to Micah as if she were 85.

Micah didn't know whether or not to help the woman walk. She just stood outside, dumbfounded. Frozen. The woman lifted up her head, smiled a wet toothless grin at the awestruck girl, and began walking towards her.

"I'm told I need to give you this," the woman said in a voice as frail as her body. She slowly reached her wrist towards Micah and waited for the scan. Micah gingerly brought hers closer, being careful not to make skin-to-skin contact, and activated the INSAV. Room 30. End of the hall. Of course.

"Well, Ma'am, it looks like we have you in one of the farthest rooms, but it's one of our best. I promise. Would you like me to get you a wheelchair?"

"Oh, no. Don't worry about me. I've been walking my whole life, no use getting lazy now."

And how long is that life? Micah wondered, not knowing if it would be offensive to ask. "Alright, well… would you like my hand at least?" Micah offered out of courtesy, but prayed to herself that the woman would say no.

"Why yes, that would actually be quite lovely. You can never be too careful of what you may encounter on the road," the woman said with a wink.

She stretched out her hand towards Micah and waited. Micah looked at it and slowly inched her own towards the alien-like body in front of her. She was almost scared to touch her, afraid that if she grasped too tightly the woman's skin would peel off like that of an overcooked potato. She let the woman place her hand on top of her own and gently curled her fingers around the sides. Her skin didn't feel like anything she'd felt before. It felt like thin, hot leather that had been left out to dry for too long. Still, Micah smiled and slowly began walking forward. She began the small talk she tried to engage all of her patients with.

"So tell me, what brings you here today?"

The woman let out a small laugh.

"That's very kind of you to ask, but I think the correct question would be what doesn't bring me here today. I don't know if you can tell just by looking at me, but I'm quite old."

"Now, I wouldn't say that."

"You're right. 50 would be old. 55 would be senile. 76 is ancient."

Micah was amazed. "So you're 76. That's something to be proud of!"

"It's a curse and a blessing. I'm now cursed with the most ridiculous of health problems, but I guess I'm blessed for being here for so long. If you see that as a blessing."

Micah didn't know if she did.

"I'd sure say it is."

"Tell me, how old are you? You look too young to be out of school yet."

"Oh, yes. Yes. I am. My dad works here so I get to volunteer after class. I'm just 18."

"18! Oh my, I remember when I was 18. A lot was different then, but a little piece of me likes to believe that certain things stayed the same." The woman slowed her walk and seemed to become lost in memories of the past. They were quiet for a moment, both focusing on the small steps the woman was taking down the hallway. They were halfway through but had slowed down to half their initial pace.

Micah thought of the woman's life. If her historytext was right, when the woman was 18 there would have still been parks in Sector 15, like the stories her grandmother used to tell her. This woman probably went on many picnics with her family, too. Micah wondered what the sector looked like before the transition into the concrete jungle it had become.

"Are you sure you don't want that wheelchair?" The woman was now beginning to breath heavier, deeper.

"No, no. We're almost there. Aren't we?" Her eyes had begun to droop and the wrinkles in her brow became stronger in perseverance.

"We are, it's just right there," Micah responded, pointing to a room on the left. Micah had to distract her in some way to make the rest of the walk easier. She took the plunge.

"Tell me about those things that used to be full of trees, and bushes, and plants. What were they called?"

The woman's thin lips curled into a smile. "Parks, dear. They were called parks. And they were wonderful. Parents would sit and let their kids run around the entire area. We had special toys and equipment for them, too. There were these great things, they were called swings, and there were seats attached to ropes that would fling you high into the air. They don't have those anymore, do they?"

Micah racked her brain, trying to think if she had ever seen this strange contraption.

"No, I'm afraid they don't."

"That's a shame. They were wonderful. That was a time where everyone could play and enjoy themselves together. Even the white people."

At this Micah was alarmed. Her historytexts taught her that since the creation of the underground, over 150 years ago,

Nightcrawlers weren't allowed to interact with Daymen at all.

"Do you mean you were allowed to be outside at night?" Micah asked.

"Oh, no. I've never been allowed to do that. No, when I was a little girl some of the Nightcrawlers would come out during the day and play with us. I remember I had quite a few friends who were Nightcrawlers. I, of course, knew there was something different about them, but that didn't matter when we were playing hide and go seek. I mean, they were always chosen to hide first, but that's beside the point."

Micah was confused. Neither her historytexts, nor P's letters, had mentioned anything about this.

"I'm sorry, but I don't understand. I thought there have always been laws against that."

"Of course there were laws, but no one really cared about them. The policemen didn't see it fit to arrest someone for wanting to play outside. If they were stealing something that was another issue, but back then Daymen stole too. As long as they were back underground by about mid-day no one really seemed to mind. It's not like today at all."

Micah couldn't believe that, again, she was lied to. It now seemed that everything taught to her through 15 years of school was just a product of someone's imagination.

"When do you think that stopped?"

"It hasn't been that way since I was a little girl. Maybe seven? I can't really remember the exact time. All I recall is waiting for my friends at the park one day and they never showed up. I cried and cried to my mother, I didn't understand what was happening. All she told me was, 'the bad men have gone away.' She was holding me, rocking me back and forth as she was saying this over and over again. I didn't realize until later that she was crying, too."

"Did you ever ask your mother about it again?"

"I did, once. When I was about 16. She told me that I never had any light skinned friends on the playground. She told me I was making it up. She told me to stop thinking about it. But, I couldn't make something up like that."

"You never saw them?"

"I didn't even know their names. But, that's in the past. There's no way to go back there now." The woman was now inching down the hallway, grasping Micah's hand with all her might. "You know what, I think I will take that wheelchair now."

"Of course. Can you hold on here by yourself for a minute?"

"I think so."

Micah ran to the end of the hallway and grabbed a spare wheelchair. She brought it to the woman and gently placed her body down. She then silently wheeled her the few feet she had left to walk and placed the chair into the far corner of room 30. Micah bent down in front of the chair so that the two could be at eye level.

"The doctor will be with you shortly. I'll make sure to find him right now."

The woman looked at Micah and nodded. Micah turned and began walking out of the room. When her fingers were gripped around the doorknob she heard a small voice from behind.

"Wait, Miss. I forgot to tell you something." Micah flipped around to once more face the woman.

"You have the most beautiful eyes. They remind me of something, but I can't quite remember what."

Micah knew exactly what they reminded her of. But, she didn't dare say. She didn't know who might have been watching.

The old woman could get away with telling her story because she was... well... old. If Micah was questioned about it she could always tell the government that she didn't believe a word she said, who knows what happens to your brain after you reach a certain age. But, internally, Micah didn't question a thing. Some memories were forever. She simply gave the woman one last smile, said thank you, and closed the door to be on her way to the next patient. She didn't even bother to look up the woman's name later that day.

9

MMicah and her father had to leave at least 20 minutes before the sun set in order to get back to their home before dark. This was usually an enjoyable walk, yet today seemed to be the first bitingly cold day of the season. They walked quickly, without speaking, which Micah appreciated. She didn't want to have to lie to her father yet again about how her day went. After they had scanned into their building, scanned into their apartment, and thrown their bags next to the door, Micah plopped onto the couch next to her brother as her father sprung into the kitchen to help their mother with dinner. Gabe was eating a small bag of chips and, without asking, Micah plunged her hand into it and emerged with a small handful of BBQ'd goodness.

"Thanks," she said, shoving a few into her mouth. "Delicious." Gabe had his eyes glued to the TV. He was watching the nightly news, which ran constantly for 3 hours during the last few hours into the night. They were showing a story about food conservation.

We can all do our part. Save your rinds! Save your scraps! Boil everything down into a broth and then send your leftovers down to the Department of Conservation. Remember, everything can be saved. Everything can be re-used. Martha Dlack is here to give us a few tips on how you can help out at home.

Thanks, Tim. Now as you can see here I have a large bucket of potato skins to my left, and a little bit of moldy cheese to my right. I'm going to show you, and everyone at home, how to make this into a delicious soup.

Micah watched as the plump woman on the screen diced up the skins and peeled mold off the cheese. She then placed all of it into a pot with cream, broth (homemade of course), and a few other items. Micah turned to try and joke with her brother.

"You'd think with the whole food conservation effort obesity would be a thing of the past," she joked, grabbing another chip. Gabe angry crumpled up the bag, stood up, and turned towards the table.

"I think dinner's almost ready."

What's wrong with him? Micah thought, getting up to follow suit.

Dinner went as usual. These days the family wasn't as energetic as they used to be. Whether it was the weather, or stress at each of their jobs, the Davis family had stopped trying to pry into each other's lives and ate most of their meals in silence. Sometimes someone would interject with an attempted joke, or Mrs. Davis would begin talking about a novel she was reading, but otherwise the meals came and went like the rising and setting of the sun. The family dinners were necessary, but no one paid any special attention to them anymore. Ever since Micah had begun working at the hospital her parents didn't seem worried about her at all, and ever since Gabe's shifts had been switched he hadn't actually been able to make it to many of the meals. Those that he could attend would be spent constantly shoving food into his mouth as if he would never receive another loaf of bread or glass of milk. This afternoon was the one night a week he had off.

Gabe, as usual, excused himself early. Mrs. Davis was next to follow, and Micah and her father together cleared the cups and plates. When Micah finished she, as usual, went straight to her room and immediately looked for a note in the floorboard. For the twelfth night in a row there was nothing. She undressed herself, replacing the now comfortably tight blue shirt and still ugly red jumper with a long white t-shirt, and slid into bed. She laid there for about an hour, attempting to read a lesiuretext, her historytext, to mentally go through some old letters, but gave up on everything and ended up staring at the ceiling. Suddenly she heard her door slowly creak open and Gabe appeared behind it. He walked forward, sat on the foot of her bed, and threw her a tattered ball of paper.

Micah was frozen.

"Read it," He demanded, looming over her bed.

"How the hell did you get this?" She questioned in exasperation.

"Read it," He repeated, unresponsive.

Slowly, with shaking hands, she uncrumpled the letter and began reading it to herself.

M,

Can't write anymore. Too dangerous. You must come here. I have secured a passage at the intersection of 15th and Q. If you can get there tonight at 3 someone will be waiting. No need to respond with a letter. Only your presence.

                                                                P.

Micah's hands were shaking even more than before. She looked up at her brother.

What had she done.

He stared back. Waiting. For an explanation. For an excuse. For an apology.

"I can expl..."

"You can't."

"It was a mista...."

"No it wasn't."

"I'm sorry."

"No, you're not."

She just sat, hands clutching the yellowing paper.

"Well... what do you want me to say?"

He didn't respond, but stood up and began pacing across the room. Every time his eyes would pass the small crevice where the letters were placed by P for Micah to find they would stop, focus, squint, and continue. He was looking for an answer within the wall. Finally, still pacing, he spoke.

"There's nothing for you to say. With one action you have disobeyed every major law that I work to protect. Do you know what you've done by writing these letters? You've given a giant fuck you to your family, to your government, and to your home."

"Gabe, what do you mean these letters? This is the only one, and I haven't responded."

He stopped walking and looked straight at his sister.

"And now you *lie* to me. God, Micah. Dad should have punished you after finding out about The Red Knob. Maybe then you wouldn't be the malicious, cold-hearted bitch that's standing in front of me today. I found your pen, dumbass. You really thought that putting something under your bed would keep it hidden forever? That's probably stupider than actually writing. You told him about us, about the aboveground. Do you know the consequences of that?"

"I know, they're bad."

"They're not bad, Micah. They're lethal."

At the word lethal her hands became clammy, her forehead hot, her stomach tight. Her brother had one of the most important jobs in the sector. As a trash collector he was closest to the Nightcrawlers and closest to the law. He had singlehandedly sent dozens, hundreds of people away to be hung. She didn't know whether or not his bond to her as family would preside over his bond, and oath, to the law. She felt a single tear of fear slide down her cheek. The face of the boy she saw in the street took over her mind.

"What are you going to do."

"What I have to."

"No, Gabe. You can't. Not to me."

He looked down at the worn carpet, eyes fixating on anything but his sister.

"Micah, I have to. Did you even think of the position this would put me in? If anyone else finds out about these letters *from* anyone else it won't just be you who's hung, but me, Mom, and Dad. We'll be charged with conspiracy."

He looked back up at her with determination and disgust.

"Did you even think of that?"

"Gabe, I…"

"You didn't. If you did you wouldn't be doing this."

"But you can't give me up. I'm your sister, Gabe. Your *sister*." She was sitting at the edge of the bed, letter thrown to the ground.

"Micah, I have to."

"But, you don't. What if I find a way that you don't have to."

"I don't think there's a way."

"But there is," she stuttered. "Think about it. They've invited me down. They'll tell me things, things that no one else can find out. I can find out who has power down there, I can figure out who controls everything. I'll give you names. Faces. Descriptions. Schedules. Once I'm done you can bring everything to your supervisor. You'll be the most important trash collector in history. You can bring down everyone. The entire underground will fall apart. Isn't that what everyone wants?"

Gabe glared at her and continued pacing. His eyes unrelentingly rested on the slit between the wall and the floor.

"You're sure that you can give me names? Places? How can you be sure?"

"You've read the letter. He wouldn't have invited me down unless he was comfortable with me."

"I know that. It's why I don't believe you."

"Gabe, look at me." Micah got up from the bed and walked over to her brother.

"You know you would never forgive yourself for turning me in. I could never forgive myself for getting our family in trouble. If we can pull this off, everyone gets what they want."

Gabe pulled away from his sister and turned towards the full-length mirror. Micah looked at her own reflection behind him, searching his face for a decision. She first thought he was looking at the mirror, but then noticed he seemed to be trying to peer through it. He was looking for something that didn't lie in front of him, but Micah couldn't tell if he found it. His gaze suddenly focused on his sister's reflection in the glass. Without turning, he spoke to her.

"If you promise it can be done."

"I promise."

"If I feel this is going the wrong way at all, I'm pulling you out and putting you in jail."

"I understand."

"This is either the stupidest or smartest thing you've ever done."

"I guess we'll have to wait and see."

10

MMicah had never been surrounded by this much darkness before. The advertisements that ran endlessly around every building were blank, their vibrant colors reduced to nothing. She felt that the darkness wasn't just around her, but inside her. There wasn't any difference between her skin and what lay around it. They blended together seamlessly into one indistinguishable shade. She kept rubbing her hands together and brushing her feet against the floor to remind herself that she was still there. She could feel her heartbeat pounding against her chest, she could hear it thumping in her ears and feel it push against her wrists. She hadn't been swept up by her surroundings yet. Yet.

She was standing at the intersection of 15th and Q. She didn't know what to expect. She had no idea what she was waiting for. She was just standing, waiting. Hoping. Thinking.

Don't say anything when you're on the corner. Don't speak. Don't even breathe heavily. If someone comes by and finds you, you're done. You understand?

I understand.

Gabe had dropped her off at exactly 2:55. After the talk with his sister, Gabe walked to the depot, picked up a truck, and picked up Micah. He had switched shifts with another trash man who was working as a night guard. Between 2:30 and 5:00 the trash men collected all debris from the day. It was perfect timing. He brought her to the corner, dropped her off, and continued on his shift.

She stepped out of the truck into complete darkness. No one would know. They said nothing more to one another. There was nothing more to say. He would be back at 4:45 whether or not she was there to meet him.

When she was younger the darkness would terrify her. Even though it was mandatory to have a light on in every apartment at all times, when her parents would turn off all but the night light in the hallway she was always overwhelmed with a feeling of terrifying solitude. She would huddle her toys together to create a plush army and imagine them fighting the creatures that could come out of her window and from underneath her bed. But, there were many nights where even they couldn't protect her. She would then grab her best warrior, a pink rabbit named Willis, and scurry to her parent's room. She would throw open the door and push herself between them. Their bodies were fortresses to her fear. With Willis at her face and her parents at her sides she was protected against everything. Every once in a while her mother would wake up when she got into the room.

"Are you scared again, boo?" she would ask, motioning her towards the bed.

"I can't see," she would respond, tears welling in her small eyes.

"Honey, don't be scared of what you can't see." Her mother would say, stroking her hair. "Without the darkness you wouldn't be able to dream."

"I would!" Micah would plead, curling further into her mother. "I can!"

Her mother would kiss her forehead and curve her long body around her daughter's small figure.

"Sometimes to create real magic we have to start from scratch. Sometimes the darkness is the only place where your mind can truly be free."

Micah's mother would ask her daughter to tell her a story.

"See with your head," she would say. "Tell me what you see with your head." Micah would make up stories of princesses and dragons, talking frogs and superhero doctors. Many times she would drift off this way, sealing the end of the stories in her dreams.

Standing in the darkness now, she tried to remember these and tell them again to herself.

There once was a unicorn who rode rainbows to fight battles against real horses. There once was a frog king who lived underground and had all the gold in the world.

She tried to keep herself company with these stories, but her mind was racing a mile a minute. She couldn't focus on anything without images of the underground bombarding her brain. She had only heard awful things about it. It was, according to everyone she had ever known, hell on earth.

In the five minutes that she stood on the corner she imagined absolutely every alternative to what could be lying below her, including who could be lying below her. She couldn't believe this was the night when she would finally discover who P was. Lying in her bed she had imagined so many possibilities.

She listened to the sounds that surrounded the darkness. There was a dripping of water coming from above and landing somewhere to her right. Maybe they would take her through the gutter. She moved closer to the sound and waited for the screeching of metal against concrete. Suddenly, something grabbed her arm. Her heart pounded. A face leaned into her left ear.

"Be quiet. I'm taking you down now. Walk slowly and grab my waist." It was a woman's voice, but spoke in an accent Micah had never heard before. It was rough, sharp, with elongated vowels. Each word ended quickly and there was a slight pause before the start of the next.

Her hand was led to the woman's hips and together they gently walked to the left. They went slightly down the sidewalk before it turned into a set of stairs. Micah had no idea where they came from-- the stairs seemed to be located exactly where she was standing before. There were 7 tall steps, 1 2 3 4 5 6 7 Micah counted, before the land flattened out. They walked for about five minutes, completely silently, down a narrow damp hallway before reaching another set of stairs.

Micah couldn't see anything. Everything was completely dark. She was guided solely by the woman's movement. This stairway was circular. They went down, down, 71 steps. Still in complete darkness they walked a little further before the woman took Micah's hands off her waist and disappeared. Micah was now standing completely alone, unable to see anything. She didn't know where the walls were. She didn't know if there were even any lights. All she could feel was the damp air and ground beneath her feet. She tried activating her INSAV. Nothing worked. Completely alone and surrounded by a darkness she didn't understand, she had never been more terrified.

Suddenly, but faintly, Micah saw a light at the far edge of the tunnel. She began walking towards it, taking small steps and holding her hands in front of her. Her fingertips itched for contact with something. Anything. As she inched closer the light became stronger and wider. She realized it framed a rectangle. A door. She finally reached it and, after taking a deep breath, pushed the thin wooden frame open.

PART II

11

The light blinded me. My fingers laid resting on the door as my eyes attempted to adjust to their new surroundings. With my body pushed against the wooden door, waiting for everything to come into focus I began to see blobs of figures. Slowly, a circle of men and women emerged. I couldn't see their eyes but could feel them looking into me. I carefully grabbed the sides of my hood and lifted it off my head. I looked around the room at who stood before me.

Sitting at the table were four bodies, three men and a woman. As I scanned the room I couldn't believe how similar each of them looked to members of my own class. Two eyes, one nose, one mouth, two ears. I had heard from my classmates that Nightcrawlers all looked completely different from one another and, while some may look a lot like us, most of them had fangs or boils all over their bodies. These rumors had been around since before I could remember and it seemed like each year they grew in intensity.

When the students were brought to the government house to

watch a hanging, the man or woman being hung always had a bag over their head by the time any spectators arrived. All students training to be segregationalists attended these fieldtrips at least once a month. We would all walk, in a neat little row, down the street and carefully line up in the town square. By the time we got there, someone would already be standing on top of the tall platform, burlap and rope strung around their neck, waiting to be thrust downward.

So, I had seen a lot of Nightcrawlers before. But, I guess I had never really *seen* them. I figured out when I was about twelve that something was done to these people to keep them quiet during the ordeal. When I was fourteen, I finally discovered what exactly that was.

My class had just arrived, as usual, to the government center and was waiting patiently for the event to start. No one was excited to go to the hangings anymore, except for the few boys who would take bets on how long the bodies twitched after dropping. Most of us were just waiting for it to be over, waiting to go back to our warm classrooms. I remember zoning out, staring at the sky and wondering yet again if there was any way I could escape on the clouds. When I looked back down there was a large thud and a gasp from the audience. The woman had fallen over and somehow her burlap sack had released itself from her face. What lay underneath was, in a word, horrendous. The head was almost completely bald with blood stained tufts of hair as the only reminder of what it used to cover. The face had jagged scars across it-- so deep that patches of skin were hanging off her cheeks. It was barely even distinguishable as a face. The man next to her quickly picked up her limp body and shoved the bag back onto her head, grabbing an extra rope and twisting it tightly around her neck. He placed the noose around her and immediately pulled his lever. While most of the time at least half the crowd leaves after the body is dropped, that day time seemed to stand still. Everyone waited for the body to stop moving. It didn't take very long. 30 seconds, maybe. This woman had given up, and everyone had seen why. When all was finally still our class began their journey back to school. Out of the corner of my eye I saw Jimmy Dijik slip Sam Deward a few pieces of hard candy.

That face, and the face of the boy in the street, were the only light faces I had ever seen in my life. Both had been massacred by the world and were as red as they were white. The faces in front of me, however, were completely clean. Their skin seemed to glimmer against the jagged rock wall behind them. I couldn't tell the exact age of any of them. There was too much going through my mind to be able to describe exactly what I saw. All I kept thinking was how different. How different. How different. But, still so similar. I separated my lips, not knowing whether I was preparing to speak or preparing to scream. I tensed the back of my throat to make a noise. But, I couldn't. What if I said something wrong? What if my words didn't have the same meaning as theirs?

I was in their kingdom. I was subject to their rules, but I had no idea what any of those rules were. My heart was fluttering, my face was fluttering, my hands were fluttering. Everything inside of me-- my confidence, my organs-- felt like they were going to turn into paper birds and fly straight into a fire. All I could do was stand in front of them, fingers still around the edges of my hood, watching everything burn.

The man in the very center of the table stood up. The cloth on his body looked rough, I imagined it rubbing against my skin. Everything was loose and held together by strings. I looked around the room again. They were all wearing clothes like this, but no one looked exactly the same. I wondered if these were their uniforms.

"M, I presume?" The man spoke slowly, focusing on his words as if each syllable was trapped on his tongue.

"M," I shakily responded, pulling my arms across my chest. I shouldn't give them my real name yet. That was something I had learned a long time ago.

"M. We welcome you." He paused, just for a moment, to trail his eyes down my covered body. "Would you like to know where you are?"

"Well... underground?" It hit me.

I was *underground*. They lived *underground*. This was the farthest from home I had ever been by myself.

"Ha, yes. Of course. Underground. Well, not quite. Our streets are a little lower than this. We brought you here to a safe spot." He was wringing his hands together. I wondered if this meant he was nervous, too.

"What exactly are you keeping me safe from?" I quickly asked, looking around the room once more. It seemed to be hollowed out in the stone. Exposed wires connected a single string of lights that ran through the center of it beginning right behind the man's head and ending above my own.

"It's not just to keep you safe." The man responded.

Was I a threat to them, too?

"We've been waiting for this day for a while," the man continued, placing his hands into two small pockets at his side. "I've been waiting for this day for a while."

"So you must be..."

"No, no. I'm not the man you've been writing. He sits near me, through this floor. He's waiting for you, too."

"I can't see him now?" I asked, my brow slightly furrowing in confusion. "I thought he'd be waiting for me."

"He is. But, as I'm sure you already know, it's dangerous for him to expose his identity to you. You already know so much about him. If you have the wrong intentions, which I'm not saying you do, all you would need is a face to lock him away forever."

My paper birds were now fluttering above a warm hearth. What if he knew about my arrangement with Gabe? All I could do was carry on with the plan.

"But, I don't have any bad intentions. I promise. Please. All I want to do is see him. I'll answer anything."

"That's what we expected. He's given us all of your letters and told us what exactly he has told you about himself. Each of us has a question to ask you about his life. If you answer the questions correctly, you can walk through this door," he said, pointing behind him.

What was this, a game show? I had already risked so much going down there, wasn't that enough for them?

"I'm sorry we have to do this, but we must make sure that you are who you say you are. Letting someone into our world because of a few words on a piece of paper isn't enough. We have to see that it matters to you as much as it matters to us."

I took a deep breath before responding. I didn't realize that being let into the underground was as difficult as escaping from it. In my mind, value was placed only on what was above. I was always told it was necessary to protect the Daymen, I never thought it would be as important to protect what lay below them. I had no idea, even after reading all of P's letters, that these people possessed so much pride in their land. To be let into it was a privilege, not a favor.

This, I realized, made the journey I just completed even more dangerous than I initially thought. If I did anything threatening to not just them, but to their land, the consequences might have been deadly. I didn't even know what they would do to me if I misanswered a question. I chose not to think about that, tried to repress my nerves, yet I could still feel my palms becoming clammy and taste my mouth running dry.

"I'm ready," I managed to squeak out.

"Alright. I'll ask the first question. Do you remember what P told you he did for a living?"

I immediately responded without skipping a beat. "He sits at the entrance to the aboveground. He helps to transport goods, but he's never been above." I took a breath and held it in, waiting for their response. I knew it was right, there was no doubt in my rational mind. But, at that moment I wasn't completely rational. I thought of everything that might have happened to me if I was wrong. What if I was hung like all of the Nightcrawlers I had seen before? I imagined my hair, pulled out in chunks. I imagined a knife slicing across my cheeks.

"You're right." The man responded, sitting down. "Congratulations. Sonya?"

The woman to his direct left stood up. It was funny, she looked like a lighter version of one of my mother's friends. This realization comforted and terrified me at the same time.

"What's the name of the pet P's family owns?"

My breathing stopped. My fingernails clutched my forearms. P never mentioned a single pet in any of his letters. I was sure I would have noticed, pets had been banned in Sector 15 for the past 25 years. Any mention of one would have definitely stuck out in my mind. I stood silently for half a minute.

"M, did you hear the question?"

"Yes, I did. But, I don't think his family owns any pets. I... I'm sorry. I don't know what to tell you. But, ask me anything else!"

I braced myself. I half expected her to pull a glock out of her pocket and shoot me square in the face. What a way that would have been to go.

She smiled and sat back down, flattening her skirt underneath the table. "That is the correct answer. On to the next one."

I uncrossed my arms and shook them out to my sides. If I got past that one I could get past any of them.

The elderly man to the center's right asked me what recipe P had sent me, which I immediately answered and told him that unfortunately I had not had time to make one. He told me that was a shame and recommended that during one of my trips down I should try it. He already believed I was who I said I was. He was already inviting me down again. There was just one more question to answer.

The last man was sitting completely perpendicular to where I was standing and, while he was seated, I couldn't see any of his face. He wore a cream shirt with a large collar that covered most of his neck and blended with his scruffy, light hair. He was sitting stiffly with his back rigidly pushed against the chair. When he stood up he continued to look at the wall to my right and slowly turned his body. His eyes immediately locked with mine and I was struck by the color. Crystal clear blue. I couldn't tell his age, but he seemed younger than all the others. He had just small wrinkles by his eyes and a thin scar that ran from his bottom lip to his chin, which was covered with a short, but thick, beard. Once he was completely facing me he began his question. I watched his lips as they slowly formed sounds and words. Red specs that intertwined with his pale beard bounced as he spoke. Yet, the entire time, he didn't break eye contact. I didn't look away.

"What are the names of P's children?"

"Amanda is his youngest daughter, Benjamin his youngest son, and Silas his oldest." The man's jaw clenched with each name that was spoken. He waited to respond, staring intensely at me. I didn't know what to do. I just continued staring back. It was as if he was challenging me, to what I didn't know. Regardless, whatever it took, I was going to win.

"Your pronunciation is a little off."

"But I'm right."

He paused before answering, his eyes still locked on mine.

"You're correct." He didn't sit back down. "I'll bring you to him."

The man in the center stood up again.

"Silas, we decided against that. She'll go by herself."

Silas.

"He's my father, I'll decide his fate." His voice raised, enough to show passion but not disrespect.

"Very well," the man sighed, turning towards the wall behind him. "Bring her forward."

Silas walked around the table and tightly grabbed my arm above my elbow. He forcefully walked around the other side until we were both standing next to the man who first spoke to me. I didn't see a door, I didn't understand what was going on. Where they were both looking was only a wall. Maybe they had lied the whole time. Maybe now was where the glock would come in. At least Gabe would get half his wish.

"Stay very still," the man said to me, as he pushed his palms against the wall. "You'll be there very soon."

I expected a door to magically appear from the wall. I don't really know why, I could see that it was made of solid stone. But, at that moment my life felt like a fantasy and visions of my imagination were intertwining with reality.

Suddenly, the ground below me began to drop and Silas and I were whizzing below. I have no idea how many stories we went, the entire time I was flanked by complete darkness. I could just hear a bell, *Bing! Bing!* every few seconds. I wondered if this was their version of an elevator.

The floor jolted to a halt with one final clank. Silas pushed open the wall in front of him and pulled both of us onto the other side of it. I looked around and realized I was in a room full of junk. Everything that I had ever thrown away seemed to be lying right in front of me. There were old toys and electronics piled right up to the ceiling, all in a neat row that led to the other side of the room. Silas pulled my arm and we began walking between rows of old computer monitors and toy trucks. The space was thin, so thin that I was practically walking behind him as he continued to grab at my arm. If it was anyone else I would have demanded he let go of me. But, I felt he was the type of person that wouldn't accept anything short of his own terms. As we got closer I realized we were walking towards a small light at the end of the room. He stopped walking and my body pushed into his before bouncing back.

"I have her." Silas stated, as if I was a package to be delivered.

"Wonderful! Wonderful, wonderful wonderful! Well, what are you doing just standing there? Move aside!"

I saw a wrinkled hand grab Silas's shoulder and push him to the left. He finally let go of my arm and I immediately began rubbing it as if it were a reflex.

The man that stood before me was, undoubtedly, the man I had been writing to. He was a spitting image of Silas. Or, rather

Silas was a spitting image of him, just 21 years younger. The man was slightly shorter than his son, but exuded an energy that made him immediately feel inches taller. His smile was, in a word, radiating. His blue eyes glimmered as he gave me a toothy grin and plopped his hands onto his hips. Even though I knew he spent his entire life as a simple worker, he had a movie star quality about him that I couldn't deny. No wonder he was always asking me about them.

We both had looks of wondered bewilderment glued to our faces. We waited so long to be able to simply look at each other and, without having to kneel down and peer in between the floorboards, say

"Hello there. You must be M. I just, wow. This really is marvelous." His eyes seemed to glimmer even more as he spoke. The voice was clear, crisp, but shared the same accent that Micah had heard from everyone else in the underground.

"Yes, but I think you can start calling me Micah." I'd given him my name. There was no turning back.

"Micah? You say?" He stumbled over the word and paused for a moment to think it over. "Well, I can't say that I've heard that one before. It's a beautiful name. You, my dear, can start calling me Patrick."

I didn't repeat the name, I simply nodded. I couldn't say it out loud yet. Saying it out loud would mean I was liable for its destiny. I took a moment to look around the room. The ceilings were sky high. They may have literally gone to what Patrick called the sky, for all I knew. They seemed to reach stories and stories up and the aisles of junk reached with them. The room must have been at least twenty rows across. All I wanted to do was run down them, letting their items zoom past my eyes. I wanted to see it all as quickly as I could. After reluctantly releasing my gaze from following the rows of microwaves, sinks, tables, and whatnots, they settled behind Patrick onto his desk. Sitting on top of it was a thin slice of dark orange pie.

"Is that..." I asked, pointing above his shoulder. His head spun around and bounced back with an even wider smile.

"It is. I was saving it just for you. Please, come come. Sit." He walked around the desk and pulled out a rusting metal chair. I followed and placed my body into it while simultaneously sliding my coat off of my shoulders. I looked down at my outfit. For some reason, probably out of habit, I had chosen to wear my uniform. Ridiculous red and white. I really didn't have much else, but I'm sure if I really searched I could have found something, anything different. I felt extremely overdressed and out of place.

Patrick pulled a decaying wooden chair up from the wall and sat to my right. He leaned in with his full body and pushed the cake towards me with one hand.

"My wife made it last night. She was very careful about her spices, it's even more delicious than usual. I just had to save you a piece. Here, try it." He pulled a metal three-pronged fork out of a wooden cup sitting on the table and placed it to the side of the plate.

"I really have to, don't I?" I asked, not looking for an answer.

"You don't. I wouldn't suggest it." A voice answered from across the table. Silas had pulled up a chair at the opposite end of mine.

"Did you get to eat any?" I smiled at him, picking up the fork.

"I ate the batch that wasn't poisoned."

My throat tightened. Patrick placed his hand into my arm.

"Micah, you have nothing to worry about. It's not poisoned. This piece came from the same pie that Silas ate for dinner. I know what he's doing, and it's really better to just ignore him. Please, eat."

"But Micah, why would I lie to you when we've just met?" Silas smirked. "We haven't found a reason to hate one another yet."

"I wish you were still young enough for me to send you to your room," Patrick glared at his son.

"I can still go there," Silas coldly replied, getting up from his chair. "Find me when you get home." He forcefully walked back through the long aisles, his shoes tapping across the hard concrete.

Patrick shook his head.

"I don't know what they say where you're from, but down here we call that being a little shit."

I laughed. I'd called Gabe that many times.

"I think I've heard that once or twice."

"I'm sorry he's being like that. He doesn't really approve of our... relationship."

"You say that like it's an affair."

"Ha, well. It is. Of sorts. When I started writing to you I had no idea it would end up like this. Never in my wildest dreams would you be down here with me today. Everything just, somehow, fit into place."

"But that's something I don't understand. You wrote to me that communication was too dangerous. How is it safer for you to bring me here than to write to me?"

"I felt it was becoming too dangerous for the both of us. Every time I sent a letter through my ceiling I was never sure who was actually picking it up. You always replied as yourself, but there was no way for me to know for sure. That's why I had to bring you here. I had to make sure there really was an 18 year old girl still living above me. I'm sorry they gave you so much trouble coming down here, but you really never can be too careful, especially with the stricter laws your people have been putting into place. I felt it was getting to the point that if I gave you any more information about myself in writing, anyone could use it against me. If someone found those letters both you and I would be in deep, deep trouble. No one else found them, did they?"

Gabe's face popped into my head.

You're sure you can get names, faces, schedules?

I'm sure.

"No, no one. I promise."

"Good." He looked down at the pie. "Please, take a bite! It's really very delicious."

I picked up the fork and balanced a small yellow, purple, and brown mound on top of it. The piece was heavier and denser that any pie I had tasted before. The second I placed it on my tongue I also knew it wasn't going to taste like any pie I had tasted before. The crust was as coarse as their clothing and the filling was as sweet as their accent. I felt like I had placed a large dollop of glue into my mouth. There was a strange, earthy taste to it and a quick kick at the end that startled my taste buds.

"Wow, that was delicious. Please tell your wife thanks for me." I looked back up at him in a forced smile, but saw that he wasn't even looking at my face. He was memorized by the small black metal circle attached to my wrist. I put my fork down and brought my wrist towards my head before pointing it out towards him.

"It's my INSAV," I explained, turning it back towards me. "It's that recording device I wrote to you about."

"INSAV. Huh," he responded, eyes still glued to it.

"Or, um, intelligence saver, I guess," I expanded. "At least, that's what it's supposed to do."

He didn't respond but simply continued staring at it, looking at his own reflection in its glassy interior.

"You can touch it, if you want."

He looked up at me as if I had just given him access to the Holy Grail.

"Are you sure?"

"Of course I'm sure, it's not going to hurt you. Here," I brought my wrist closer to him. "Take a poke."

He quickly brought one finger forth, gently poked the INSAV, and then immediately retracted. I couldn't hear it, but could feel him saying to himself the same thing I said when I first encountered the pen in Raziela's apartment.

Whoa.

I tried to change the subject, to bring the conversation back to normalcy.

"So, is Silas worried for you? Is that why he's acting like that?"

Patrick looked down and picked a small lump of crust off of the side of the piece and crumbled it in his fingers, letting the bits fall back onto the ceramic plate. "That's part of it, I think. He's worried something might happen to me if your government finds out what I'm trying to do. But, I'm really not trying to do anything out of the ordinary. I'm not trying to do something with you that I wouldn't try with anyone else. I just want to get to know you." His shoulders went up in confusion. "I genuinely can't figure out why that's so awful."

"I can't either."

He smiled at me before whisking his hands in sudden circular waves.

"But, he's also just a kid. Kids his age have very particular views about who belongs where. He's just trying to find his place in this complicated mess that we call home. There's been talk of... well... there's just been talk." He looked down at his watch and hurriedly glanced back up.

"Oh my, it's almost 4:15. We have to be getting you back before the sun starts to rise. Finish your pie first, but then we must be going."

12

II yawned as I sat huddled in the foot space of the passenger's seat of Gabe's truck.

"What did they do to you? You smell awful." Gabe commented. His eyes were as glued to the road as the taste of that pie was to my mouth.

"They didn't do anything to me. They didn't even really bring me anywhere."

"You were down there for an hour and a half, how could they have not brought you anywhere?"

"They tried. Well, one woman tried. She brought me down a long hallway and we stopped there for a while. For most of the time, actually. She then brought me to a small room, but there wasn't anyone there. I think they messed up. She said they was supposed to be there. We waited for the rest of the time before she had to bring me back up."

"Fucking ridiculous. Do they know how much I risked sending you down there? Did you even get the woman's name?"

"They do, Gabe. It wasn't her fault. It was dangerous for her, too. They want me to go back again next week."

"Next week? Are you fucking kidding me?!"

"Gabe, you knew this wasn't going to be a one time thing."

He let out a low, frustrated growl.

"Can you get the truck again next week?"

"Can I get the truck? Yes I can get the truck, no one wants this fucking shift. They'll be glad to trade it away. If I send you down again, though, you have to promise me you'll come back with information. You didn't even get her name?"

"I didn't, but I will. I promise."

"You'd better."

Because Gabe was a trash collector he had special access to the side of our building. He knew where almost all of the cameras were in the entire city and had at least an idea of how to dodge them when necessary. He just never thought he'd need to dodge them to this degree, I was sure of it.

He strategically parked the truck in front of the side camera and swiped the door open.

"Go inside, get some rest, and tell no one of this," he hissed as I slid out of the vehicle. He walked me down the hallway, scanned open our apartment door, and turned back down. I held the door while it shut to make sure there wasn't any noise and tiptoed to my bedroom. I very carefully peeled the clothing off my body and brought my shirt up to my nose. It smelled fine. He was just being a little shit. When I got into bed I looked once more at my floorboard before closing my eyes. There had to be an easier way to do this. I had to find Tyrone's elevator.

Pages 345-55

THE REVOLUTION AND CIVIL WAR
By: Ian Dale

When the underground was first created a temporary government was immediately put into place. The highest members of the Daymen elected a president, vice president, and cabinet members to control the new territory. Jerry Smyth, who was the foremost proponent for the creation of the area, was unanimously elected president. Before his appointment as UG president, Smyth held two terms as the national medical advisor and one as a member of the AG president's cabinet. He was, undoubtedly, the most fit for the job. Elected as his vice president was one of the nation's foremost financial advisors, Ashley Bricks. Together, they possessed all key traits to lead a young sector to success. With Smyth's pristine medical and political knowledge, he was the only true choice in reducing rates of cancer and putting into place a government that would protect and preserve the newly created underground. With Bricks as his financial advisor, together it was believed that they could create enough jobs and redistribute our industries to accommodate both populations.

This was, as expected, exactly what happened. Under Smyth's terms, the bipartite economy that we currently still use was created. He discovered many jobs that could be completely performed underground. For a full list of these jobs please note the chart in the beginning of this text. Initially, as stated before, the UG citizens were only given jobs as basic farmers and positions that interacted strictly with their own industries. Banking and administration for both sectors were still left solely to the AG. Smyth created a public school system that was controlled by the AG, but taught entirely by UG citizens. All stores and factories employed UG workers, but all managerial and administrative jobs were still placed into the hands of AG members. The Daymen who worked side by side with Nightcrawlers were, of course, provided extra financial compensation for these added risks. The two men stayed in power for ten years before another election took place. This extended time was necessary to accommodate the extreme changes they needed to enact. Voters in the first election were entirely AG citizens, as the government felt the UG citizens still needed time to adjust. Both won a second five-year term and were nominated to run in the election following five years later. This time, UG men above the age of 21 were allowed to vote with AG citizens and the two politicians were, again re-elected. At this point, the UG members became concerned about their representation and demanded that women and men age 17 and above be allowed to vote. This law was, consequentially, changed to accommodate their requests. Still, AG politicians were elected into power for the following 40 years. Jeffery Kneel was the first UG man elected to power. He was given the position of vice president and still reported to the AG leaders. The next election therefore provided an unprecedented opportunity to the Aboveground. Now that a UG citizen had experienced the requirements of a position higher in the government, we were able to release all hold on most UG activities. All administrative, managerial, and governmental positions for programs that existed solely in the UG were given to UG citizens. The existing job positions were redistributed and some UG citizens were allowed to emerge during the night to work above ground on small labor tasks. They were grateful for the extra work.

However, since this handover of power, the UG has disintegrated. The UG board of politicians did not know how to effectively manage their own people. Disease rates, which had been steadily decreasing over the previous 60 years, began rising again. Despite the thousands of jobs that AG politicians had incorporated into their economy, unemployment rates rose twofold. Families started to fall apart and the slums that now infamously burden the region started forming. With the turnover of power the underground that we know today began. It is a disease rampant, dangerous place without any actual form of law. Everything so tirelessly put into place by Smyth and his successors has been completely destroyed. They are now past the point of no return. It is too dangerous for members of our community to sink below and offer help. For the past 30 years the UG has been run by a powerful dictator that even we cannot determine the name of. He is protected by a large army and has tricked the people into believing his power. He has created a ruthless, amoral society. This is why, among other reasons, there are such harsh punishments for the emergence of a Nightcrawler above land. We, quite literally, have no idea what they are capable of. At the moment all we can do is wait for the land below us to completely destroy itself. Once this happens, and the people have either become so weak that they cannot fight back or they themselves have found the power within to override their dictator, we can finally help them. I hope this comes before they have completely destroyed themselves.

Nothing matched up. I went down there, I met a few of these people that were supposed to be cruel, malicious, and self-destructive. I sat with them, ate their food. Saw what they were surrounded by. Nothing made sense. But, I couldn't raise my hand and just say that. I couldn't stand up, walk to my teacher's desk, and tell her that everything she taught was a lie. I would not only be called a fool by everyone in my classroom, but probably be taken straight to the government house for disobedience. I knew that there was a thriving city underneath us, but all I could do after reading this passage was answer the assignment as quickly, and vaguely, as possible.

I learned to detach myself at school and have two sets of beliefs. Outwardly, I believed in everything they told me. My hand was able to write the words they asked for without pause. But, inwardly, I knew everything was a lie. Every time I wrote down a sentence I wrote its antonym in my head.

What was the point in which the UG lost complete control? They would ask me.

When they were given power to control themselves, I would quickly type into the screen above my arm.

They haven't lost complete control, but are probably more powerful than you or I can imagine, I would write on the screen in my head.

I began to feel, especially after venturing underground for the first time, that I was living more and more of a double life. It was becoming exhausting, believing one thing and showing another. But, this was all I could do. For now.

Going to class that entire week after going underground was practically the same as sleeping with my eyes open. I couldn't focus at all on what they were trying to teach me. I now knew, firsthand, that everything I was told was false. The only time I felt awake was at the hospital. The small talk that was required with each patient was vaguely refreshing. It forced me to wash my face, open my eyes, and bear a toothy grin. And, when I was given a twenty-minute break once a day, it gave me the opportunity to look for the elevator.

When the head nurse came to dismiss me, I would pretend, every day, to head towards the staff lounge to grab a cup of coffee. I would take the stairwell, telling her I needed the exercise, and divert my path to one of the floors I had yet to search. I was working my way up, starting at one. I was so stupid not to ask Tyrone what floor the elevator was on. But then again, at that time I never thought I would be in the situation I am today. I looked into every closet I came across, even if it wasn't labeled as a janitor's closet. I made mental notes on which ones were locked and promised myself to come back to them later. Each day I had time to look through about half the floor before going back down to make an appearance in the staff lounge. If anyone asked where I was my response was always the bathroom. Better they think I have a stomach problem than a snooping one.

I had only reached the third floor by the time the following week rolled around. That day at school I couldn't sit still, my nerves were running a mile a minute. I was more cheerful than ever before during my shift at the hospital. Everyone I usually worked with noticed.

"Look at that smiling face!" Cindy exclaimed as I greeted her walking into the building.

"Well aren't you a sight for sore eyes!" one of my father's colleagues remarked.

"Things have really turned around for you, huh?" my dad smirked when I ran into him in the hallway. He had no idea.

Gabe slid into my room at about 2:15. "You'd never believe how happy the guy whose shift I picked up tonight was," he groaned. "I don't think you understand how big of a favor I'm doing you."

"I understand, Gabe. And I can't thank you enough."

"You promise that when you come back up tonight that you'll have more information than before. You know what I have to do if you don't."

"I know, Gabe. But you don't at all think that you're overdoing this a little bit? We burned the last letter."

"You never know who might be watching."

"But I really don't think you have to send me to jail. Mom and Dad will never forgive you."

"They'll understand once I tell them what you did. But, come up tonight with a few names and we won't ever have to have this conversation again. We can forget about the whole thing."

"You and I both know what's happening is completely unforgettable."

"You can forget anything," Gabe replied, grabbing the doorknob to leave. "You just have to try hard enough."

Half an hour later I was yet again shoved into the hidden space of Gabe's passenger seat.

"I'm not even going to stop this time. I slow the van down, you jump out, and I keep going. I tell anyone that asks that I accidentally zoned out at the wheel. You tell no one that I brought you here."

"Got it," I quietly replied, diaphragm crushing against my knees. "Just warn me before we get there."

"It'll be about two minutes."

We continued in silence. It amazed me how quickly my nerves subsided compared to last week. I was ready this time. I knew what to expect. The cold air, hard floor, long hallway. I ran through the journey in my head. I was ready.

"We're here. Get out."

I reached my fingers up to the door, popped open the release lever, and released by feet from the clutches of the vehicle. I used both arms to hoist my body up against the sides of the seat and, in one motion, sprang out of the moving truck. I kept running in the dark until I crashed against a wall. I looked back at Gabe as he reached across and pulled my door closed. Here we go. Round two.

I waited to the left of the gutter again, this time a little closer to where I thought the woman emerged last week. I was completely silent, hands in my pockets, hood over my head. When she grabbed my arm I wasn't alarmed but welcomed the touch. I let her glide my body down the stairs, through the hallway, and down another flight. I counted to 71 and walked five more paces. I wasn't surprised when she let me go. I stood, waiting, for a few seconds before retracing my path down the hallway and grasping for the light surrounded wooden door. When I swung open the door there was only a single man standing in the room. He was the older one from before.

"Welcome back," he smiled at me.

"Glad to be here," I replied.

"Are you ready to see something new?"

"I wouldn't be here if I wasn't."

"Today I'm taking you directly to his home."

This was something I'd always imagined but never expected.

"I'm ready," I said, bracing myself for the floor to drop.

"Almost," he laughed. "Almost. But you have to put this on first." He grabbed a pile of white, beige, and brown garb from the table. "If we send you into town dressed like this, everyone will immediately know where you're from."

I cocked my head and gave him a small laugh.

"Won't they look at my skin and automatically know?"

"That'll be a little bit of a hint. But, there are people of your color who live below with us. They and their families have escaped over time from the aboveground to become a part of our culture. You haven't heard about them?"

I wondered what exactly he thought I was taught. The truth?

"No, no one's ever mentioned that to me."

"That's strange. We have quite a few darker skinned people living down here. As long as you put on this outfit and don't open your mouth you'll be able to walk through our streets unnoticed."

I took the pile from his hands. "Where would you like me to change?"

"As I'm sure you can tell these facilities weren't really made for this... situation. I'm sorry, but all I can do is turn around."

"I was never one for modesty," I joked, placing the clothing back onto the table and pulling off my coat. The man turned around and I began peeling off my clothes, paying special attention to the soft fabric. The clothing he had given me was so rough.

Once I had finished changing I traded my white shirt and red pants for a baggy beige pullover with quarter length sleeves that bunched around my arms towards the end and flowed to a little below my knees. There was a dark brown rope in the pile that I used as a belt, and white cloth shoes that slipped onto my feet. I smoothed the cloth across my body, twisted the belt, and pulled at the dress to create the illusion of two different pieces.

"You can turn around now."

He turned and showed a look of pleasant surprise. "That looks lovely. There are just a few more details. You have to take out your earrings and put them into this small pouch," he said pulling a bag out of his pocket. "And you have to wash off that nail polish." Out of his other pocket he pulled a small bottle filled with a clear liquid.

I took a rag and dampened it, rubbing my nails until the fabric was stained red. As hard as I tried, I couldn't erase a few small patches from the crevices between the nail and skin. I hoped no one would notice.

"Alright, now you're ready. Let's go." He placed a single hand onto the wall and the floor began to sink. I listened to the bing again. Bing, bing, bing! Only three times before the doors opened. We were again in a dark room.

"You're sure you're ready?" he asked. I could hear the excitement in his voice.

"No turning back now."

I heard the click of a small button and a panel dropped towards the floor.

My silent world was suddenly bursting with activity. Hundreds of people appeared in front of me walking in every direction. They were all wearing something similar to what he had dressed me in, similar but all a little different. Before I had another second to think he was off, scurrying down the narrow street. I almost lost him in the mix of people but found his head bobbing a few feet away. I stepped outside of the room and into the crowd.

I immediately became terrified that someone would figure out who I was. As I weaved through the figures, trying with all my might to trace the man's disappearing head, I was convinced that someone would grab my arm and pull me away. There was no way I could blend in this easily, if a Nightcrawler were in my place above ground they would have been identified within seconds. They would have been thrown to the ground by a mob and beaten until a trash collector arrived. I'd seen it before. When I was younger I'd even participated in it.

But I seemed to glide through effortlessly. Even as I bumped shoulders with countless men and women they continued walking without notice. I thought about where I was underground in relation to what was above. If I was right about my location and we had traveled just a few blocks south, we were at the intersection of 10th and G. The street sizes seemed to be the same, maybe a little bit wider, but this could have been an illusion created by the cement and steel bands that laid about five stories above my head. Some of the sections were still covered with peeling layers of blue and white. My historytext was almost right about the ceilings. Maybe they were beautiful once, but definitely not that day. When I gained a solid grasp of the man in front of me and was able to comfortably walk a few paces behind him I began looking at the storefronts around me. They were designed so similarly to the ones I was used to, but had the strangest items in their windows and neon lighting that ran around the entirety of the buildings in radiating colors. I felt like I was transported back in time 100 years but into an alternate universe. Open stores that seemed to spring from one another's walls tightly lined the streets. Many of the shop owners stood outside of them, practically in the road, monitoring the crowd and sipping small glasses of a substance I couldn't see and probably wouldn't recognize. Others were trying to bring people into their stores with unintelligible yelling and passionate gesturing. In the window of one storefront, where an older woman with frizzy black hair sat outside on a small wooden stool, I recognized practically ancient televisions, ones that I had only seen pictures of in my historytexts. They were painted vivid colors and had extravagant wiring on top. A store a little further down the road, which I eventually figured out sold nutritional supplements, had a giant red illuminated sign that read PREVENT RICKETS. VITAMIN D HERE. I had no idea what rickets were and only barely remembered learning about the vitamin in science class. Was it for bone growth or skin health? I couldn't remember and made a mental note to look it up when I got back above.

We passed places I recognized, signs for banks and a school and a few more that took me a moment to figure out. These buildings looked so similar to the ones I was used to, but I knew within their walls was something I would only vaguely recognize. To the left of what seemed to be the high school there was a large, green neon sign for "Jerry's Mushroom Café" with an illuminated picture of a strange shape appearing to sprout out of the ground. Yet another question I would have to make sure to get the answer to.

After walking for a few blocks the man turned to me and motioned to his left. He disappeared into a door and I ran in after him. He was waiting against a red brick wall, back pushed against the side. Silas was standing next to him. His hair was disheveled and white shirt streaked with faint black and brown stains. I thought about what time this was for them. Probably right before dinner. I guessed, based on the exhaustion he was trying to hide on his face, that he had been at work all day and just gotten home.

"Nice of you to finally join us," he remarked, lifting his body off of the hard wall and pivoting towards the stairs.

"I got a little stuck. That street was pretty chaotic compared to what I'm used to." I ran my fingers through my hair in an attempt to bring it back behind my ears. They stopped for a second on the holes where my earrings used to be.

He didn't want to hear my excuse, by the time I responded he was already halfway up the dark wooden staircase. I ran after him, skipping steps to catch up. I grabbed the thin matching metal handrails that surrounded each side and used them to push myself up even further, at times skipping more than two steps. He didn't look back at all as we scaled the five stories to their apartment. The walls around me were a cream textured stucco, warped and discolored by time. When my fingers weren't grabbing the rails they were racing across those walls, grazing the peeling paint. To follow a man I knew already hated me to an unknown place I had to stay connected to something.

He didn't wait for me when we reached the top and continued walking down the hallway. He stopped in front of the last door on the right, hand waiting on the doorknob. I ran up next to him and pressed my shoulder against the outer frame.

"I guess I'm not used to these stairs, maybe it's the lack of altitude," I tried to joke. He blankly stared at me and opened the door.

"Lynn, we're here," he blindly screamed into the room.

Leading with my head, I slowly spun my body around the doorframe and peered into the apartment.

The door led directly into what looked to be a living room. There were two small mismatched floral couches on opposing walls and a low glass and metal table between them. On the far wall, balancing on a tall, narrow stand, was a small television. This must have been the TV that Silas had fixed for his family. Patrick had made such a big deal of it in his letters, I imagined it being bigger. There were pictures at every height in every frame imaginable all over the walls. Some of them were family pictures, but most were archaic landscapes, ranging from oil paintings to what looked to be drawings by her children. I was sure that, if I squinted my eyes enough, these swirling pictures would transform the walls into a pastoral paradise. There were paintings of rolling hills, sprawling fields, and colorful gardens. I had never seen paintings like this before, everything displayed in my apartment was art created in and portrayed the sector.

I stepped inside and heard movement through a door on my far left. There was a strange odor, much stronger than the smell of the pie from the week before and the crowded streets I had just snaked through. A woman's hurried voice leaked through the mustard yellow kitchen door.

"You got her! Oh my, this is so exciting! Your brother and sister are in your room changing, you should go too. You look a mess."

"She's already seen what I look like. I don't need to clean myself up."

"Oh, oh! I can't believe I… where is she? Did you set her down in the room? Oh no, I hope you put her on the good couch," the hurried female voice squealed.

"I'm sure she can seat herself."

"Your father warned me you might be like this," she playfully scolded.

The door swung open and a small woman with a smile as plump as her body emerged from behind. She was wearing a long, dark blue skirt and loose faded pink top. In her right hand was a blue and white striped cooking cloth. The smells and sounds from before intensified and I caught a glimpse of Silas standing over a small burner before the door swung back shut. Her eyes were glowing as brightly as her husband's from last week. I was still standing against the wall, face next to a large painting of a garden with small yellow flowers and a central red bench. She gasped at the sight of me.

"Well look at you! You must be Micah! I'm so sorry Silas didn't welcome you to our home. I like to call this place the garden because, well, just look at all of these paintings! I've been collecting them since I was a little girl. They're all so old, but slap a new frame on something and it's just like new! Please, sit, sit. On the red flowered couch, not the blue one. Yes, yes. It's much more comfortable. I can't tell you how happy we are to have you here. I'm sure Patrick has told you. Would you like something to drink? Water? That's really all I have to offer. Here, I'll get you a glass. No, don't get up. You look so comfortable now! Right at home. I'll be right back."

When she was through the doors I laughed a little bit to myself. Different place, different color, same mothers. She quickly rushed back with a green glass full of liquid.

"Here you go. I don't know if it will taste the same as where you're from, but hopefully you'll be able to drink it. Dinner's almost ready, Silas and his siblings should be bringing it out. They're so nervous and excited to meet you. Nervous-excited I call it. We all are." She pushed her legs in front of me between the couch and glass table and plopped her body next to mine.

"Patrick has told me so much about you. It means so much to him that this has worked out as it has. I can't believe you're actually down here. He'll be back in a minute, he usually gets home from work very late, but always in time for dinner! The kids should be ready by now, Amanda! Ben! Are you dressed?"

Two small voices replied from the hallway on the far right side of the room. "We're ready, is she here?"

"She's here!"

I heard fast thumping running closer and closer to me until it stopped right before the end of the hallway. I could see a small set of feet paused at the edge.

"Amanda, what's wrong?"

"We're scared of her."

"Well that's crazy. We talked about this. There's no reason to be scared."

"But what if she doesn't like us?" the little boy peeped.

"That is impossible. Come on! She's very excited to meet you."

"I am!" I chirped in. "I've heard so much about you guys."

They waited a few seconds before jumping out from behind the hallway.

"You two are cute as a button!" Their mother exclaimed, tightly clapping her hands. "Aren't they, Micah?"

The two children looked, as their mother had described before, nervous and excited. Amanda was a little taller than her brother, but I knew from the letters that she was a year younger. Her long, light brown hair was tied with bulky beaded bands into two high ponytails that cascaded onto her shoulders. She wore a necklace and bracelets that ran up to the middle of her arms and matched the hair ties. Her jewelry was extremely colorful and emphasized even further the bland colors of their clothing. She wore a long brown dress much like my own, minus the synching at her waist. Her brother was, as well, wearing a matching necklace. He was the only one in the family to have hair almost as dark as mine but it was tightly cropped around his face. They both stood next to each other, her hand around his arm, as if they were presenting themselves on stage. They had the same clear, blue eyes.

"You look wonderful." I replied, fidgeting on the unsupportive couch. "I love your jewelry."

This seemed to be the key that unlocked Amanda's heart. She sprang from her brother and tumbled onto the couch next to her mom, falling into her lap.

"We made them especially for today! Silas got the beads from his shop. I told Ben only girls wear necklaces, but he didn't care."

"They're very beautiful," I said, looking up at Ben, who had further sunk into the wall after his sister's departure. "I think they look great on both of you."

"Dad says you're from up there," she said, pointing to the ceiling. "And that we're not supposed to tell *anyone* you're here."

Their mother's face became bright red.

"No, honey. You can tell people that you had a visitor, remember? Just don't tell them where she came from. People don't like where she comes from."

"Up there!" Amanda screamed, standing up on the couch. "You come from waayyyyy up there."

"I do," I replied, almost embarrassingly.

"Bad people come from up there, but you're not bad," Ben yelled from the other side of the room.

"That's right, Ben," their mother said, motioning him towards her. "She's very good." He squeezed in front of her and she wrapped her arms around him. "Why don't you go grab the bowls from the kitchen and bring them over," she asked, planting a giant kiss on his cheek. He nodded and scurried across the room through the swinging door.

"We're having a shitake carrot stew," Amanda proudly remarked. "I picked it out for you."

"And what a good pick," her mother beamed. "Can you tell her how we made it?"

A look of confusion sprang across Amanda's face. "We... um... I don't know. We just did."

"You don't remember cutting up all the mushrooms with your special knife?" her mother enquired. Amanda just shrugged. "I guess." Their mother laughed. "Why don't you go grab the silverware?" Amanda exaggeratedly nodded, bounced off the couch, and hopped into the kitchen. As if on cue her brother followed close behind.

"I don't think they really understand what all of this is," Lynn explained, wiping off the table with her blue and white cloth. "They're just excited to have someone over for dinner."

"I would be too, if I were them," I replied, setting my glass down on the rim of the table. "Is there anything I can do to help?"

"Oh no! Don't be silly! You're our guest. Guests just get to stand there and look pretty. Oh, that rhymed! I continue to amaze myself! I'm going to go check on everything and I'll be right back." Lynn gave the table one last sweep before joining her family in the back room.

As I sat by myself I couldn't help but wonder, what in the world was shitake carrot stew? My family had, of course, made stews before, but ours were filled with meats and other things like celery, spinach, and noodles and were always complimented with a fruit of some kind. My father loved to put pineapple in his. I prayed that the stew wasn't going to taste like the pie from last week. The odors coming from the kitchen smelled a little better than before, but I didn't think I could sit through a whole meal with a taste like that in my mouth. I thought I could detect a hint of sweetness but that may have just been wishful thinking. I looked around the room once more and counted the landscapes around me. 23. There were 23 pictures of the natural earth in the living room of a family that would never actually see it. I wondered if they hung these pictures in desperation or imagination. Were sprawling hills and valleys something they wished to see someday, or just a piece of the past whose beauty they wished to appreciate?

The door swung open and Ben slowly walked forward,

precariously balancing a pile of white bowls as big as his torso on his forearms. I got up from the couch and walked towards him.

"Here, let me help you with that," I said, bending down to take a little bit of weight off his load.

"I have it!" he exclaimed, continuing to walk towards the table. I backed up and walked next to him, prepared to grab anything that fell from his grasp. He surprisingly made it to his destination, dropped the bowls with a controlled thud, and began setting them up around the coffee table. His sister was close behind with spoons, and their mother followed with six cups. By the time the entire table was set everything was so cramped that there was barely any glass peeking below. The only noticeable space left was a circle large enough for a big pot.

Lynn took a step back, surveyed her family's work, and called towards the kitchen.

"Silas, you can bring it in now! We're ready."

He pushed the door open with his back and, with cloth covered hands, brought forth a large steaming lidless pot. Lynn quickly folded her cloth and placed it in the center before Silas dropped the meal onto the table, slightly spilling a little stew over the edge of the metal container.

"Dinner!" he screamed, grabbing his younger sister and spinning her upside down. She let out an uncontrollable giggle. He swung her onto the couch and her dress bounced as she fell. She quickly sat up and straightened her back in preparation to eat.

"Micah, sit next to me!" she said, beating her hand against the couch where she wanted me to sit. I hesitated but then snaked over to her. The rest of the family followed suit, filling up the remaining couch space. Ben sat with Amanda and I, and Silas on the opposite couch, opposite side. Lynn left a small spot next to her on the edge.

"Patrick should have been back by now, I'm sure he just got caught up at work." I couldn't tell if she was worried but with that remark my mind started racing.

What if the government found out what he was doing. What if they know about the letters. What if they're coming to get me. Should I escape? Should I leave?

The front door creaked open and he came barreling forth, throwing a blue scarf and burgundy overcoat to the floor. Ben sprang up and threw his body around his father's legs.

"Daddy! We were waiting for you to eat! Come sit down, I'm starving!"

"I'm starving too! And it looks like you guys made quite a feast. Amanda, did you help your mother out at all?"

"I did! I cut the mushrooms!"

"Ah, I'm so excited. I could smell it in the stairwell! I'm sure we made our whole building jealous."

Amanda beamed with joy. I realized that this stew, which my family would eat on a light day and Gabe would still complain about being hungry after devouring, was more than just a meal for them. It was an event and, for their parents, a sacrifice.

"How was the shop today?" Patrick asked Silas, sitting down next to his wife.

"Same old, same old. Did a lot of repairs today."

"You're in high demand," he said, spooning the stew into his wife's bowl. "And you've got quite a skill."

Silas laughed and grabbed the ladle from his father. "It helps to pass the time before the meetings."

Patrick's demeanor suddenly became very stern. "We can talk about that later. Micah, I'm so glad you could make it down again," he smiled at me, reaching his hand out for my bowl. I handed it over and he spooned the brown, black, and orange mixture up to the brim. When he handed it back I let the flavors waft into my nostrils, breathing in their earthy scent. There was something warm and inviting about what he had just handed me even though it was full of ingredients I had never seen before.

He reached for Amanda and Ben's bowls and filled them halfway before finally completely filling his own. "How was your week?"

"It was fine, uneventful," I responded. I felt like I was talking to my own father.

"You say it was uneventful, but you have to remember even the simplest things you do are unexpected to us. I'll ask you again," he laughed, filling his spoon with a helping of stew. "How was your week?"

I picked up my own spoon and swirled the chunks within my bowl. They were all about the size of my fingernail and varied between square and circle, brown and orange. The broth was dark brown and had little pieces of green leaf floating throughout it.

"My school days were fine, I really enjoyed volunteering at the hospital this week."

"What a saint," Silas sarcastically remarked, taking a loud sip of his stew.

"That's very nice," Patrick responded, glaring at his oldest son. "Ben told me when he grows up he wants to be a doctor, isn't that right Ben?"

The little boy nodded, spilling back into the bowl some of the soup that he had carefully placed into his spoon. "I wanna wear a big white coat," he said, as if this was the most important part of the profession.

"Then you'll be just like Micah. Did you know that's what she's going to be, too?"

Ben dropped his spoon and looked up at me with wide eyes.

"You're a real life doctor?"

"I'm... trying to be." My stomach turned as I lied. It didn't hurt because of the food, which I still hadn't tasted, but because of the dishonesties I was telling to an innocent five year old. I realized that, as much as Patrick knew about me, I was still partially a fabrication to him. But, telling him the truth would ruin everything.

"Nonsense, you're about to be!" Patrick remarked, grabbing his wife's cloth to quickly wipe his face. "Four more months, right?"

I tried to think back on what I had told him. In reality I had three more months of school before being given a one month, once in a lifetime break in which I was supposed to "prepare for my career". I must have told him in my letters that I had four more months of schooling before becoming an official doctor.

"Yeah, four more."

"Will you volunteer at the hospital for all this time, as well as attend school?"

Luckily this was one part of my story that didn't require a lie.

"I hope so, yes. At least I would like to. We'll see how things go."

Silas again grabbed attention from the other end of the table. "It's really wonderful that you're able to help so many people." He said, looking straight at me. This was the only nice thing he had said since we first met. I wondered if he was finally coming around to my presence.

"Even though there are thousands of families starving and not getting the medical attention they need underground, I'm really happy that you can supply everyone above with the attention they think they deserve. You're quite the little martyr."

Nope.

"What's a... martyr?" Amanda asked, stumbling over the foreign word.

"It's a word your brother made up. I told you he's full of bologna." Patrick quickly replied.

"You're full of bologna and cheese!" Amanda mocked at Silas. He smiled. "At least I'm delicious."

"I wouldn't eat you," Ben confirmed.

"Well I wouldn't eat *you* either," Silas laughed, poking his brother in the side.

The meal continued this way for about a half hour more. Patrick would ask me questions, I would try to respond as vaguely as possible, and Silas would either remark with a quip or not remark at all. Ben and Amanda were silent for the rest of the meal, focusing on finishing their seemingly large bowls. When they had finally licked them clean Lynn rose, grabbed her children's scarce remnants, and sent them off to wash up.

"Ben, can you read a book to your sister tonight?"

"But Mommy, you always do it!"

"Not tonight, sweetheart. Mommy's going to sit with Daddy, Silas and Micah."

"I want to stay up with you!"

"If you go to bed right now, tomorrow night I'll let you stay up for an extra fifteen minutes."

The two children accepted the bargain and sulked away.

"Now that Ben and Amanda are asleep we can have dessert," Lynn said, walking over to the tall stand supporting the television. She opened a small drawer on the bottom and dug through a mound of stray papers to pull out a tiny, tin square from underneath. She excitedly brought the package over and filled the void on the couch next to me where her youngest kids had been sitting.

"Lynn, are you sure you wannna bring this out tonight? You've been saving it for a while," Silas asked.

"Positive," she responded, ripping off the silver wrapping. Underneath lay a fist-sized piece of chocolate. I was surprised-- chocolate was kind of rare aboveground but was part of a handover at least once a month. Whenever my parents were able to buy some from Mrs. Dern I was grateful but didn't treat it like gold. From the looks on the faces around me it seemed like Lynn had saved this piece for a very, very long time.

"Good a time as any," she said, breaking the chocolate into four equal pieces and handing one to each of us. "It's going to go bad soon, anyways."

"You don't get to eat this a lot?" I asked, already knowing the answer. I was looking for an explanation more than anything else.

"You might say that," she said, smiling. "Some might even say it isn't allowed down here, but I have my ways. Would anyone like a cup of coffee with their chocolate?" Patrick and Silas nodded their heads yes.

"And you, sweetheart?" she asked me.

I thought about the amount of time I was going to have to stay awake after this. A whole other day.

"If it isn't too much trouble."

"Never too much trouble," she hummed, walking back towards the kitchen.

"Maybe not for her," I heard Silas mutter under his breath. His father heard it, too.

"Silas, can you put your political beliefs aside for one meal, please. Let the girl visit in peace."

"If I can't visit her land in peace I don't see why she's allowed to visit mine." The fight they were about to have was entirely because of me. I felt like I had to step in.

"If I could bring you up I would, but it's not a place you'd want to go. I really don't think you'd like it."

"You can't decide that for me."

"You're right. I can't decide for you because I don't make my laws. With the way my people are right now if you came above you'd be beaten and hung. It's awful. Disgusting. But know if I could change them I would."

He didn't know that this was exactly my destiny. To create the laws meant to destroy him. My profession wasn't there to help him. It never would be.

"That's why she's down here." Patrick attempted to explain. He was defending me like my own father would. "She wouldn't be sitting with us unless she wanted to help. Don't you see what she's risking just to be at this table right now?"

Silas sat, unresponsively sulking. Patrick looked up apologetically.

"Silas has had a few bad experiences with the aboveground. He has... had... a few classmates who haven't returned." I looked over to Silas as he sat staring at the small piece of chocolate.

Suddenly it all made sense. Ever since I first arrived below ground he was the only one who had disapproved of me. But, the truth was they all should have disapproved of me. I realized that when I descended down those stairs I should've been descending to my death. All that my people have done to theirs is kill and beat, slaughter and decapitate. Every one of us was guilty, even myself. I had watched hundreds of men and women be killed as if they were roaches and our city needed to be fumigated. I thought back to my school field trips to the government center, to the news I heard every morning and the shows I watched at night.

Eight more Nightcrawlers hung for trespassing! Ten more sent to the government house! Special end of the year mass hanging!

Silas's disappearing classmates must have at some point just been a number in my head, one of the dozens I heard about every day. I'd never been forced to put faces to these numbers before. I knew they were people, I knew that they had families and friends too, but I pushed all of this away so I wouldn't have to be confronted by it. To everyone above, and to everyone I knew, Silas's friends were just bodies to be hung. I looked back down at the chocolate in my hand. I was all of a sudden disgusted. I felt undeserving of it, of the meal, of the clothing they had put onto my body. They had given me all of this and all my people had given them was pain. Why had they not killed me yet? My body should be hanging from their ceiling. Yet, I had never experienced anything but kindness in my two journeys. That is, from all but Silas. Maybe he was the only sane person in the entire room.

I wanted to push the table away and bring myself to my knees in front of him. I wanted to beg for his forgiveness for something those associated with me had done. Although I never tightened the noose on a Nightcrawler's neck, I had never loosened one either. All the pain that I had witnessed suddenly hit me like a brick. My hands began shaking and I placed the chocolate onto the bare table. I looked back up at Patrick.

"Have you all had someone close to you who's been killed?"

"Everyone down here knows someone. It's become a part of who we are."

"It shouldn't be," Silas said, focusing on a water spot on the table. "We shouldn't have to live like this." He spoke quietly, lost in thought of those who had passed and tracing his fingers across the scar on his chin. "I shouldn't have to pick between living in fear and not living at all."

Patrick placed his hand onto his son's shoulder.

"We don't live in fear all the time," he reassured me. "But it is becoming more and more often."

Lynn came back with four cups of coffee. "I can see you've already begun the discussion," she murmured, placing one in front of each person.

"Lynn, show her." Silas pushed, leaning back in his seat. "Show her what they did to you."

"Not right now, I don't want to ruin a good piece of chocolate," she responded, tucking herself into her own body on the couch.

"Please," I practically begged. "What did we do?"

"Oh honey, it wasn't you. I know that."

It didn't matter that it wasn't me. It could have been my mother, or my brother, or my father. It could have been my friend, or my banker, or my grocer. I had no idea what happened to her but whatever it was I already knew it could have been done by absolutely anyone in my life.

"It's not as bad as it looks," she said, standing up. She turned around and slowly pulled up her shirt. Across her lower back were giant scarred slashes than ran from hipbone to hipbone. All I could do was stare.

She quickly put her shirt back down and sat again on the couch. "Really not as bad as it looks."

But, it looked pretty bad.

"How did that happen?" I stammered.

"It was my fault really," she began.

"It wasn't. Don't ever say that." Silas defended.

"I guess it doesn't matter whose fault it is. A few years ago I went to visit Patrick at work and may have gotten a little too close to the entrance of the AG. I wasn't really looking where I was going. It was dusk, I had completely forgotten, and didn't realize that the portal was right in front of me. I was trying to find him and went up to ask someone if they knew where he might be. I didn't look at the person before I asked; they had their back turned to me. When they turned around I realized it was… someone from above."

It seemed like another word had been replaced by this description.

"The man immediately threw me down and beat me with his baton. I shouldn't have asked him, I should've looked where I was going."

"Don't say that," Silas pleaded. "Don't ever blame yourself."

"There's no use in discussing details now," she sighed, picking up her cup of coffee. "What's happened has happened. I was in bed for a few weeks afterwards, but I'm fine now. I'm lucky he didn't take me up and hang me, it's happened before. God knows it happens all the time."

"I don't understand how you can dismiss it like that." Silas's fists were beginning to clench. "They shouldn't be able to get away with all of this."

"Sometimes you have to pick your battles," she sighed. "I'm saving my anger for another day." She picked up her chocolate and took a small nibble from the side. "Hmmmm, nothing like chocolate."

"But the day is today. The time is now." Silas remarked, his cup of coffee suspended in both hands below his face. Lynn laughed.

"Did you learn that little saying at one of your meetings?"

He took a small sip, letting the liquid rest on his tongue before responding. "I've learned a lot of little sayings at these meetings. I've been telling you to come."

"Oh, it's for young folk, not people like me who have a family to worry about."

I tried to piece together what they were talking about. Was Silas part of an exclusive group? I took a large breath and asked.

"Silas, I hope this isn't crossing a line, but you've mentioned your meetings a few times. What're they about?"

Patrick immediately responded before his son had the chance to speak.

"It's something he does after work. He meets up with a few friends. They grab drinks and chat."

"Dad, why don't you want me to tell her?"

"Tell me...what?"

Were they hiding something, too?

"We aren't just a small group that sits around and drinks. It's a pretty large one and we chat about a lot more than our social lives."

"What do you chat about?"

His body suddenly straightened and he confidently pushed out his chest.

"We chat about the coming revolution."

13

II was sitting on the floor of my room. Back against the wall. Knees up. Head hanging.

I was waiting for the sunrise. That was it. That's all I wanted. Just to be in the moment when it's halfway up the sky. I wanted its soft rays to drape across my skin. And then, I wanted it to stop. To be stuck in the in between. To be caught between the two places it belonged, below and above. I wanted it to sit there with me, both of us with no idea of where to go next.

Gabe was pacing inside my room when I got back. He saw me open the door and furiously ran towards me. He angrily grabbed my arms, pushing my body into his and squeezing me tight, throwing my head into his shoulder with one hand.

"I drove by twice. I didn't see you." I expected the words to drip with frustration. Instead, they were riddled with fear and concern. "I thought they'd taken you."

I wrapped my arms around him, too.

"No, Gabe. They would never take me."

"I didn't mean just them, I meant... never mind what I

meant," he finished, pulling away and regaining composure. "What the hell happened? I drove by three times. You were never there."

"I lost track of time."

"I… there aren't excuses for what happened."

"I know."

"You could have gotten both of us killed."

"I know."

"Don't you know how worried I was?"

"I know. I'm sorry."

"Why do you keep thinking that sorry is enough to solve everything? I'm risking my career for this. We're risking our family."

"I know. I got caught up with theirs."

He sat down on my bed as his head fell into his hands.

"I just kept thinking of everything that could have happened to you. I really thought you were gone."

I sat down next to him.

"If you were so convinced why didn't you turn them in? Why didn't you tell your superiors that the UG had taken me hostage? You could have lied and said they snuck into our building and took me from my bed. You know they would've sent a swarm of trashmen down looking for me. They never would have found out what you were doing."

He didn't respond at first, but kept his head pushed into his hands. I tenderly put my hand onto his back and gently rubbed it with the tips of my fingers. He finally brought his head up and looked at me with defeated eyes.

"I didn't think the Nightcrawlers had taken you."

It was as if a veil lifted from over my brother. I had always seen him as a one sided individual. Ever since I could remember all he had wanted was to be a trash collector. In preschool he would come home every day with a drawing of himself in their uniform, in elementary school his fascination had graduated to short stories, and by the time he was thirteen he was already shadowing men on their shifts. The job was made for him. It was the perfect fit. He never doubted it. Or at least I thought he never doubted it. His statement completely amazed me.

"You thought I was captured by trashmen?" I asked. I couldn't believe he had even alluded to it.

His jaw tightened. He couldn't respond.

"Is this something that's happened before?"

"No," he defensively retorted. "Not yet."

"Why were you so worried, then?"

He got up from the bed and walked to the other side of the room. He faced the wall but I could still feel the intensity on his face.

"A few weeks ago we were given a new order. To turn in... anything.... we found at night."

"Anything," I repeated unquestioningly. He nodded.

"Anything. Before, if we found someone walking around above ground at night we had always been required to call it in, but never arrest. With this new law, no one's safe. Everyone's a suspect."

"You were worried I'd been arrested by your colleagues." It wasn't a question, it was a matter of fact.

"I checked every radio. I drove down every street. Nothing was called in, but that didn't convince me that nothing had been found."

"I shouldn't have scared you like that. It won't happen again."

He twisted around.

"It's not happening because you're not going down there

again."

I pretended to care about this forbiddance.

"But Gabe, I was so close to finding out names of their major leaders."

"I don't care about that anymore. I don't care about any of it. All I care is that you're safe."

"You're not worried about the letters? What if someone gets wind of what we've been doing?"

"Micah, didn't you hear me? I don't care about that anymore. Thinking that you were gone just... it just really made me realize what matters. You should have called me out on my bullshit a long time ago. When it comes down to it you know I could never turn you in."

Until that very moment, though, I didn't. My brother always acted as if his job was more important than his family. He was barely home and, when he was, it was all he ever talked about. He had told me countless times that he couldn't wait to "find someone to be with and leave this fucking apartment." I guess I discovered the reason he stayed. We meant a lot more to him than he was willing to admit. He walked back to the bed and sat down next to me.

"I never should have told you that I was going to turn you in. When I found the letter I should've burned it and forbidden you from speaking to him again, but that was it. I could never give them my own sister."

I hugged him from the side and laid my head onto his shoulder.

"I don't know what I would do without you," I whispered.

"I know exactly what I'd do without you," he laughed. "Be a lot less fucking stressed right now. What did you talk to them about for such a long time, anyways? And how did you get back here safe and sound?"

*　　*　　*　　*　　*　　*　　*　　*　　*

I choked a little bit on my sip of coffee.

"The coming what?"

"Revolution."

My loose body became suddenly alert on the floral couch.

"You shouldn't have told her that," Patrick scolded. "Not yet Silas. Not now."

"We have to stop saying not now! The only time is now! Now is all we have!"

"Keep your voice down," Lynn hissed. "Amanda and Ben will hear you."

"What type of revolution?" I asked, leaning in closer to Silas.

"The normal kind," he responded. "Guns, bombs, government overthrow. Exactly what it sounds like."

I should have been appalled. I should have stormed straight out of their apartment, gone right up to my streets, and told the closest trash collector everything I knew. But, I wasn't. I didn't. Intrigue filled the gaps in my mind where repulsion should have taken its hold.

"It's come to that?" I asked, looking at each of the family members in the room. Patrick and Lynn just looked down.

"Not yet," Silas replied. "But soon."

I laughed.

"I thought the only time we have is now."

"Sometimes now needs a little planning," he smirked back. He was warming up to me, just the slightest.

"When is this... revolution, as you call it, going to take

place?"

"We don't have a specific date yet. Things like revolutions aren't planned like school dances."

"Then enlighten me, how are they planned?"

"Slowly. With support. With escape routes, and plans B, C, and D. We have to make sure we're prepared for everything."

"You're revolting against the aboveground?"

"That's exactly what we're doing."

I was confused. My historytexts had all told me if a revolution were to take place in the underground that it would be against their own leader. I figured this was false in some way, but hadn't figured out exactly how.

"Why don't you revolt against your own government? Aren't they the ones keeping food and supplies from you?"

He looked back at me with a look of complete surprise.

"I don't know who told you that, but they've been lying. Our government is doing all they can to help us, it's the aboveground that's destroying everything. They've been sending down less and less food, giving us barely any supplies. Look around this room, do you see anything vaguely new?"

I didn't. Everything looked at least twenty years old.

"When did all of this start?"

"About sixty years ago, when they lost hold of all underground political power. To maintain some form of control they started reducing our resources. They've made it so that we're still dependent on them."

"You can't make your own resources?"

"Everything is transported above ground. Sometimes, in sectors far, far away, they're able to sneak raw materials underground. But, by the time the goods get to us, if they do get to us, they're either awful quality or a small quantity."

This was the first time I had even remotely thought,

We are singlehandedly destroying them. They're dying not because of themselves, but because of us. Because of me.

"You know about all of this?" I asked his parents.

Patrick scraped his thumb against the rim of his mug. Lynn burrowed her tired head into her husband's shoulder. Neither responded immediately.

"We know there's a plan. Everyone down here knows there's a plan. But, Micah, know I didn't bring you down here for the revolution. I genuinely want to know what it's like up there," he said, looking up to his ceiling. "If we're going to revolt, I needed a secure sign that your people are as awful as everyone believes they are. I wrote to you expecting to either get no response or to have the trashmen knocking at my door. For three days after I wrote to you we had our men here waiting with guns. We were all terrified."

"No one expected you to respond as you did," Lynn said as she clutched her husband's hand. "We all prepared for the worst. But you, you really are the best that could have happened."

"After we started communicating I stopped going to the meetings. I distanced myself from the group. I could no longer be a part of a movement that would destroy something as sacred as your family."

Patrick looked worn, as if he had told this to many people many times.

"If you exist there have to be more like you. Everyone above can't be bad. I can't stand the thought of hurting someone innocent."

"But we're all innocent," Silas vehemently argued. "She may be innocent, but so was Skylar. So was Alex. So was Lynn." He looked to his stepmother, who tiringly smiled back. She looked towards me and placed her hands on the table.

"We brought you down here as a warning," she said. "For you and your family. You have four months to get out. You can't tell them why, but you must."

"You don't have to help us," Patrick stated. "But for your kindness this is all I can offer you. This is happening whether we want it to or not, Silas has made that very clear."

I stared into my coffee cup as if, somewhere in its kona depths, there was the answer to what I should have done next. They had basically just told me that, no matter what I did, my entire world was going to be destroyed in less than half a year. They had offered a warning for my family, but that was it. It was kind, but a warning would never be enough. Where did they expect us to go? Travel between sectors was completely banned unless you, as an individual, were given special permission to leave. All immigrants arrived at their new location completely alone and were forced to give up everything they had ever known in order to do so. I realized in order to save those I loved I only had one choice. I looked up from my coffee cup and stared straight into Silas' eyes.

"Do you know about the elevator?"

Their looks of worry and explanation were suddenly replaced with confusion. Patrick and Lynn had no idea what I was talking about, but I could see as Silas shifted his body forward that he knew just the one.

"I might."

His blue eyes glimmered. He was beginning to see where I was going.

"What's she talking about?" Lynn asked. "I don't see how this connects."

I continued looking solely at Silas.

"What if I help you. What if I sneak medical supplies down when no one's looking. You said it yourself that the underground is short on everything. If you show me the elevator, I can help you. But, you have to help me."

I could see the wheels turning in his head as he thought it over.

"How are we going to help you?" He said it in a way that seemed like we were already making plans, not suggestions.

"If I sneak you as many supplies as I can then you protect my family. When the revolution comes," I continued, "you bring us down here. You help us become part of the underground."

"Micah, Silas, I don't know if this is the best arrangeme...."

"How many supplies can you get?"

"My father is a head doctor. I can go almost anywhere and get almost anything."

"Supplies of any type?"

"Including food."

He didn't need to think it over. We knew what we needed from each other.

"When will you sneak it down?"

"Immediately. A little at first, but more and more as time goes by. I'll need to test the waters, but by the end everything I can get my hands on will be yours."

"And you promise to tell no one of this until you absolutely have to? Not even your family?"

"I promise."

"Silas," Lynn interjected. "Where will you keep them?"

"We'll figure it out," he responded, breaking my gaze for the first time. "That will be the least of our worries."

"Micah, we didn't intend this when we brought you down. I

never thought you'd say that you'd help," Patrick explained.

Silas stood up and walked around the coffee table until he was looming over me. I twisted my body to face his.

"Micah, do you understand that by agreeing to help us you're going to be a part of punishing every person you've ever known. We're not just looking to take over the aboveground. We will kill every single person in the government that has hurt one of us. Do you understand?"

I thought of my classroom. My classmates. My teachers. My historytext. My field trips. My INSAV. I thought of all they had ever told me. I thought of the boy's gaze as he lay dying in the street. I thought of the woman's face as she lay defeated on the ground.

"I understand," I replied, popping the piece of chocolate between my lips. I let it slowly dissolve and coat my entire mouth.

"What time were we supposed to send her back?" Lynn abruptly asked her husband.

"4:00."

I looked up at the clock. It was 4:20.

Shit shit shit shit shit. Gabe was meeting me on the corner at 4:30. I stood up and ran towards the door. "I'm too late!" I yelled. My heart was pounding against my chest. There were those paper birds again.

"I'll take you another way," Silas said, grabbing his coat. Together we flew down the stairs, out onto the road, and into the building across the street. We scaled five flights and Silas barreled through the door on the top. He ran to the end of the hallway and pulled a leaver down from the ceiling.

"People have been making escape paths for years," he quickly explained, climbing up a thin ladder that had sprung from the top. We climbed it hastily and suddenly I was running down another dark hallway, this one at a slight incline. He grabbed my hand and we ran even faster. We reached the end and he turned, a full ninety degrees without warning, and my ankle grazed the wall. He pushed open a door and we were in the room from before, the older man standing there once again.

"Where were you!" he exclaimed, throwing me my uniform. I quickly changed without modesty.

"We lost track of time," Silas responded, picking up my stray clothes from the floor.

"Well hurry, hurry!" The man demanded. "The sun will be rising soon!" I flung on my coat and turned towards the door to leave.

"Wait!" Silas grabbed my arm and spun me around. "I need to give you this." I looked down at the sheet of paper he had thrust into my hands. It was a pocket-sized blueprint of the 5th floor of the hospital with a red dot in the corner. I nodded thank you and began running.

The hallway was completely dark. I tried to figure out where in its path I was, but missed my timing of the first stairwell by a few seconds and slammed into its angling. I quickly picked myself up and ran up the stairs, counting to 71. I ran down the second hallway as quickly as I could and counted the second set, 1 2 3 4 5… I stopped. I listened for sounds from outside. I heard nothing and gently pushed the top open, sliding my body into the darkness above. I closed the latch and swiftly scurried as far as I could into the shadow of the wall. I tried to control my breathing. I listened for the sounds of Gabe's engine, but knew I was already too late.

Shit shit shit shit SHIT! I thought to myself again. After everything I had just gone through, that was it. I was in my final moments. A trashman was going to find me and know. All I could do at this point was try and walk the four blocks home as inconspicuously as possible. I pulled up the hood of my black coat.

I tried to think of all the princesses I imagined when I was younger. They would always glide across the floor and tried to do the same. I had walked a single block before I heard a yell from across the road.

"Hey! You there! Come here!"

Do I run? Do I go to her? Do I faint? If I ran, where would I run to? There were trash collectors everywhere that time of night. I uncontrollably let out a small whimper and headed towards the uniformed man. Maybe I could drop Gabe's name and get away.

"What're you doing here this late at night?" She demanded.

I knew I had to think of a response quickly, but nothing was entering or leaving to my mind. Why was I such a great bull shitter at every other time in my life except for right then?

"I was... taking a walk." I stuttered. Taking a walk? Who takes a walk?

"Taking a walk?" she asked disapprovingly. I nodded. "Identification, please." My shaky hands reached towards her and I pushed my INSAV against her wrist. They both blinked and my information appeared above her device. I watched her eyes as they scanned over my name.

"Micah Davis, is it?" Again, I nodded. She closed the screen and shoved her hand into her pocket. "Come with me."

That was it. I wasn't even going to be able to say goodbye to my family. She walked five paces in front of me in the direction I was initially traveling, a quiet whistle leaking from her lips. I kept my head down the entire time. It took everything within me not to cry. If I was going to go down, I was going to do it nobly. At least, as nobly as I could manage. Once we got to the government house I'd be sure to tell them who my family was. There was no way anything would happen to me. At least, that's what I told myself.

With every trashman we came across the woman I was following stopped her whistle, gave them a quick nod of her head and continued walking. No one seemed to be confused as to why there was a dark skinned girl following her.

We turned down my street and I looked up to give my building one final look. I hated that place, but at least it was home. And, I reminded myself, it was a home that would be destroyed in less than four months.

The woman stopped in front of my building and turned around towards me. I was confused. Was she letting me stop to get something? Did they add a new jail somewhere on one of the floors?

"This is your stop," the woman said, reaching her hand out of her pocket. She reopened my information from her wrist to double check. I looked up at her bewilderedly.

"I..." I began to speak, but realized there was no use. I wasn't going to argue with her and was relieved enough not to search for an explanation. She pressed her wrist against the scanner and unlocked the door.

"Go ahead," she said, holding the entrance open.

I had no words. I walked inside and completely past my apartment.

"Micah," she loudly whispered to me. I turned around. She was stopped at my door. "Isn't this where you live?"

What.

She motioned me towards the door. I stood on the other side

of the frame and she scanned her wrist. It opened my home. It shouldn't have done that, no matter who she was.

"Wha..." I began.

"Shhh....shhh. You don't need an explanation. Just be thankful you've made some friends in the right places."

With that she pivoted on her left foot and whistled down the hallway.

*   *   *   *   *   *   *   *   *

"What did you talk to them about for such a long time, anyways? And how did you get back here safe and sound?" Gabe asked me.

My lips tightened before answering. "It took a while for them to warm up to me, I didn't get much out of them. And somehow I managed to make it back on my own."

When he left I continued sitting on my bed before eventually crawling across my floor and burrowing against the wall.

DIET OF THE NIGHTCRAWLERS
By: Ian Dale

The diet of the underground is extremely different from our own. As stated before, there are no family units. Consequentially, the meaning of a "meal" to the Nightcrawlers is completely different than the definition it carries above. These people do not sit and have civilized meals as we do. They hoard their food from one another in secret locations and eat solitarily. Sharing of foods, something we all commonly practice, is nonexistent. After children reach a certain age, approximately 7 or 8, they are told to fend for themselves. They may continue to live under their parents' roofs, if they are lucky enough, but it is extremely unlikely that these adults will provide nutrition for their children. The children are taught to, just like their parents, keep all food they find or buy to themselves.

This practice is partially a cause for the intricate youth gangs and slums that are discussed in the earlier chapters. When the children feel unwelcomed by their family, they react by escaping to a community of youngsters who they believe understand how they feel. The youth they find, however, seldom provide more support than the home they ran away from. Here is an account from Samantha, a young girl of a slum existing below the south side of Sector 10.

"I am completely alone and have no one to turn to. My family cast me out when I was 6 years old and this slum is the only place that would take me. It was wonderful at first, I always had someone to play with and we all shared with one another. But, then things got tough. I had no one to help me, and because of this, couldn't give any of my friends help. They ended up not really being my friends, anyways. I would give anything to be in a world where families exist. All I want is a warm bed and someone to read me a story before I fall asleep. Why is that too much to ask?"

Samantha's story is not unusual. After interviewing approximately 100 youths in slums across 45 sectors, we were told similar stories over and over again. Wherever you live, there is a child living below you who is hungry, alone, and fighting for their life. By becoming a segregationalist you can save them. You can help create laws that will protect not only our people, but through this eventually provide a better life for these children. You are on a path of righteousness that cann......

I stopped reading and copied the last answers of my assignment off the boy sitting next to me. There were two more pages of lies that I was supposed to sit through. With every false description Ian Dale made of the underground I had a flashback to sitting in Patrick's living room and eating with his family.

After children reach a certain age, approximately 7 or 8, they are told to fend for themselves.

I saw Amanda and Ben emerging from the hallway, smiles as wide as their faces.

The children are taught to, just like their parents, keep all food they find or buy to themselves.

I tasted the chocolate that Lynn had saved for so long.

Three more months, I reminded myself as I slyly looked over my shoulder at my neighbor's paper. Three more months and I can leave this school. Four more months and this school will be destroyed.

This thought brought me a sick joy. I hated myself for finding pleasure in the knowledge that everything around me was going to be demolished, but I also hated everything around me for what they were doing to everyone below them. All my memories were in these city blocks, every single birthday, every single holiday, every single triumph and downfall. I had never known anything else. They had never let me know anything else.

But I had always wanted something more. Not a day went by that I hadn't wondered what lay beyond the walls of my sector. I never understood why I was the only person who seemed to feel trapped within them. No one else appeared to mind knowing that there was an unreachable world just a few minutes away in every direction. They were content living every day of their small lives in this small sector. They never questioned their occupations, never questioned the choices that were made for them. Maybe they did, at one point in their life, but chose to follow a path that was given to them instead of creating one of their own. I looked around my room. If I were to stand up, right then, and scream to my classmates that everything they were told was a lie, would they even care? Would my proclamation plant a seed of doubt in any of their minds? Or, were the roots of the government so strong that they stole all nutrients from any other ideas before they could even take root?

It wasn't their fault that they lived like this. They had no idea what existed below them. They had no control over who they were destined to become, just as I had no control over the letters that appeared below my floorboard. Any one of them could be in the position I was that day, any one of them could have lived where I lived and received what I received. But, would they have responded in the same way? How many of my classmates would have chosen to write back to Patrick instead of turning him in? They were all typing so intensely into their computers, they didn't seem to doubt a word they wrote.

No, I was meant to receive those letters. I was meant to respond as I did. Maybe when the revolution comes my classmates will fight for what is truly right. That will be their opportunity, just as Patrick and his family were mine. Eventually they'll have a choice to make, and on that day they'll finally be in control of their own destinies.

I didn't want any of them to die. They didn't choose to be born into the positions that were thrust upon them. But, neither did the Nightcrawlers. The thousands of underground citizens who had already died didn't choose to be born with light skin, just as I didn't choose to be born dark. The revolution, whenever it's going to happen, will be confronting all of us with a choice. Do we accept the world we were born into, or do we risk our lives to change it for the better? For many of my friends this will be the first, and most important, choice they'll ever have to make.

Four more months.

"Alright everyone, INSAVs closed! Time for our monthly field trip."

I had completely forgotten that day was one of those days.

I didn't speak to a single person on the walk there. Once we made it to the government center I stood as far in the back as possible without drawing attention to myself. But, I also made sure I could see the man's rope encompassed around his neck.

Before that day, I had always thought these deaths were meaningless. Before I began receiving letters from Patrick, every person hung in front of me wasn't even a person, they were just an excuse to step outside my classroom. The bodies before me didn't hold life and therefore didn't hold meaning.

After writing with Patrick these deaths were meaningless in a different way. They were deaths that would never be avenged and had no true cause. Yet, that day, I realized these hangings, which I had witnessed once a month every month for my entire life, had more meaning than anything I had ever witnessed. Every hanging that took place was fuel to an underground fire. These people weren't just bodies captured for no reason, pulled from their families as they walked to work or back from the store. They were prisoners of a war that only those underground knew had begun. They were soldiers, dying victoriously for their land. They were true heroes.

With as much respect as I could muster, I watched the man drop. He was giving up his life so that one day those he loved could have better ones. The very least I could do was appreciate his final moments.

The girl next to me was picking her nails. The boy to my right was digging a few pieces of candy out of his pocket in preparation to hand them over to a victorious friend. Everyone walked back to the classroom chatting as if what they witnessed was just another part of the school day. And, I guess for them, it was.

Throughout my entire shift at the hospital that afternoon all I could think about was my break. I smiled and chatted, held children's' hands and patted mothers' backs as I walked them down the hallway, but not a bit of me cared about any of it. As I walked them down to room 4- 7- 23- 22- 11- 5, I was secretly counting down in my head the minutes until my break. Just one more hour. Just forty seven more minutes. 10 more.

The last five were the worst. Time inched slower than ever before. I would look up at the clock expecting the hand to have traveled swiftly on its teleological path, yet it seemed stuck at a spot one minute after I had looked before. I wanted to jump onto a chair, pull it off the wall, and manually move the hands myself.

Finally, the time came. I found my substitute and headed straight for the stairwell.

My shoes reverberated against each step as I climbed, echoes melting into the bare walls of the stairwell. Every movement I made felt sharp and unnatural. I grabbed the railing as I ascended the stairs, but even my grip felt strange. Once on the landing of the fifth floor I paused and leaned against the wall, reaching into my bra to pull out the small note that Silas had handed me right before I ran out of the underground. I peered down the stairwell once more to confirm that I was alone and unfolded it. My fingers shook as they analyzed the note, tracing the path I was about to take. The elevator seemed to be in a narrow hallway halfway down the main one and to the left. I quickly folded back the piece of paper onto the original creases and shoved it down my shirt. I would burn it once I got home.

I opened the door and walked down the hall with false confidence. I couldn't appear to anyone that I didn't belong there. I couldn't second-guess myself. I smiled at a passing doctor who locked eyes with mine. He smiled back as I turned left down the second hallway. I counted the doorways that I passed, right hand outstretched waiting for the fifth. Once in front of the door I immediately grabbed the knob, half expecting it to be locked. The device turned as I pushed it and the door opened. I slid inside, closing the door as quietly as possible. I was in. Finally, I was in.

The room was completely dark, but at this point I was used to these situations. I slipped my fingers across the wall, searching for a switch. My left hand stumbled upon an angled bump and I pushed it up. The lights flickered at first and then the room was completely illuminated.

It was small and square. Each wall was about a body and a half's length across. I didn't understand. There wasn't anything close to an elevator in the closet, each wall was completely covered by a tall, metal-tiered storage rack. On these racks were basic cleaning supplies of every kind-- extra mops, hard soaps, liquid soaps, cloths, buckets and brooms. Hidden in the far left corner was a large sink that ran to the floor. I walked over to it, checking to see if there was anything trapped behind or within. Nothing. The sink was simply stained with soap scum. I didn't understand and pulled out the map once more, retracing my steps. Down the hall, first left, fifth room on the right. Labeled "Janitor's Closet". Everything fit except for what was inside.

Was this a trick by Silas? Was this his way of getting me out of the underground, by convincing me that there was something I could do to save my family? My stomach turned. If there wasn't an elevator in that closet my family was as dead as the rest of them. I peered into every shelf, looking for clues in the items they were holding. There was nothing out of the ordinary. I walked around the room, even pulled at the sink thinking it might be false.

There was nothing.

I walked back to a corner near the door and let my body slide down it, bringing my knees to my chest. How was I so stupid to trust someone like that? Defeated, I let my legs loosen and slide across the floor. My right leg became trapped against the shelf I had nuzzled my body next to and pushed against it at an away angle. Amazingly, the shelf pushed back and slightly swung forward, inching away from the wall it was burrowed against. I paused in amazement before bringing my left leg behind the moving shelf and pushing with both limbs. With the strength of both my legs the shelf moved away on a hinge to reveal the wall that lay beneath. There wasn't a noticeable door, but as I leaned my head closer I noticed a faint crease that ran up and around in a large rectangle. If there was an entrance it was either behind this wall or masked to look like it was a part of it. The shelves were so tall and full of supplies that I noticed none of this when I originally looked behind them.

I wondered if there was a theme to this mystery and pushed the wall inside the crease with all the weight in my body. It, just like the shelves, pushed open to reveal another level of darkness. There was no going back. I continued pushing until a gap large enough to slide my body through was created and I ventured to the other side. The door immediately swung shut behind me and I was again surrounded by almost complete darkness. But, across a murky room about ten feet in front of me, I saw the faint glow of one small button. I scurried towards the pulsating orb. I couldn't believe I'd missed this, why didn't I know it would be hidden? Everything else was. I took a deep breath, pressed the button, and stepped back to wait.

At first it seemed like nothing was going to happen. There

were no noises, no creaking of a cage as it rattled towards my floor. It was so dark that I couldn't even see if I was standing in front of an elevator door or just a blank wall designed to look like one. I changed my mind about what I said before-- this was the slowest that time had ever trickled.

Without warning, a vertical sliver of light appeared before me and continued growing until I was standing in front of a bright elevator car large enough to tightly hold two people. Its interior was entirely one color, a light beige that traveled from the ceiling, to the walls, to the laminate floor. There were no railings, no moldings, no car door. I smiled as I stepped into its clutches, allowing it to take me to wherever my final destination was going to be. The only thing that differed from the uniform interior was two buttons on the front right hand side of the car, a 5 and a U.

With a firm thumb I pressed the U and watched the elevator doors as they trapped me within. My time was now.

The elevator sank for less than a minute before opening again. The ride was calm, almost too calm. I expected bumps, creaks, and interruptions, but the trip was as smooth as the drinks I used to down at The Red Knob. I watched myself sink through layers of concrete, dropping further and further from safety but closer and closer to my resolution.

I don't know what I expected to be in front of me upon my arrival, but I at least expected... something. When the doors opened I was in yet another room. An empty room subtly lit by a single green overhead light. Although this room was slightly lit, there didn't seem to be much that needed illumination. It was just an empty room with a simple wooden door at the other end. I laughed to myself, stepped out of the elevator, and headed to the other side of the room. Behind this door would probably be another hallway, leading to a stairwell, another room, another stairwell, and finally my destination. That seemed to be how everything was organized down there.

I turned the knob wholeheartedly expecting the door to open immediately. It didn't budge. I tried shaking it, turning the knob in the opposite direction, lifting up when I turned, lifting down. Nothing. I raised my now sweaty hand and bent down to be at the same level as the handle. Did I need a key like the one Raziela had shown me before? I looked for a small hole by tracing my finger around the metal frame and eventually brought my hand back up to the circular knob, feeling around it for any answer.

The back of the knob was rough, with small bumps equally spaced. I brought myself back up and looked at the golden fixture from straight above. Hidden on its opposite side was a design that had rivets and numbers completely surrounding the back of the knob. Numbers 1 through 60 encircled the fixture, with small rivets at every fifth number. On the knob itself, next to these numbers, was a single red mark.

So it was a code. But why wouldn't Silas have sent me with one? I tried to remember as much of my conversation with his family as I could. Did any of them ever mention any numbers? We talked about my school, and how I had four more months of training. I turned the knob so that the mark matched up with the number four and tried pushing in the door. It was still locked shut. I thought about what time they had asked me to go down to the underground during my two visits. I turned the red mark to match up with the 3, then the 0. Again, the door was as solid as a rock. Now flustered by frustration, I reached into my bra and ripped out the small note, clutching the sides with two thumbs. My eyes raced across the page, looking for anything.

There were no numbers to be found. I let go of the page with one hand and pushed on the door once more, mentally begging it to open. I was running out of time, my break would be over in less than ten minutes.

It was then that I saw it. Vertically written, on the place where my thumb had been, were three digits. 46-15-4. They glowed purple in the green light, it must have been written in an ink that would only show up in that room. I happily sighed and entered the combination. Without turning the handle I pushed against the door and it opened without effort. Behind it was a man with a tight black mask over his head, pointing a large rifle directly at me.

I threw my hands up, dropping the page.

"Silas sent me down!" I yelled.

He inched closer to me, still directly pointing the gun at my nose.

"Silas who," the man grumbled, tightening the grip on his rifle and shifting his weight forward.

"Silas..." I began. After all my interactions with his family I had never learned their last name.

"Silas for the revolution!" I exclaimed. It was all I could come up with. This didn't seem to help matters, but instead heighten them. He pushed the barrel against my face.

"How did you get down here?"

"I've been down before, just not this way. A girl first brought me down, I never saw exactly who she was. She brought me to a room with three men and a woman. This guy Silas was there," I tried to explain. "He's Patrick's son. I was writing to Patrick."

That seemed to be the only phrase I needed to say. The man dropped his gun and backed away from me.

"I know who you are. I didn't expect you to be coming

today."

"I'm sorry, I didn't mean to alarm you. I wanted to make sure I knew the passage. I thought Silas would have told you."

The man laughed.

"Silas likes to only communicate the big details to me," he said. "We knew we'd be expecting you eventually, but he never told me when."

I wasn't important enough to mention? I had only risked my life twice to meet him in his territory, and once again to blindly follow his directions.

"We never decided when," I apologized.

"Did you bring anything?"

"Not this time. I just wanted to make sure I knew where I was going."

The intensity in his body was reclaimed.

"You risked coming down here without any supplies?" He sounded furious.

"I'll bring some next time."

"If there is a next time."

I paused and shifted my feet. We were still standing on opposite sides of the door.

"Is there anything specifically you want me to bring? I promise I won't come down without anything ever again."

The man grunted and pulled a folded note out from his left pocket. It was on the same type of tattered yellow paper as the map Silas had given me.

"Right now they're asking for stitching supplies. Can you manage that?" He sounded doubtful.

I thought about where this was stored. On the third floor there were a few kits in each of the first ten rooms.

"How much?"

"As much as you can manage," he answered as if the response should have been obvious.

Our demeanor with one another reminded me that this was an arrangement, not a budding friendship.

"I'll be back tomorrow, same time."

"If you don't get anything don't bother coming down. Ever."

"Alright, I promise I'll be here on time."

"I'm sure." He remarked. There was a long pause. "You should probably leave now."

"Oh, yes. I'll be on my way out. But, can I ask you a question first?"

"Doesn't mean I'll give you an answer," he murmured.

"You've been waiting here for me, all day, not even knowing if I'd come down? Not even expecting that I'd come down?"

The man laughed, pulling his mask further down his face and straightening his eye and mouth holes.

"You think you're the only one who comes down here? If I were you I'd pay closer attention to your surroundings."

There were other Daymen who snuck supplies to the rebellion?

"How many of.... us... are there?" I apprehensively asked.

"More than you think," he smugly responded.

Great answer that told me nothing.

"Can you tell me who any of them are?" I knew what he would say before he even opened his mouth.

"Now why would I do a stupid thing like that?"

He backed away, grabbed the side of the door, and quietly but powerfully closed it.

I went back into the elevator, pressed the number five, travelled to the top, replaced the shelves, closed the door to the janitor's closet, and continued the rest of my shift.

15

Taking supplies from the hospital wasn't difficult. While the world seemed to be running short of everything else, our hospital had never suffered. Every single person that ever walked through those doors always received treatment, no matter what their situation. They may have had to sit in the waiting room for an hour, and the treatment they received may have not been top notch, but they received at least something. I'd always thought that this meant our government was running smoothly and that they cared about their people. But, recently, I'd begun doubting myself. In my mind it was quickly becoming simply a way to subdue the people. If we believed, truly believed, that we were being taken care of there was no reason for us to question anything. If they could give off the appearance of concern there was no reason for us to be concerned. I was realizing, though, that in order for my people to feel like they were being taken care of the safety of another population was being completely compromised. In order for our children to be given flu shots the children below couldn't even have access to cold medication.

The underground man behind the door began asking for the simplest things-- acetaminophen, ibuprofen, penicillin. Gauze, disinfectant, banana bags. They weren't asking me to steal large pieces of equipment or even strong medications. They wanted the items that had always been available to me. Maybe they were asking some of the other helpers to grab these objects, but no one in the hospital ever acted like anything important was missing. I never heard a peep about medication from the pharmacy being stolen or equipment from the rooms vanishing.

I began walking around the hospital always on edge. This was a consequence of my decision, always believing that there may have been someone lurking behind me. There was always the chance that someone would follow me down the hall or see me sneak into the closet. Then, everything would be ruined. My life, Patrick's, Silas's, Lynn's, Amanda and Ben's lives, would be compromised.

Four months. Four more months, I had to tell myself every day of the first week that I started sneaking down supplies. I prepared an explanation in my head for everywhere I went. I mentally accounted for every hour, thinking of how I could twist the truth without suspicion.

After the first week, though, my nerves started to break. My shoulders became relaxed when I sat down instead of being tight and stiff. I was becoming more comfortable with my double identity and ability to conceal it from hundreds of people. I started to feel a little jitter of joy instead of a bolt of fear when I pulled off a trip.

The entire first week the man behind the door never took off his mask. I never asked for further explanation of who he was, never asked him another question. We made our exchange in silence. I accepted his head nod as a sign that our arrangement was still valid. We didn't need to share words. As long as he knew why I was doing what I was doing nothing else mattered.

The second week that I went down, to drop off a large bucket of cough drops and throat soothers, as I opened the door the man wasn't there. This was even the time that I had planned to finally break our silence with a "Hello," just for kicks.

Silas stood in his place. He was sitting in a chair, slouched back, reading a fraying hardbound cloth book. I hadn't seen one of those in a long time.

"What're you doing here?" I asked, slamming the bucket I was holding with both hands onto the ground. "Where's the mask guy?"

"He's taking a break," Silas replied, not looking up from his pages.

"What're you doing, standing in for him?"

"You might say that..." He was lifting the book away from himself in anticipation to close it. "There. I had to finish that chapter, it's my favorite part. What did you ask me?"

"Why are you standing where King Kong should be?"

"Who? Oh... Frank. Frank wanted to switch shifts."

"You do this in shifts?"

"Yeah, some of us. Half an hour once a day every day of the week. I just happened to be switched into this one. He usually does the late night."

Late night? I didn't realize this was a twenty-four hour operation. Maybe Silas would answer the questions King Kong didn't.

"How many people actually come down here? 20, 30?"

Silas flipped his book over, analyzing the back cover.

"A handful. A few handfuls would be more accurate."

So more than a few. That means I would've interacted with at least one of them. There was someone in that hospital, right then, that I'd met before who was in the exact same position as me, attempting to balance between two worlds just as I was. I may not have been able to externally share this burden, but at least internally I knew that someone was carrying just as much weight. I thought Silas might be kind enough to help me identify at least a finger of this secret handful.

"Can you give me any descriptions? You don't have to share names, just faces."

He smiled and stood up, letting the book in his hand drop to his waist.

"Now you know I can't give you that."

It was worth a shot. I didn't need to ask him anything more, he would only respond in falsely witty clips anyways.

"Alright. Well, here's what I have for today. Frank told me this is what you guys needed."

He pulled a list and pen out of his pocket. He pulled up his book and pressed the paper against it, checking off a box near the middle.

"So what do you need for next week?"

He scanned the list with his pencil.

"More for stitching," he responded. "Anything you can get your hands on."

I nodded and turned around to leave.

"Wait," he called, list still spread in front of him.

"What else do you need?"

"I want you to come to one of our meetings."

My questioning eyebrows accompanied a confused response. "Your meetings?"

"The meetings about the revolt. I want you to really

understand why we're doing this. I don't know what they tell you... up there," he said, swirling his pen in the air. "But I want you to know the truth."

That's all I really ever wanted. I didn't ask to be swept up in this movement, I didn't want to be part of a revolution. All I wanted was to understand a mystery that I never thought would be solved.

"When is it?"

"This Saturday night."

"I can't come at night, remember? I almost got caught last time."

"You can't come through the hospital?"

I thought about my schedule. There were a few night shifts. No one ever wanted to take them in fear that a band of Nightcrawlers would bust through the doors and barrel across the halls. And, Sunday was the one day a week I had off of school. My parents would think I was noble for sacrificing my day away from schoolwork to recover after working an all night shift.

"I might be able to come."

"Good, you don't have to tell me either way. I'll be here waiting between 10 and 10:15. If you don't come I'll just leave without you."

"Sounds like the best way to do this."

"Good," he smiled, pulling the list off the cover of his book and tucking it back into his pocket.

I looked at the cover. The letters were unreadable upside down and in large, red cursive. I remembered books from when I was very, very little, but they had been banned before I had learned to read and replaced with electronic versions on our INSAVs. I was told the books were all burned because they held lies. They told everyone that the state of literature had deteriorated and that every text had to be digitalized and revised. That way they could update and edit with each piece that was released. They took total control. I was so young that I'd never known it any other way. I constantly re-read novels, watching as the stories altered and transformed. When we had a shortage of oranges, oranges were taken out of every single story. When they started growing again, they were written back in. Before a few months ago I thought this was a favor.

"What's that book called?" I asked, trying to look at the title from straight above.

"Oh, my mom used to read it to me when I was little. It's about a little girl who falls down a rabbit hole one day and is brought to a magical world. Alice in Wonderland. Have you read it?"

I'd never heard of it before.

"It sounds interesting," I said, turning to back away. "Does she ever get home again?"

He paused before answering and stared at the cover before raising his eyes to look at mine.

"Why don't I just let you borrow it sometime? It might help to explain where I come from."

"So you're not going to tell me the ending?" I laughed, feeling like I was getting pulled into yet another mystery.

"No, I'll just wait until you get there yourself."

I playfully shook my head and walked away, devising how I was going to sign up for a night shift and concocting a way to get out of it.

The signing up part ended up being easy. There were half as many nurses at night as there were during the day and everyone helped out with rounds instead of standing by the elevator or running supplies. We were assigned to help a small set of rooms instead of doing one job on a single floor. This was hopefully an easier situation to sneak away from than during the day. I just needed to find a way to take an extended break.

When I got home that afternoon I immediately told my mom what I'd done.

"I'm working the nightshift at the hospital on Friday."

It was a statement, not a question. The knife she was using to dice a chicken breast dropped onto the hard counter.

"Honey, I don't think that's the best idea."

"Its as good of an idea as any."

"You're about to graduate. This is one of the most important times in your life. I don't want this volunteer work at the hospital to be taking over school. You should go out on Friday, sleep at a friend's house. There's no reason for you to be working all night."

"I've already signed up for the shift," I told her matter of factly.

"Micah, I don't think you understand how dangerous it is out there at night. We're getting more and more reports every day of Nightcrawlers coming above ground. What if something happens to you?"

"I'm sure it won't, mom."

At least not from the Nightcrawlers, of that I was positive.

She sighed, pressing her weight into the counter through her palms.

"Does your father know about this?"

"Not yet, but I don't see why he'd have a problem with it. He's worked night shifts before."

"Yes, but he's needed. He's the only one who can do his job, I'm sure there are lots of girls who can take your place on

Saturday night."

"I'm sure they could have, but I've already signed up for the shift and it's almost impossible to find a replacement."

I was going to the shift; there was no way she was going to win this argument.

"I really wish you had asked me before you did that."

I went up and hugged her from the side, letting my head drop onto her shoulder.

"Next time I will, I promise. What are you making for dinner?"

She brought her left hand to my shoulder.

"Chicken tomato stew, I even found some canned pineapple for your father. Here, grab the can opener and you can help me make it."

On Saturday I went home immediately after school. It was the first time in a long time that I didn't head straight to the hospital. When I got back my house was empty except for Gabe who taking a nap in his room. I brought out a change of clothes, made myself a turkey, lettuce, and tomato sandwich, and sat down on the couch waiting for the clock on my wall to hit 5:15. I turned on the wall projection. We only had one channel and it was showing a string of interviews with prominent figures. I watched the interview with the Administrator of Agriculture.

We are researching new hydroponic techniques to grow more in the small amount of farmland left in each sector.

That's all he ever said.

After he spoke, though, an older man with tufts of graying hair and a plump build strolled onto the screen. He walked slowly but proudly, eventually sitting in a leather chair next to the other interviewee and across from the perfectly made woman in pink who was interviewing them. It was Ian Dale. I knew it was him. That face had stared back at me in every class I had ever attended.

"Dale, how nice of you to join us this afternoon. How is your family?" She casually asked him as if they were old friends.

"Oh, good, good. Nothing to complain about there."

"This was quite a big year for you, wasn't it?"

He laughed. "It was a little busier than usual, you might say that."

"Don't be so humble!" She exclaimed, hair bouncing as much as her voice. "For those of you at home who haven't been following Mr. Dale's career, he recently received a *lifetime achievement award* for his revolutionary historytexts. He's written sociologicaltexts for almost every study. Even if you didn't recognize this man when he walked onto the screen, I am absolutely positive that you have read something of his. Let's all give him a hand!"

There was a rousing round of applause from the studio audience. Dale blushed.

"Thank you, thank you. I'm lucky to be able to do this type of work."

"Now, not many people would say that," she assured with a flick of her wrist towards him. "Some of the subjects you have studied were quite dangerous. Can you tell us a little bit about them?"

"Which dangers would you like me to talk about? I guess there were a lot of them."

"Tell us in a few words what it was like to spend time in the underground. I think that's the question we're all dying to hear the answer to." She proclaimed, turning towards the studio audience.

There was a murmur of agreement.

He immediately responded as if he was reading a page of his text.

"It was pretty much as awful as you'd expect it to be. Nothing was clean, everything was crowded. Even more crowded than our streets and stores. The people were, in a word, moral less. But, it's not their fault! It's the fault of the dictator that has taken over the land."

"Did you ever encounter this dictator?"

"No, no. Fortunately not. He didn't even know I was in the underground when I was doing research. My presence would not have been approved of."

"So you *snuck* into the underground?"

There was a large gasp from the crowd as Dale shrugged his shoulders and smiled through his teeth.

"I had to. Our people deserve to know the horrors that lie beneath them. They need to know the extent that our government is reaching to help both parties."

"Did you ever learn the name of this dictator, at least? That has been a huge point of contention with politicians in the last few years."

Dale sighed. "No, no. I didn't learn that, either. The people are so terrified of him that no one even mutters his name. He is destroying their homes, but there is nothing they can do about it."

"Is there anything we can do about it?"

"All we can do is sit back and wait for them to ask for our help. Even in all the time I was down there I couldn't understand their loyalty. They are starving, yet they refuse to rebel. I tried talking to them to let them know that we are here to help, but they didn't believe me. They've been told that we are monsters, when really it's their leaders who are the monsters.

We have to wait until they are either too weak to fight back, or until they have an extreme change of heart."

"How tragic." The woman looked into the camera, grabbing at her heart as if she was wildly affected by the Nightcrawlers' unfortunate position. "For more on this story, you can check out our INSAV page, or find Ian's book on your INSAV."

She bared a perfectly white, toothy grin to end the show. "Everything completely accessible, right on your wrist. Thank you for joining us today, see you next week." Orchestral music accompanied the end credits. I turned off the projection.

When I got to the hospital everyone from the day shift was in his or her final rush before leaving. I checked in with Cindy at the front desk who told me I would be working rooms 15-20 on the 3rd floor.

The hospice floor, good a batch as any. I headed up and found the main doctor from the day. She gave me a surprisingly short list of tasks. I had to check their vitals once every two hours and hand out a few medications. The head nurse might hand me a mop if things got too slow, otherwise the night shift on this floor was pretty laid back. "I hope you brought something to amuse yourself," she joked before running out of the hospital.

It was going to be easier to sneak away than I thought. There were only four other nurses on this floor, including the overweight lethargic woman that introduced herself as the head one.

"I usually just sit in the lounge for most of the break," she told me. "At this point there's not much we can do for these people, but it's always good to have someone watching over them."

The hours rolled by. I tried to stay clear of the other nurses so that they wouldn't notice when I eventually would have to leave. I could hear them chat chat chatting away in the other room, but chose to sit in the suite of one of my patients. I read her chart over and over again out of boredom.

Ruby Demith, age 57. Cause of hospice-- old age. I wondered if that was actually what she was dying from.

Finally, it was 9:55. I listened in to the controversy developing in the staff lounge.

"I can't believe she did that to you!"

"I know, right? What a BITCH."

"She should have at least told you she was going to sleep with him."

"Some people just don't get it."

Four voices still complaining about what they were complaining about two hours ago. Perfect.

I simply walked up the stairs onto the fifth floor and slid into the closet. I couldn't believe how easy my heist was becoming.

At the last moment I decided to place my brown eyes into their case. Why should I hide something that they accepted?

Even though I was five minutes early Silas was waiting for me at the bottom. He looked relieved when he saw me and immediately turned around to begin walking down the hallway.

"I'm glad you're here, now I won't have to be late to the meeting."

"Is that the only reason you're glad to see me?" I tried to joke.

He turned back to give me a tight lipped smile and small laugh but didn't respond. Guess we weren't on that level yet. I tried to ignore this and asked him more questions.

"How many people are going to be here?"

"It's a big meeting, so probably a few hundred."

I suddenly became very nervous.

"You don't think any of them will find out who I am?"

"At the meeting it doesn't really matter. As long as you're with me no one will question where you came from. But, not everyone on the street is a full supporter of the revolt, it's there that we'll have to be careful."

"What will you be talking about at the meeting?"

"Why don't you just wait and see?"

I couldn't. I wanted to know everything right then. I wished that I could just take a pill and immediately gain all the knowledge I was about to be confronted with.

We unsurprisingly walked down more dark hallways before he stopped me to change.

"Place your clothes in this corner, no one will take them," he reassured me, handing over a pile of underground garb. It was so dark that I couldn't see and began changing blindly. I listened for movement but he stood completely still.

"I'm done," I said after piling everything he had handed me onto my body.

"I know," he responded, pushing open a door to the street. He grabbed my hand and pulled me through the crowds. Everyone seemed to be moving quicker today, as if the entire underground knew a secret that they could only expose through their speed. Even the shop owners seemed like they had more energy. We walked about six blocks through masses of people before sneaking into two thick, black metal doors. They were heavy; he had to let go of my hand to open one with both of his own. The building he was bringing me into seemed more stable than the rest. The walls were made of a dark stone and had bands of black steel running in crisscross patterns across the front and sides. Directly inside and through another door was yet another long and dark staircase. We tumbled down the shoot, quick feet vibrating against the black metal of the stairs. It led to another heavy metal door. Immediately after the room was unsealed I heard a bustling of activity from inside contrasting the eerie silence I had been surrounded by in the staircase. It sounded like there were millions of flies bouncing across the room. I followed him in and realized these flies were actually hundreds of men and women.

The room felt like it had a subtle electric current freely running through it. Everyone was speaking, not a single voice was silent. No one was yelling, whispering, or speaking over one another. The voices were all operating in chaotic harmony. The people stood in no particular direction, creating loose circles with their bodies. Silas and I laced through these groupings until we reached the front of the room. On a long, narrow stage was a horizontal wooden table with four chairs neatly tucked beneath.

"Stand here," he told me, letting go of my hand once more.

"I have to go get the others to start the meeting, but here…" he said, scanning the room.

"Emily! Emily" He yelled across, waving a hand in the air.

"Silas! Hey! Glad you made it!" The woman began twisting her way through the crowd towards us.

"Me too. Any way you could keep my friend Micah company while I go get the others from the back?"

"Of course!" She came and stood right next to me, arm outstretched. I didn't understand what she wanted. She must have realized this was a custom I wasn't used to.

"Oh, I'm sorry! This is a handshake," she said, grabbing Silas's hand and swinging it back and forth within her own. "It's how we say hello."

"You know where I'm from?" I asked. I expected most Nightcrawlers to hate me. She smiled at Silas.

"I've heard of you before," she responded.

"Alright, I'll see you guys in a little bit," Silas said, moving towards the front of the room. He disappeared through a door to the side.

Emily and I awkwardly stood next to one another for a few seconds before I spoke.

"How did you hear about me?" I asked.

"Silas and I are close," she said, peering over the crowd. "He's been talking about this for weeks."

He'd only asked me to come down a few days ago. This was something he planned?

"Is this a big meeting?" I asked her.

"One of the biggest. I've attended almost all of them, but there're a lot of people here who have never been to any. I only recognize about half of these faces. It's great. This is exactly what we could have hoped for."

"What are we going to talk about?" I figured maybe she might answer some of the questions Silas refused to.

"We're going through everything today. Since there are so many new people, including you, we have a lot to explain. Silas is so excited that you're here."

"Really? He didn't seem like it."

She laughed, a full-bodied laugh that made her long blonde hair shake against her shoulders.

"He's not the best at showing emotion. But believe me, he talks about you a lot."

I was confused.

"In what way?"

"It's a big deal for you to be down here. I think he's proud of it."

"Why is he proud of it?" I inquired. It was his father who communicated with me, not him. He didn't really have a right to be proud of something he didn't exactly do.

She looked at me quizzically. "What do you mean? He brough...." The room quieted to a hush as the door on the far left opened and figures began to emerge from within.

They walked out in single file, one after another. When the first man hit the stage the room erupted in cheers. I recognized him as one of the people who had first greeted me in the small room on my first trip to the underground.

Actually, I recognized them all. They were all in the room that day. Silas was the last to walk out. They each stood behind a chair and, after soaking up their admiration, brought the crowd to a hush by sitting down. Everyone was turned towards them, waiting to be told any news.

"Brothers and Sisters, thank you all for coming tonight. I know you have busy schedules, and I cannot tell you what it means to us to have each of you here tonight. We are going to begin this meeting by introducing ourselves." The man stood up and walked around the table until he was standing on the edge of the stage.

"My name is Barrett Williams, I am one of the founders of this organization. It was I that our leader came to when he realized something must be done to combat the aboveground. I act as his right hand man, conveying all information to the people. It was he who called for this mass meeting. It was he who decided it is time that we share our plans with all of the citizens. He sees how hard you all work for your families, and that even your greatest efforts are no longer enough. He knows that it is finally time for us to fight back!" The man's voice had escalated throughout his speech and ended in a powerful roar. The crowd once again erupted in cheers. He sat down, and the one woman of the group took his place.

"My name is Sonya Murry. I am in charge of all militaristic, medical, and nutritional supplies. I have been working night and day in preparation for the coming months, gathering every good that we may need. We are storing all of this in a safe location that will be revealed right before the revolt. We are trying to gather enough weapons for every citizen and creating all that we can from the few resources we have. If you have any scrap metal, please make sure to find a way that we can receive it. The earlier the better. We are making weapons out of absolutely anything. This is all we are asking for. The medical and food supplies are being taken care of with other methods."

She turned her head and, although I couldn't tell for sure, felt that she was looking directly at me.

"If you have extra food, save it for your family. The coming months will be tough. There is rumor from the aboveground that they will be further reducing our rations. Through these struggles we mustn't give up hope! If we come together as a unified society anything is possible. By the looks of our crowd today, it seems like we are on our way."

She, as well, turned to sit down in her initial seat and received a large round of applause. The man sitting to the left of Silas took her place next. He was the oldest of the group, the one who had spoken so kindly to me in the first room. His voice was quieter than the rest, it felt as if the entire room leaned forward and stretched their ears to hear him speak. While the others spoke to the crowd in declaration, he spoke in conversation.

"I am Dustin Kroll. My job is to plan each attack. When the time comes, I will divide each of you into battalions." He paused to look around the room. "I can already see looks of worry on each of your faces. Here, let me demonstrate," he said, bending down to a young man in front of him.

"You, sir. What is your name?"

"Ha...Harry." The boy nervously responded.

"Harry, would you please join me up here?" he asked with an outstretched hand. The boy hesitantly grabbed it and was hoisted to the stage.

"Everybody, please say hello to Harry."

"Hi, hello Harry," the room responded in waves.

The man looked back at the boy, who stood, red faced, clutching his hands together in front of him.

"Harry, are you planning on fighting with us?"

"Wouldn't be here if I wasn't'", he proudly, but anxiously, responded.

"That's what I like to hear. What area of the sector are you from?"

"The southwest corner."

"Ah, yes. Anywhere near The Mushroom Palace?" He asked.

The boy nodded emphatically.

"Right above it."

"Their marinated Portabellos are to die for," the man said to the crowd before realizing the implications of his chosen speech and turning back to Harry.

"Harry, do you have siblings?"

"Two sisters and a brother."

"Are they going to fight too?"

"My whole family is ready," he responded, pointing to a mass in front of him. "We're all here tonight."

"And what is your last name?"

"Jorgensen."

The man smiled down at them.

"Jorgensen family, I'm giving you my promise right now that you will not be separated in battle. You will all fight together in the same battalion. Your passage to the aboveground will be near your home. You will gather your weapons a week before."

The man looked back up at the crowd.

"This is how you will all be treated. Everyone standing in this room is now part of a symbolic family. We are all each other's brothers and sisters. But, we need you to know that your biological family is valued as well. You will fight together. You will be able to support one another. Our intention is to separate the aboveground from their ignorance, not sons from their fathers. Harry, please go be with your family."

When the boy hopped down from the stage the audience screamed louder than for either speakers before him. The man clapped back at them before sitting down onto his seat. Silas took his place. He was obviously the youngest of the group, but walked with a demeanor of confidence and determination larger than them all.

"My name is Silas Durand. I mediate communication between all parties, including yourselves. All requests come in through me. If you are kind enough to donate your scrap metal, as Sonya mentioned, I am the man that will send someone to pick it up. To let you know of all future meetings, I will send out a message with times, dates, and locations. When the time finally comes to begin our war, I am the one who will ring the first bell."

I was astounded. I had no idea that Silas meant so much to this revolution. I thought he was just a basic missionary, one of hundreds who attended the meetings and believed in the cause. But, he was so much more.

"I also watch over the aboveground railroad. Some of you

may not know this, but for decades a network of noble citizens from above have been risking their lives to help us in our increased time of need. They risk capture by the trashmen every day to provide for us extra food and resources. These people do this out of the goodness of their hearts. Some of them are even here with us today." He paused to nod at a few key figures scattered across the room.

There must have been other Daymen down there with me, as well. I turned around to see if I recognized any of them, but their faces were muddled in the thickening crowd.

"They, and their families, will be protected. Not all Daymen are bad," he continued, this time looking straight at me. "They have as much good in their hearts as ourselves, it is sometimes just locked further away inside a series of boxes that no longer have a key. They can be good, they have the potential to be good, but not today. Not now. Not after what they've done to us." Silas' voice cracked as he struggled to get through his next words.

"When Brother Tyrone was killed I made him a promise. Some of you may be wondering why I'm even up here. Some of you went to school with me, some of you sent your children to school with me. You may not remember me being the brightest, or most charismatic. There are hundreds of men and woman who could be standing in my place right now if it weren't for one simple detail. I made Tyrone a promise. A promise that I would continue his mission and continue the work he had risked his life completing. Through him, a previously unparalleled aboveground network was created. The railroad he created is three times larger than anything before. Before he was captured and taken above I told him I would continue that dream." He stopped. The room was silent and tense, waiting for what he would say next. Everyone seemed to be on the tips of their toes, faces flushed with compassion and purpose.

"My mother always told me that you need to fight for what you believe in. I believe in this sector. I believe in these people. I believe we deserve to be free, to be able to feel the sun on our faces. You deserve to have a choice of life or death. You, we all, deserve this revolution."

This was a side of Silas that, before this moment, I didn't know existed. Our encounters had always been filled with tension. He had always seemed so rough, so stuck in a world within his own head. I never understood it. I never understood why he was the one person I had met in the underground that wasn't immediately struck by me. From the second I met him he had treated me as if he already knew me, as if we had pushed passed the point of friendship and onto judgment. But, now I understood. My presence to him was not unique, but part of a string of interactions that he risked his life to make possible. While he was the only Nightcrawler that continually brought me down I wasn't the only Dayman that he accompanied. He had always been critical of my beliefs because he had to be. If someone were brought down with false intentions it was he who would be responsible. If I had turned out to be a lie, someone who only wanted to expose the secrets of the underground, it would be he who would face the consequences. He didn't just carry the weight of himself on his shoulders, but that of an entire community. It must have been exhausting.

He slowly looked around the room once more before looking up at the ceiling.

"No one deserves to be trapped in a world they didn't choose."

He delicately placed both hands into his pants pocket and

walked off the stage and through the side door. Barrett stood up once more.

"Thank you all for joining us today. You may all go if you so choose, but are given the option to stay and get to know your fellow brothers and sisters. Sonya, Dustin, and I will be walking around to answer any and all questions. We will have another meeting the same time next week. Please, tell all that you know. Thank you."

The silent room cheered once more before everyone began turning into one another to begin their conversations.

Emily tapped me on the shoulder.

"I'm going to mingle, but you should go back and see him. I'm sure in a few minutes he'll take you back up."

"Go see who?" I asked, looking around the room. I didn't know if she was talking of another Dayman or of a new escort.

"You know who I'm talking about. Silas. He always sits in the back room after a meeting. He'd want you to go back. Let him know I'll be waiting for him at Jerry's," she said, walking into the center of the crowd and yelling into the dissipating group.

"Molly! Molly! Wait for me, I'm coming!"

I snaked through the stationary circles of discussion and opened the side door. It was a small room, with only enough space for a loveseat and low wooden table. The shelves that embraced the walls were completely covered in books of every kind, shape, and color. I had never seen so many before in my life.

Silas was sitting on the right of the couch, arm draped over the side. From his hidden hand I could see a flowing sliver of expanding white mist and noticed a filled ashtray on the table. He was staring straight ahead, but didn't seem to see me. He was lost somewhere in his own world. I couldn't even imagine the memories that world held. I quietly walked in front of the coffee table to his right.

"Spare a smoke?" I gingerly asked.

My voice seemed to snap him out of an inner delirium.

"Sure, sure." He said, reaching into his pocket to grab a thin metal box. He seemed calmer than before, as if this meeting allowed him to release an anger that had been boiling inside since he met me. He handed me the cigarette and square silver lighter from across the table. I walked around and sat down next to him.

I crossed my legs and flipped open the lighter. It was one of those refillable ones, the kind that used to offer a lifetime warranty. I flipped it around in my hands, feeling the fluid design that was indented into it. There was an inscription on the bottom of one of the sides.

"For Tyrone"

Tyrone. The name clicked.

Sitting at the bar by myself.

Intertwining our bodies.

Reminding him of someone.

Looking for him in the street.

No. There was no way.

I flipped open the lighter and brought its flame to the end of my cigarette. I breathed in harshly, gripping its round edges with the center of my lips. Smoke filled my lungs and I let the flame down, holding its sweetness in before releasing the grayness to become nothing.

"Tyrone," I read out loud, continuing to twist the lighter in my fingers.

"You were close to him?"

"We were like brothers," he said, taking the zippo from my

outstretched hand and shoving the butane filled device into his pocket.

"What was he like?" I asked, leaning back into the couch. Silas's eyes lit as he remembered his friend.

"He was ruthless," he said, taking in a drag. "Never took no for an answer."

He looked into his hands, laughing quietly. "It's probably what got him killed."

"I can't even imagine," I said, drawing circles with my index finger into the arm of the couch. "To lose someone like that."

"It's his own fault really. Motherfucker got too damn confident. He didn't look like us. He and his parents had escaped from the aboveground when he was really young. He looked like you," Silas said, staring into my eyes. "He started going above ground to do the stupidest things."

You don't even know, I thought.

"There was a point where he was above there more than he was down here," he continued unfazed by the changing expression on my face. "He got careless."

"How did they find him?"

Silas took a long puff of the slim rod before answering. "He started getting careless about who he confronted for the railroad, too. Someone turned him in. I was with him when it happened." He said, getting trapped again in his own mind's eye. "We were walking to work. We both worked in the warehouse, fixing things. I had gone into a shop really quickly to grab a piece I needed to fix an old telephone. You know, the one with the circular dial?"

I didn't even know what a telephone looked like, but nodded as if I did.

"I just needed the circle dial. I had everything else. The phone was beautiful. We found it at the overflow pile. No one else had recognized what it was. No one's allowed to use phones down here anymore, just like how it is up there."

He looked at me for confirmation and I nodded back. I didn't have any form of communication that wasn't attached to my wrist. He continued.

"I knew we could never get it to actually work, but we were so excited to restore it. I looked everywhere for this extra piece and finally found one at a little resale shop right next to the warehouse. He waited outside, said that he wanted to listen to the sounds of the world, or some shit like that. I just thought he was being a dumbass. Too lazy to just walk into a fucking store with me. When I came back out they had him cuffed against the floor. I couldn't even try to save him. If they had known we were associated I would have been as gone as he was. All I could do was stand by and watch as they beat him. Watch as they," he took another pull from his cigarette,

"Sliced at his back and kicked him across the face. They beat him in front of everybody. I've seen the trashmen take a lot of people up to the gallows, but never like that. He didn't even walk away. They had to carry him."

He took a last angry puff before slamming the butt into the swollen ashtray.

"They didn't have enough fucking dignity to let him walk away. He was beaten like a dog and carried away like an animal."

He pulled out another cigarette from his coat and we sat in silence. I couldn't respond. His anger was more justified than I had previously thought. Here was a story about a man, a man he thought was his best friend. This man was my first connection to the underground, and now I was discovering that he was a part of it. At least a larger part than I already knew.

"You're the reason his dream is coming true," I finally said, trying to comfort him. He just continued staring forward. "You give him meaning."

"I'm not," he responded. "I don't. His dream was to live in peaceful co-existence. Fucking... he thought he could convert you all," he said, swinging his hand across his body. "He thought he could change the world with words. If he even knew about all the weapons we're gathering...."

"He couldn't," I responded, placing my hand onto his arm. "My people wouldn't listen to his words unless..."

"But you did," he said.

My stomach jumped.

"I've met him?" I asked, disregarding my first thought.

I knew the answer.

"Maybe, I'm not really sure I guess." He suddenly became taken aback. "I'm sorry, I shouldn't have said that. You just remind me of a girl he told me about once. He never told me her name but..." he stopped, looking deeply into my eyes. He seemed to be searching for something. I watched as his pupils gently swirled around my irises. "He always told me he was going to save her. I'm sure it wasn't you. It couldn't have been you. It's just... your eyes. I don't know, I guess they kind of look like hers would have. They're so blue."

When men told me this I usually pulled away. I usually looked to the side and took another sip of my drink, or got up to excuse myself to the bathroom. But, at him I just stared. I wanted him to unlock whatever it was he was searching for.

"Can you come down next week?" he asked, finally looking away. "There's another meeting, but I would love for you to stay later. Some of us hang out afterwards. I want you to see that we're more than just an angry proletariat. We have fun, too. I want you to see why we're fighting so hard to save this society."

I thought about how I could sneak away for more than a few hours. Now that my parents believed I worked the night shift at the hospital, I could tell them I was working again next week without actually signing up for anything. I could tell them I was leaving for my shift, sneak into the hospital, and sneak into the closet. It would be difficult, but well worth everything if I could pull it off. I just had to pray that my dad wouldn't look at the hospital roster.

"I want to see that too," I said, standing up to leave. I had been down for about an hour, someone might have been looking for me. "Is the meeting time already planned?"

"Sunday night, early on. It's an early meeting so everyone can celebrate afterwards. We're hosting a gathering. The best soldiers are soldiers that care about one another, and the best way to get someone to care about another person is to get them drunk." he joked. "I can be ready to pick you up at sunset."

"I'll be there," I said. "Could you bring me up now? I'm sorry to be in a rush, but I'm getting nervous that someone might notice I'm gone."

He stood up, as well, and began walking towards the door.

"Of course, of course. Let's go out the back." He grabbed my hand and we walked into the crowd and to the other side of the room. Everyone patted Silas's back or stopped him to share a handshake on our way over.

We walked through the smaller door, up the stairs, and back onto the street. He grabbed my hand tighter to keep us together in the crowded metropolis. As we weaved through the street, I felt like each shop owner or idle bystander tried to lock eyes with Silas. Women sitting on the floor washing plates out of buckets stared as we walked by and mustached men drinking their strange beverage brought the cups down from their faces when he passed. Had they done this before and I was too intimidated to notice? I didn't feel that their glances were threatening, but each possessed a solemn intensity that I couldn't quite pinpoint. I put my head down and burrowed through the crowd with him until he brought me back to the door we emerged from earlier that night. Pushing in front of him, I reached into the corner for my clothes. There was nothing but air where the pile used to lay. I shuffled across the floor with my feet, searching for it anywhere. All I felt was dust.

I turned to where I thought his body was quickly, accidentally pushing him against the opposing wall in the process.

"Silas, my clothes aren't here. My stuff isn't here. I can't go back up there like this."

I thought about being stuck down here forever. Never being able to say goodbye to my family, all of my mother's fears about the underground stealing me finally coming true. He laughed and placed both hands onto my tense arms.

"Relax, relax. After a meeting like that you think we aren't prepared for something like this? One of the men probably just brought them to the front, thinking that they were left here by mistake. I'm sure your clothes are at the entrance," he calmly reassured me. "I'll take you to the end, and if we don't find them I'll give you a replacement. We have a lot of those, too."

I was still shaking as I grabbed his hand so he could lead me through the dark. I knew he told me that everything would be fine, but a small piece of me still believed that something awful had happened with my clothes that would come back to haunt me. That I would re-emerge onto the fifth floor of the hospital in someone else's uniform and the entire staff would be standing outside the door of the closet, my clothes in my father's hand.

When we finally reached the door, though, my clothing was neatly hung up on the other side. Frank was guarding them. I ran up and uncontrollably gave him a giant hug.

"Thank you thank you thank you!" I said as my body squeezed into him. "I've never been more grateful for you in my entire life."

What crept onto his face was the first sign of actual emotion I had ever seen. Through the sliver he had created in the mask for his mouth was a large, toothy grin.

"I'll move your clothes more often," he joked. "Didn't your mother ever teach you to not leave your stuff sitting on the floor? They'll get dirty."

"I guess she didn't remind me enough," I laughed back.

I quickly changed and walked to the elevator.

"Sunset," Silas reminded me as I stood waiting.

"Until then." I responded, slyly. And then I remembered the message Emily wanted me to give him.

"Oh! Emily told me to tell you to meet her at Jerry's." I said as the doors opened.

"Thanks, I'll head there right now."

Moment ruined, but message delivered.

My mom didn't care that I asked to work the night shift again. If I made it back once, I guess she assumed I would make it back again. My dad beamed with joy when I told him.

"The nurses from last night gave you rave reviews," he told me that night at dinner after I woke up from sleeping the whole day.

"They said you were so attentive to your patients, and that you even sat with them for most of the night," he said, crunching an ear of corn into his teeth. "They were really impressed. It made me one happy poppa."

None of the nurses had even noticed I was gone. When I raced back to the third floor they were still sitting in the exact same spot that I had left them, this time with a deck of cards. I simply walked back to Ruby Demith's room and sat in the chair next to her bed, getting up every so often to check on the rest of the patients. When the sun rose I simply walked back home.

We were getting ready to take our final exams at school. It

didn't matter whether or not we passed, our careers were set in stone. We would all start at the bottom, with a cubical in the government house and work our way up towards a nice corner office at the top. The next two weeks at school were going to be a breeze. All I had to do was show up and fill in a few bubbles through my INSAV. The test didn't even have any essays. Whoever condoned this method of examination probably should've been fired a long time ago. Then again, they were probably the same people that created all our other laws. I knew how well that was working out.

I was a zombie for the entire week. I barely skimmed my readings, never participated in class discussions, and even began eating alone at lunch. A few strands of hair were constantly encroaching my face, I never had the energy nor desire to fix my appearance. I didn't care about anything above ground anymore. My heart lay beneath.

I started going through my day imagining what Silas was doing during the night. I thought of him sitting in his warehouse, tinkering with an old toaster. I imagined him guarding the elevator, reading the book his mother had given him. In my mind he was always moving, always thinking. He was alive in his head at the night and alive in mine during the day.

Waiting for Saturday wasn't very hard when I didn't care about the time in between.

Even a tour of the segregationalist's office couldn't awake my senses. It was a tradition, in the last few weeks of school, for the graduating students to take an extended tour of the government house. We all dressed in our best uniforms and scurried down the street, bright faces barely able to hide our excitement. Or, rather, bright faces barely able to hide their excitement. I simply went out of obligation.

The day finally came. I woke up and walked to school with my father. He gave me a kiss on the cheek before turning towards the hospital. I read my text. I wrote my notes. I ate my turkey sandwich. I ignored Renee when she tried to sit down next to me. I walked home, watched the news, and left my apartment at exactly 5:20.

So there would be no trace of my presence, I simply followed someone into the hospital when they swiped their INSAV and ducked underneath the check-in booth when I passed Cindy, who was busy calling forth another patient anyways. I took the stairs up to the fifth floor and walked with my head down, hair hiding my face as I snuck to the janitor's closet. I walked in and quietly closed it. Everything was becoming too easy.

Silas was again sitting in his chair reading his book when I arrived at the entrance.

"I thought you told me you were going to let me borrow that," I said to him upon arrival.

He looked up at me and laughed.

"Hold your horses," he said, standing up to stretch. "I'm almost done re-reading it. I'll give you my copy soon."

"You make it sound so... magical," I said, looking around for a change of clothes. "Is there any way I could get changed here? I don't want King Kong to get mad at me for leaving them on the floor again."

"Yeah," he said, grabbing a pile of cloth from under his chair. "As long as you don't mind changing in front of me."

"They don't really teach us modesty up there," I joked, stripping off my coat and unbuttoning my shirt. "They teach us about math, and physics, and chemistry, but definitely not modesty."

He laughed, a distant far away laugh, and suddenly seemed to notice that I was getting undressed. I saw his eyes look me up and down before turning around.

"I'm really excited for you to come today. My dad and Lynn will even be at the meeting."

"What? He changed his mind about the whole thing?"

"He's always had his mind made up, he's just finally ready to show everyone."

I was excited to see his family again. We hadn't spoken since I ate dinner in their apartment and was briskly forced to leave.

Today he had given me a long, button up, green and white striped shirtdress that tied around my waist and fell a little above my knees. The shoes were not as bulky as what were normally given to me and gently slipped onto my feet. They even had a small, plastic flower in the center of the loop that went around my big toe. The fabric was thicker and cleaner, and the shoes more comfortable. The outfit seemed fancier than usual, not that I really knew what was required to be classy down there.

"Where did you say we're going after the meeting?" I asked him, trying to figure out if my enhanced outfit was intentional.

"We're having a large gathering at the meeting space. We're turning the room into a concert hall. There will be lots of drinks and dancing, a few guys from the north end are bringing their instruments and jamming. It should be a lot of fun."

I guess I had assumed that if they didn't have food or medicine the underground wouldn't have music, either.

"What kind of music are they going to play?"

"I don't think you have a name for it where you're from. We don't really have a name for it here, either. It's just a bunch of people who beat on anything they can get their hands on. We have to learn to make due with what we have."

"Which isn't a lot."

"Exactly. I think one of the guys is planning on bringing his washboard."

"A washboard?" I didn't even know what that was. Silas could tell by the tone of my voice and began laughing.

"Yes, a washboard. It's what poor people use to clean their clothes. You'll see."

I couldn't even imagine what he was about to bring me to. I tried to think of what sounds a ....washboard... might make, but my thoughts kept becoming interjected with the sound of my clothes dryer at home. I sure hoped that wasn't what I was about to go listen to.

"That dress looks really great on you," Silas said as he stretched out his hand towards mine.

"Thanks," I said, grabbing it to walk down the dark hallway. We normally walked in silence, but tonight Silas was chatty. He made jokes about his family, told me stories from his childhood.

He told me that when he was little he strung a rope between his bedroom window and the window of a friend who lived across the street. They had attached the rope to both their beds as tightly as possible. He was halfway out his window before he heard his mother screaming bloody murder from below.

"Silas! What are you thinking! Are you an idiot? Did I raise an idiot!"

I heard him laugh in the dark.

"You go back inside. You.... Go!" She screamed at him. She couldn't reach him way up there, and he knew he would have made it to the other end before she could have walked up the stairs. But, he chose to listen to her anyways.

"Do you regret it?" I asked him, genuinely curious.

"Every day of my life," he jokingly responded.

When we arrived at the meeting it was even more crowded than before. There seemed to be twice as many people as last week, and they were consequentially twice as loud. My ears were buzzing with incomprehensible words as we slowly twisted and turned our bodies to get to the front. He gripped my hand even tighter than before to make sure I didn't get lost in the crowd. We finally stopped when we found Patrick, Lynn, and Emily, who were standing together pushed against the stage.

My surrogate underground parents smiled when they saw me and pulled me between them so that I snuggly fit in the front row. Silas gave them each a pat from behind and Emily a quick kiss on the cheek before disappearing into the front room.

"I'm so happy to see you here!" I screamed to Patrick in an attempt to be heard over the stirring crowd.

"I should be saying the same to you," he said back in a normal tone. "How did you get down here at night?"

"I told everyone I was working the night shift at the hospital," I said. "No one will notice I'm gone."

He looked concerned. "Are you sure about that? This will be an awfully long time for you to be gone."

"I'm sure, as long as my dad doesn't check the hospital roster and see that I'm not on it I'll be fine."

"Lynn, does that sound safe to you?" He asked his wife over my head.

"Safe as any other decision!" she responded, looking around the corner to see if anyone was coming out of the door yet. "Ohhhh, this is so exciting! Silas is such a wonderful speaker, isn't he. Just like his father," she smiled to her husband.

"Oh, honey. You're too kind. You ain't so bad yourself," he said back to her, smiling down at me.

"It's all the singing I do in the shower!" she said, humming to herself. "Helps to keep my voice *sharp*. Wait, wait! I think they're coming out!" she exclaimed, clapping her hands together.

The door opened and suddenly everyone was clapping, an entire auditorium full of people celebrating the same cause. Barrett, Sonya, Dustin, and Silas walked out after one another in the same line as last week. Instead of heading directly behind the table they stood in front of it and cheered back at the roaring crowd. They were smiling with their whole bodies.

Finally they stopped clapping and moved their arms in downward motions to bring the room back to silence. Lynn was one of, if not the last, person to stop moving her boisterous hands. Silas had to give her a special look. It was as if he was a 5th grade kid in an elementary school play with the mom that everyone knew because she couldn't stop cheering. She was as happy in the audience as he was on stage.

All but Barrett re-took their positions behind the table and sat down. He remained standing tall and moved towards the center front of the stage.

"Brothers and Sisters!" He began, arms raised high. "I welcome you all to one of our final meetings before the revolt!" The room again erupted in uncontrollable screams of joy. He, again, moved his arms downward in a sign of silence.

"Today is a great day, but we must not forget why we are here. We are here to win our freedom, our independence! We cannot do this by ourselves. I would like you to take a moment and look to the person next to you. Go on, don't be shy."

He gave everyone a minute to observe their surroundings as he looked down at the crowd.

"The eyes that you just looked into are the most important eyes in this entire room. This person, who you may not even know, may save your life. They may dress your wounds. They may protect your children. We all have the power to save lives. We must not forget, though, that this also gives us the power to take them. This is what we are here to talk to you about today."

He began pacing across the stage, hands tightly held behind his back.

"While our ultimate target is freedom, our initial target is to combat the lies that are spread in the aboveground every day. They have been told that we are disgusting (he paused at each descriptive word), that we are a disease ridden, amoral, uncompassionate society. They have been told we are less than human. That we are scum. The scum that resides below the earth."

There were boos throughout the crowd.

"They've been told that we are destroying ourselves! That we have no family! No friends! No empathy!"

Lynn cupped her hands around her mouth and let out a large "Boooooooo! They're the scum!"

"They've been told that it is our government, not theirs, that is failing us! They don't know about our suffering, our pain. Our children that starve in the streets. The families that go months without a single bit of fresh food."

The room erupted in disapproval. I was squished even further against the stage, my stomach digging into the hard wood.

"There's one man responsible for all of this. There is one man that has single handedly destroyed any truth about our once beautiful and rich society."

He, and each of the members sitting on the stage, pulled a large sheet of paper from their shirts and held it up above their heads with both hands for all to see. On it was the picture of an older, dark man. I recognized it immediately.

"Ian Dale!" Barrett screamed, shaking the picture. "Ian Dale has destroyed our society! He has convinced his people that ours are evil. But the truth is, he's the evil one! He's the one who will go to the *real* underground for his actions!"

If I thought the crowd had erupted before, this was the Mt. Vesuvius of emotions. Every single person in the room, big or small, was screaming at the top of their lungs at the picture, cursing it with all they had.

Barrett stood on stage, smiling. He stood still with the picture raised over his head as the crowd's voices poured into him. With a fire in his eyes, he grabbed the middle of the picture with both hands and tore it in half.

"Down with Dale!" He screamed, pumping his paper filled fist. "Down with Dale!"

The entire room began chanting it with him. "Down with Dale! Down with Dale! Down with Dale! Down with Dale!" I was even chanting it.

I didn't know if this was meant to be the end of the meeting, but at that point there was no more control over the crowd. They were chanting incessantly, without thinking, letting bare emotions shape what their mouths spoke.

I had never been surrounded by this much emotion before. Everything aboveground was tamed, organized, and precise. Nothing was as out of control as this meeting. I had never screamed for anything in public, never been around someone who cared enough about something to chant for the downfall of a man they had never met. I realized most of these people probably didn't even know who Ian Dale was. Their hatred was solely fueled by Barrett's commands.

These people were as cut off from the aboveground as most Daymen were from the Nightcrawlers. Just as everything I had previously known about them was told to me in my historytexts, everything they were told of the above came from Barrett and his crew. They were blindly following a leader because it was their only choice. They were starving and their society was dilapidating, but they didn't really know why. The revolution offered a solution to a problem they didn't know the cause of firsthand. It was their only option to escape from insufferable pain.

I wondered if anyone in the room doubted Barrett as I had doubted my government. Was there anyone there who thought to themselves that he might not have been telling the truth? Or were they all blindly following him as the Daymen unquestioningly followed their own rules?

I realized how special my position was. I was one of the only people in the entire room that was given the opportunity to choose which truth to believe.

These people didn't realize how lucky they were to have a leader that passionately communicated reality with them. They didn't realize that there was a world above them full of people who lived their lives with no concern for the underground because they were told not to have concern for the underground. That was it. That was the only reason. My people didn't care because they were told not to. These people cared because they were told to. How strange, the transformation of equal power, when placed into different hands.

The men and woman on stage looked at one another, as if to debate whether or not to try and control the crowd. Silas was the first to shrug and get out of his seat. He walked to the front of the stage where we were standing and hopped down in front of me.

"What a night, huh?" He said into my ear before hands from all around me reached out to touch him. He grabbed hands back, moving along and through the crowd until he reached the side and snaked his way towards the front room.

The other members simply walked off the stage, the older man smiling to himself and shaking his head.

"Kids," I was sure he was saying to himself. "Kids these days."

As they walked into the room another set of people came out all holding large, strange objects in their hands.

Lynn immediately switched her chanting of Dale's name to screams for this group. She beat her hands across the stage, letting out loud whoops that curved up at the end.

"I looovvee thhhemm!!!" She screamed to her husband. "We've seen them before! Remember!!" I don't think she actually cared whether or not he remembered. Before Patrick had a chance to answer she was back to her whooping and beating.

The group hopped onto the stage and put their instruments against the wall. Four of them lifted the long table and brought it down the steps and against the wall of the auditorium. They immediately sprung right back, grabbed their instruments, and began tuning. There were six players, four men and two women. The men ranged in age and weight from full, thick black beards and tight stomachs to straggling graying strands and bulging middles. The women were much of the same breed, minus the facial hair. I couldn't see how these people went together as a band. The women each held a small, stringed instrument in one hand and a small shaker in the other. None of the instruments matched one another, some of what they were holding didn't even appear to be instruments at all. The men held larger string instruments in one hand and a drum of some sort in the other. Everything was of a different shade and a different breed. But, this didn't seem to matter to anyone else in the room. Before I knew it the entire building's voice had transformed in the same way as Lynn's.

There was no preparation that the music was about to begin. The musicians all looked at one another, the oldest man counted to three, and they started playing. I couldn't even tell if there was a melody at first. The youngest man began plucking his instrument like there was no tomorrow, fingers flying across the strings. The women were beating their shakers and dancing around, skirts twirling in the air. Everyone on stage was beating or playing on something, even though I didn't know what most of those somethings were.

When the beats began on stage so did the beat of the audience. Suddenly everyone was moving in different directions, but to the same rhythm. No one had moved from their places, there were still bodies shoved against mine as I was pushed into the stage, but now I could push back. I began to move with the crowd, swaying and jumping as they twirled and twisted. People began grabbing one another, men and women, men and men, women and women, and spinning each other in small circles, coming together to sway again. Lynn and Patrick put their hands over me as I danced underneath, dipping my knees and moving lower as I giggled. They brought their arms around and pushed into one another in front of me, holding each other's arms and backs and moving with the music.

It didn't matter that I didn't understand their music. It didn't matter that I didn't know what instruments they were playing or that I couldn't understand a word they were singing through that fucking accent. I understood their rhythm. I was an outsider moving with them all as if I was one of them. I let myself drop back into the crowd. I let myself be swarmed by them as they moved. It was chaos. More chaos than I had ever experienced. This chaos, though, was different than the chaos my dad told me about after having a rough day at the hospital. This chaos brought me comfort. I loved getting lost in them, in all of them, as they moved around me. I felt like nothing, but I felt like everything. I danced by myself, with whoever grabbed me. I spun in circles, dipped onto the floor, swayed with the rhythm. I spun with them, dipped with them, swayed with them. I was a part of them, and they were a part of me.

I couldn't even tell when a song started or stopped. It all seemed to mold together, one giant mass becoming a single entity. I didn't pause when, out of the corner of my eye, I thought I saw the stringy hair of Raziela Davidson moving with the underground. My eyes saw her, and told me to run to her, but my body wanted to stay where it was. I didn't even realize, at one point, when Silas had come up behind me, swaying with my body.

I didn't want to turn around, I didn't want to know who had placed their hands onto my hips, sliding them to my stomach. To have an identity would be to separate myself from the group, from the collective being we had become. I closed my blue eyes and slid my hand up the arm behind me until it reached the face that was breathing into my ear. I let my hand rest on his neck before bringing it back down and letting it sit on the belt of his pants. We danced like this for, I don't know how long. Sweat was dripping down my arm onto his. When I finally opened my eyes I looked down at the hands that gripped my waist and I knew. They were the same hands that led me through the dark. The same hands that gripped their book so tightly.

I slowly turned around. He was looking straight at me. It was as if his eyes already knew where to go in order to meet mine.

He smiled, wrapped his hands around my ears, and brought my face into his.

We stopped moving with the music. No part of me pulled away. I let myself become wrapped in him. Everyone else around me was still moving, the music was still moving, but we were standing still.

When we pulled away my nose still touched his. I could feel a smile grow across his face and I pulled at the buttons of his shirt, bringing his whole body into mine. We kissed again, this time moving with the music and the community around us.

We danced for a while longer, until the oldest musician had pulled out a riveted metal board and played it across his body with spoons.

"I wanna show you something," he whispered into my ear, lips brushing against the outside of my lobe. I nodded and let him take me through the crowd to the front right side of the stage. He opened a small door and took me up another thin, metal circular staircase. At the top was a room as large as the one we were just in, with ceilings much lower. Across the entire area, as far as I could see, were rows and rows of books. I ran into the center of one of them, spreading both hands so they were touching the delicate pages on either side of me.

"What... is this?"

He was standing at the far end of the row, hands in his pant pockets.

"It's a library," he said, walking towards me.

A library. That's what we called the collection of electronic documents on our INSAVs. But to be surrounded by this much unchangeable history, to be able to feel with my fingers the original work of someone from hundreds of years ago. I couldn't believe it. I couldn't believe a place like this existed.

"You can read all of these?" I asked.

"Any one you want," he said, reaching towards me and tucking a stray hair behind my ear.

"How does this… where do they…"

"We get all your leftovers, remember?" He said, pulling a book out from the shelf to his right and turning it around in his hands.

"A lot that your people throw away comes to us, if we can sneak it down. A lot of the books you thought got destroyed came down here. They're all in these walls," he said, looking around him. "Everything you'd ever want."

I placed my hands on top of his as he gripped his book.

"The Social History of the East African Peoples," I read on the cover.

"Absolutely anything," he smiled.

I couldn't believe he had brought me here. It was the most magical place I had ever seen. Within this room were hundreds of stories, hundreds of imaginations.

"Sometimes the darkness is the only place your mind can truly be free," I heard my mother's voice echo in my head.

I pushed Silas's body against a shelf and pulled the book out of his hands. I pressed my body against his and stood on my tiptoes to bring my lips to his.

"Thank you," I whispered before kissing him.

He breathed into me as we connected, wrapping his arms around my back.

"Anything," he said, once we had pulled away. I backed up, cocking my head to the side.

"Anything?" I asked.

"Anything."

"Alice in Wonderland?"

He smirked, grabbing my hand once more and bringing me to a row towards the back.

"C….C….C…" he said to himself, looking for the title.

"Carroll…. Ca…. there it is," he said, pulling a green hardbound book from the bottom shelf. "Now you have your own copy to read."

He placed the book into my hands and I couldn't look up from its cover. The letters on the front were so… permanent.

"Do you want to read it now?" he asked.

It was all I wanted.

I sat down on the floor and, with my back against a shelf, turned the first page.

* * * * * * * * *

We must have fallen asleep on the floor. When I woke up my head was on top of Silas's shoulder, and his head on top of mine. Our books were still lying open in front of us. I jumped awake and shook him. There was something wrong. Something felt off.

He jolted awake, rubbing his eyes. I picked up his wrist and looked at his watch. It was six a.m. My fake shifted had ended 20 minutes ago. No. no. Not again.

"I have to go, I have to run." I exclaimed, leaping to my feet. He looked down at his watch, too.

"Oh no," he said. "oh no, no no no no this is bad. This is really bad."

"Show me the fastest way to get out," I demanded. If I run I might be able to convince my parents that the hospital kept me late."

We left our books open on the floor and ran down the stairs. The meeting room was now dead silent, the remnants of a celebration strewn across the floor.

When we got outside of the building the streets were completely dark except for the bright, multicolored neon lighting that laced around each of them.

"They turn the lights off during the day," he quickly explained to me as we ran. "They don't want anyone in the streets when the Daycrawlers are awake."

So they had a name for us, too.

He brought me down a small alley and we were at the building door. We ran inside, air whipping across our bodies. When we got to the door Frank was sitting in the chair, teetering on the edge of lucidity. I quickly changed my clothes and pulled back the locked door. Standing on the other side, walking out of the elevator, was my father.

17

I froze. I couldn't move. I couldn't blink. I think a piece of me thought that if I stood completely still I would be camouflaged.

"Dad.... I.... what are you doing. Here." Was all I could muster out of a frozen mouth.

Frank came to consciousness and looked out the door.

"Denzel! What do you have for me today?" He asked standing up and moving forward.

He knew my father's name.

"Just my daughter, apparently," he said, moving towards the man in the mask. "Frank how many times do I have to talk to you about that mask?" my father asked.

"Oh, sorry," Frank tenderly responded, pulling the black cloth off. He had a wide face with small, beady eyes and a bald head. Exactly what I had imagined so many times.

"I just like how it feels. It's like having a blanket on your face."

"But then I can't *see* your face," my father said. "I like being able to look at people when I talk to them."

253

I was astounded. Aghast. Confused. Relieved. Terrified?

"You know them?" I asked my father. "You... help... them?"

"Don't say it like that, Micah. You sound stuck up," he responded, standing in the middle of the room.

"How did you... why... what?" There were no complete sentences coming out of my mouth anytime soon.

"He brings us surgical stuff," Frank replied for him, pulling the list out of his pocket. "Today you're down for.... surgical pliers. You got 'em?"

"No, Frank. I don't come down until later, remember? Same time, every day."

"Oh, yeah. Sorry. I'll be seeing you later then."

My dad was doing exactly what I had been. The entire time. He knew. He knew? He knows.

"That was quite a stunt you tried to pull," he said, turning towards me. "Tricking your mother and me like that."

"But... how did she... know?" I wasn't that late. I was still convinced I could have made it.

"What do you mean, how did she know? Your mother figures out everything. When you weren't home exactly 15 minutes after your shift she threatened to go down to the hospital herself. I calmed her down, told her I would go look for you. When I got there and asked if your shift was over, the head nurse told me you didn't have a shift. I figured it out after that. You think I haven't noticed how you've been acting? Brooding around the house, not talking to anyone. I can put two and two together. I'm not an idiot. You're lucky I woke up in time to catch her."

I couldn't answer him. I couldn't believe what was happening.

"Are you angry?" I asked. I felt like I was in middle school again, getting caught after cheating off of Renee's test on the solar system.

"You're not a child, Micah. I'm not angry. But, if you're going to sneak around you need to get better at it. I thought you would have learned that after what happened with The Red Knob."

I, literally, couldn't believe the words that were coming out of his mouth. I was 90 percent certain he was about to spontaneously combust.

"I'm... sorry?" I responded questioningly. He shrugged.

"Not really much to be sorry about. Let's go home. Frank, I'll be back later with your pliers."

In silence I followed my father into the elevator, through the far room, past the shelves, out the janitor's closet, down the stairs, and out the door to our home. He refused to speak to me, refused to turn around as I walked three paces behind him.

When we arrived at the apartment my mother bolted up from the front couch and flung her body around mine. She was still wearing her pajamas, same colors and items as her day clothes, just made out of looser, more comfortable fabrics.

"Oh my god!" She screamed, crunching my head into her body. "I was so worried about you! Don't you ever do that again, I thought they'd taken you!" She finally unleashed me from her grip and I bounced back.

"Where were you?"

"She had fallen asleep in the staff lounge," my father answered for me. "I found her passed out on the couch in front of the wall projection."

"I must have passed out by accident, I'm not used to staying up that late."

My mother quickly brought me into her body again.

"You poor baby! That night shift is awful, you shouldn't do it ever again. You know what, I'm forbidding you from doing it ever again. A girl like you who's going to graduate soon shouldn't be staying up that late anyways," she cried.

"No, I…" I began interjecting. If I couldn't volunteer at night anymore, I couldn't go down to the underground again. I had sworn to Gabe that I would never step foot there, there was no way he would help me after what happened last time. My father might be able to help, but I would never be able to sneak down for more than an hour, and never again at night when everything was happening.

"I don't think that's the best idea, Jane." My father said, letting his hand rest on her shoulder.

"Micah's the best night nurse they have. She's really got a knack for it. The head nurse especially asked me today if she could begin working with them every Saturday. I was so proud of her, I couldn't say no. If this is really what Micah wants to continue to do before she starts her new career we should let her. As good of a time as any."

My mother was furious that my father was disagreeing with her forbiddance. She always tried so hard with my brother and me to show us that they were on the same page, even though we could always tell by the tone of their voices that they would go to their room that night and fight for hours.

"That's great, but don't you think it's becoming a little *dangerous*," she emphasized, gripping my arms a little tighter.

My father's shoulders raised and dropped in a tired, frustrated sigh.

"How about this, every morning after her shift is over I'll walk over to the hospital, pick her up, and bring her back home. That way we know nothing happened to her on her way back. We'll know for sure that she's safe. You trust me with my own daughter, right?" he asked, searching for guilt from his wife.

She pouted and looked back at me before responding with gritted teeth.

"Micah, honey, is this really what you want?"

I nodded emphatically.

"I love it so much, Mom. Please don't take this away from me."

She thought about my response, glared back at her husband, and then finally released my arms.

"Fine, fine. But you're picking her up every day," she pointed to my dad. "I'm going back to bed to read a leisuretext and enjoy my day off."

She angrily twisted around and stormed down the hall, slamming the door once inside.

I had so many questions to ask my dad, I didn't know where to begin. He not only knew about the underground, but lied to my mother about it in order to keep me associated with them. He was not just protecting himself, but protecting me and, in the process, protecting all of them. I wondered how long he had been helping the underground, if he had met any of them personally and had been brought down as I had. Maybe he had been to some of the same meetings I had snuck down to see. Maybe we were there together.

"Well, I'm going to go join your mother," my father said, pushing his shoes off with the toes of his opposite foot. "Get her to calm down before this becomes World War IV."

But there was so much I wanted to know.

"Wait... Dad," I said, nervous of what his answer might be. "How do you know all of them?"

"Same way you do, I suppose. I help out."

"But... how did you start? How long has this been going

on?" I was walking towards him with each question, my inquisitive face leaning towards his.

He motioned me over to the couch and we both sat down.

"It started a while ago. Probably about ten months. I've been bringing them surgical supplies almost every day since then. Everyone thinks I just go on a coffee break for too long. No one's ever asked. Not like they would challenge me, since I'm almost everyone's boss. But, it's a little more dangerous for you to be doing this. People will question you if they have to."

"Dad, I was fine. No one cares what I do."

"You think that, but you never know when someone might be watching. You're in a vulnerable position, you're easily replaceable. If you're going to keep doing this you need to become sneakier."

I smiled at him.

"But I was so good at sneaking off to The Red Knob," I half joked, half justified my skill.

"You weren't actually all that good, we found out eventually."

The smile quickly dropped from my face.

"Just like someone will find out about this if you aren't more careful."

"Ok, I'm sorry. How do I get better? I thought I was doing everything I could."

"You're lucky you have me," he said, brushing invisible dirt off his pants. "I can lie to your mother so you don't have to lie to the hospital, or in the hospital if someone actually ever catches you. The consequences aren't as... final... this way," he said.

I couldn't believe what my dad was offering. A conspiracy, a conspiracy against his own wife so his daughter could continue doing something illegal and, to many, immoral.

"Would you really? What would you tell her?"

"I'll tell her that you signed up for a shift. I'll tell her that I saw your name on the shift myself. I can even falsify some schedules. It's important that you keep going down there," he slowed down, focusing on the last sentence.

"Why?"

"There's a lot to learn about them," he said after a short pause, raising his head. ""Especially if they're going to be successful in their endeavors."

I thought about the coming revolution. This was the first time that I had talked to somebody about it aboveground. It felt strange, like the entire event was a filthy word. But, it was a filthy word I couldn't get out of my mind.

"What will happen to you then?" I wondered. Did he have a deal with them similar to mine?

"I'll continue doing my job. Just.... there instead," he explained, pointing to the ground with closed hands.

His arrangement with them was not just donating tools to save lives, but saving lives with his skills, as well.

"You're going to be their doctor?" I questioned in disbelief.

"Shhh....shhhhhhh, keep your voice down," he said, moving closer to me. "She might hear you. But yes, that's the plan. I'm hoping you have something similar?"

"Something similar," I nodded.

He breathed a sigh of relief.

"Good, good. I was praying it wouldn't be a challenge to get you down. Your brother and mother, on the other hand, I'm a little worried about."

"You don't think they'll come with us?" I couldn't imagine life without my mother or Gabe.

"We'll have to wait and see. Maybe we'll just have to drag

them down with us."

I grimaced at my father before getting up to walk back to my room. I needed time to detox from this night. Too much had happened too quickly. I began lethargically travelling down the hallway when I realized my dad had avoided one of the questions.

"Dad, how did it all start for you?"

He continued to sit on the couch, thinking. It didn't seem like he was trying to think of an answer, but of which parts of the truth he was choosing to tell me.

"There was a woman who used to work at the hospital. She showed me one day," he said shortly. "That's all you really need to know."

I was too tired to think of the implications. I didn't really care whether or not he was trying to vaguely, or not so vaguely, tell me that he had had an affair. After last night, and seeing him at the foot of that elevator, all I cared about was getting into my bed.

"Oh," I responded, walking down the hall. I immediately slid into bed and fell asleep.

While my eyes were closed my dreams raced. I was standing on top of the tallest building in the sector, something no one has ever been allowed to do. I don't know how I got there, or how long I'd been there. All I remember is trying to look past, beyond what I've always known. I stood, completely still, letting the wind violently whip my hair across my face. But, I didn't brush it away. It was foggy, I was squinting but I couldn't make out what lay beyond the wall.

Suddenly I heard a horn, low and powerful, bellowing from far away.

When I awoke, my nostrils were greeted with the scent of

chocolate chip cookies. It's one of those smells that you can always recognize, regardless of where you are or who's making them. The second that sweetness hit my nose visions of delicious batter crept into my mind and the taste became irresistible. My bed was so comfortable but a cookie sounded so good.

I tumbled out of my sheets and walked to the kitchen. My mom was leaning against the stove, picking at her fingernails. She looked up and smiled when I entered.

"Hi boo, I'm making you some cookies."

"Wow, thanks." I grumbled, trying to awaken my voice to the same level as my taste buds.

"I'm sorry I got so worked up this morning. I just get worried about you."

"It's fine, mom."

I waved her apology away, opening a cabinet above me and pulling out a glass. "I'd be worried too."

"You're just at *such* an important time," she said, cracking open the oven to check on her creation. "A few more minutes."

"You keep saying that," I said, filling up my glass in the sink. "I get it."

"No, I don't think you really, really do," she said, pulling out a cooling rack. "These are the moments that shape the rest of your life."

"Did you get that off of a graduation card?"

I was making fun of her. She was being so emotional and I had just woken up. Not a good combination.

"No, honey. It's the truth. You know I met your father in my month break after graduation. And I know that you know if you don't find someone soon you'll get put on the government's single list. Then they can pair you with whoever they want. I'm still waiting to get a notification for Gabe, it could come any day now. When I was your age I was trying to find someone to start a family with."

"I know, mom. But I don't have to decide right away."

"Well... I know. It's coming up soon. Have you at least thought about it? Have you met anyone?"

I thought about the arms wrapped around my waist as we moved with the rhythm of the people around us.

"Not yet, but I have *time*."

"You may think that, but you never notice time slipping away until it's lying in a pile underneath your fingers."

Where was she getting all of this? She didn't watch daytime projections, the only true answer in my mind.

"Do you want me to go on a date with someone?" I defensively asked her. "Fine, I'll go on a date with someone."

"No, honey. I don't want to force you to do something you don't want to do. I just... want you to discover all your options before it's to late."

She opened the oven and set the steaming cookies on top of the electric burners.

"There are lots of guys in my class, I'm sure I'll find someone. Plus, I've met a lot of people at the hospital."

Both of these facts were blatant lies.

"Have you ever thought of looking anywhere else?"

"Mom, where else is there to look? That's pretty much everyone."

She was quiet, focusing on scraping the cookies off the pan and onto the cooling rack. What was she trying to allude to?

"Well... you know... there are... places. Meeting places. I hear lots of girls your age go there, have you ever thought of checking them out?"

I couldn't believe it. She was talking about The Red Knob. For my entire childhood she had told me to never step foot in there, to avoid it at all costs. Now she thought I was old enough? She still had no idea that I used to go there all the time, had cut my ties with them, yet now she was trying to get me to go back. It reminded me that she had no conception of my reputation within its walls, and how re-attending the club would be stupider than being forced to spend the rest of my life alone.

"I think I know what you're talking about," I responded slowly, slurring my words towards the end. "I don't think it's much of my scene."

"Oh, that's silly. I think it can be anyone's scene if the time is right. And I think the time might be right for you."

"Mom, really. There's no need for me to go there. I can find someone on my own." I couldn't tell her that I already had.

"I just want you to think about it, that's all," she said, dropping the barren hot pan into the sink. "I'm not telling you to use the back rooms or anything, but checking it out wouldn't hurt, would it?"

She lifted a cookie off the cooling rack and its sides immediately began dripping down her fingers.

"Cookie, sweetheart?"

I grabbed the treat and pushed the swinging door open to sulk on the couch.

PART III

18

The test to leave school is a joke. It takes an hour and a half, a fraction of the fraction of the 15 years of knowledge it pretends to be quizzing me on. There are questions on how Nightcrawlers look, act, what we need to do to protect ourselves from them and what to do if we're captured. It's funny taking this test-- I feel like someone's quizzing me on a novel. None of the "correct" answers are actually valid in real life. The past few months have taught me that. Our test, and our education, is based on the sick imagination of a single man. Treating my text as fiction is the only way I learn how to get through it.

I graduate the next Thursday. My mother is in the audience beaming, my father thinking. My brother is sitting with his feet hanging over the edge of the aisle, I can see his black shoes invading the chair-made path from my seat on the stage. They call my name, I stand up, bow my head to my professor. They transfer a diploma onto my INSAV. I hold it out to the crowd and smile.

"Graduate of Sector 15 High School, Segregation Department. Micah

Marie Davis" it says. They clap. I sit back down. We go through each of my classmates in the same manner.

After everyone has received their diploma they tell us they've prepared a surprise. I'm unexcited, nothing they could have created is possibly more exciting than the discoveries I've been making over the past few months. The head of our school is glowing behind the podium, her face tilted upwards and body expanded as if the secret is about to leak through her body.

"We have a guest speaker," she tells us, searching the room for signs of curiosity. "He's been very influential in all your lives. Without this man, none of you would be sitting here today. It is my honor to welcome him here today. Everyone, please give Mr. Ian Dale a round of applause."

The blood drains from my face. My arms go limp, dropping onto my numb lap. My lips part as I see a hand part the curtain that's hiding him from the stage.

He walks out, slowly. With each step it seems as if the cheers get bigger. I look at my classmates. They're ecstatic, most of them are standing and all are clapping, but I can't move. My ears start to ring and everything around me is muffled.

Down with Dale! Down with Dale! Is all I hear. I'm remembering the meeting in the underground, I feel like I'm there again. He's right in front of me. After all this time, he's right here.

The ringing stops and my head jerks back into cognition. I see that now everyone is standing, everyone is clapping as loudly as they can. I stand as well to avoid suspicion and clap as lightly as possible.

He looks exactly like he did on my wall projection. Exactly like he does on the back of the historytext. Same tufts of greying hair, same plump build. Just like us, he's wearing the segregationalist uniform. After nodding to the head of the school he takes over the podium and looks around at the crowd still erupting with sound. He's taking us all in, I can tell that he's proud.

"Thank you, thank you," he finally says, voice roaring over the noise. The claps begin to diminish and gradually everyone sits back in their seats.

"Well, nobody told me Sector 15 was going to be so passionate!" he smiles, and everyone around me smiles back.

"When the head of your school wrote me about how proud she was of this graduating class and all you have done to make it here today, I knew it was my duty to come and see for myself. And my, was she right. Just by looking at you all today I can see that there are young people sitting in this room right now that are going to make a difference not just in this sector, but in the world. I cannot tell you how proud I am to be an instrumental part of this success.

"Many of you might not know this, but I first wrote your historytexts as just an assignment from the government. They wanted an account of the underground, and many before me had turned down the position. They feared it was too dangerous, that they wouldn't come back alive."

He pauses for effect, once more scanning the students directly in front of him.

"Well, here I am."

Everyone around me laughs, leaning their awestricken bodies towards the stage as if it will allow them to sooner hear what he has to say next.

"Just as I knew I had to come here today, I knew it was my duty to solve the mystery of the underground. Before my historytexts were published, we barely knew anything about the Nightcrawlers. As you all know, after their independence their situation deteriorated and safe communication became nearly impossible. But, I needed answers. We needed answers.

"I cannot be more proud that the answers I have uncovered are the cornerstone of the education of segregationalists throughout this and many sectors. We can now try and manage the underground, try and save it from itself. If I, and other historytext writers were not willing to take this chance, there may not have been any nightcrawlers left to study. Only through you will their situation get better, only through you can we teach them to stop committing these horrendous crimes which plague both the above and underground. They may appear to be savage now, but through strict laws and education we can transform them into respectable citizens that contribute to society instead of burdening it. We truly can become separate but equal, but they need your help. We need your help.

"If you take nothing else away from your education, I urge you to remember this. There is nothing more important than the truth. No matter what it takes to find it, no matter what you have to do, never stop searching. Only then will you be able to help those in need. Only then will you be able to help the Nightcrawlers help themselves. Thank you, and congratulations to the graduating class of Sector 15."

As quickly as he had come, he walks off the stage and back through the curtain to a roaring crowd. I can't believe anything I've just heard. I can't believe he was right in front of me, I can't believe what he just said. As my classmates move to be with their families, I sit completely still and continue staring at the podium. He was so close.

My mother is suddenly standing in front of me.

"Can you believe it!" she exclaims, sitting in the empty chair to my right. "Ian Dale! Here! At your graduation. You must be so proud."

I'm not. I'm disgusted. Throbbing pains run through my stomach and I can't focus my eyes.

"She is," my father responds for me, standing next to my seated mother. "I think she's in disbelief."

I nod without looking at either of them.

My mom wants to celebrate my graduation. She tells me she's making a big feast, that she might even invite a few people over. She asks me if there's anyone I want to include. "No," I politely respond.

Hours later, I'm still shaken by Ian Dale.

When we get back she immediately begins cooking. Roasted eggplant, a chicken Caesar salad, marinated asparagus and tomato soup for the first course. She cuts up a rainbow of fruit and drops the pieces into a pitcher of red wine.

"This is a special night," she tells me, eggplant sizzling to her right and soup boiling to her left. "This is the first day of the rest of your life."

If only I could tell her how wrong she truly is.

My father, brother, and I sit on the couch waiting for our meal. My brother is sipping a thick, dark ale and my father and I nurse glasses of my mother's sangria. I can tell he needs to tell me something, but can't. Halfway through a game show Gabe gets up to run to the bathroom and my father turns to me.

"You need to tell Silas that Dale is in the sector. I told your mother you're signed up for a shift at the hospital tomorrow night."

I nod, staring into the depths of my wine glass.

"Thanks."

"I told her you're signed up for night shifts at the hospital every day this week."

The liquid in my glass sloshes violently as I jerk my body towards him.

"She's letting me do that?"

"I told her it's what makes you happy. I said it would be a great graduation present. She thinks you're pretty strange for wanting to volunteer your week after graduating, but I kept telling her how well you're doing there. I reminded her that you won't be able to help at the hospital after your real job starts."

"Did she ask to see a schedule?"

"Made one up this afternoon. Your name is in a slot for every night. Tell him as soon as possible."

We hear the door of the bathroom open.

"I will," I whisper, turning back towards the projection. A woman loses 5,000 dollars for not knowing the difference between affect and effect.

"Micah honey, can you come help me set the table?" My mother bellows from the kitchen.

I set my glass down on the surface to my side and walk into the kitchen to grab the plates. I feel hollow, I need to get back underground.

"Five settings," she says, taking a spoonful of soup out of the pot and blowing on it before taking a small sip. "It needs a little more basil."

"Four, you mean," I blankly correct her, grabbing plates from a cabinet above me.

"No, five. I invited someone, remember?"

I pause and my heart jumps, the last plate suspended in midair above my head.

"Who did you invite?"

"Oh, just someone I think you'll get along with very well."

"Mom, I hope you're not trying to set me up." I pull five

forks, spoons, and knives from the sliding drawer to the right of the sink.

"I wouldn't call it that," she rationalizes, pulling the asparagus out of the oven. "Could you tell your father and brother that dinner's almost ready?"

"If you tell me who you invited," I say, standing my ground with a large pile of cutlery weighting down my arms. I can't handle any more surprises today.

"I really think you'll like him. We talk about you all the time, I told him you were graduating and he asked if there was anything we were doing to celebrate. I told him about this dinner and, well, it just kind of happened."

"But *who* is it?"

"Do you remember me telling you about two men a little while ago? They were new to the sector and were brought in to help with some law reformation."

I know exactly who she's talking about, and neither of those men would have forgotten me by now.

"Yeah, but I remember you saying they were a lot older than me. I don't think something like this is really going to work out."

"Oh, honey age doesn't matter. Your father is seven years older than me and we get along just fine. Give it a chance."

I had given that a chance. A long, long time ago.

"I'm not going to like him."

"Give it a chance."

I turn away from her and push past the door to set the table.

I'm filling the dinner glasses with water when we hear a knock on the door. My father gets up from the couch to answer it, looking back at me before twisting the knob.

"Shawn!" he tells the man after opening the door. "What a

pleasure to see you."

The man looks a little plumper than I remember. He's wearing an orange bowtie with swirling yellow accents today.

"The pleasure is all mine, Dr. Davis," he says, placing his hand onto my father's shoulder. I'm very excited to spend time with your family. Jane tells me this is a very special night."

"Ah yes, well, graduations are pretty special," my father says, moving to the side so Shawn can enter our home. "Micah's worked very hard. I don't believe that you've met. Micah, this is Shawn." He extends his arm towards me. I'm standing behind the table, half filled jug of water balancing in my right hand.

Shawn and I look at one another. He knows I know, I know he knows. I expect to see fear and surprise in his eyes. He seems smug, though, and almost relieved. He remembers me, I'm sure of that, but what exactly he remembers I'm not quite sure. The night we had together wasn't anything special, but I can never be positive of what goes on in the minds of the men I sleep with. It seems that I can never really be sure of anything, now. Shawn comes straight up to me, walking in front of and ignoring Gabe who sits mesmerized on the couch.

"Nice to meet you, Micah," he smiles at me.

So we're going to play this game.

"You too... Shawn, was it?" I begin to extend my arm to shake his hand and have to stop myself, pretending to rebalance the pitcher of water.

"Yes ma'am."

"Nice bowtie, Shawn."

He looks down at his neck and tugs at the colorful cloth with one hand. "Thanks, I try to wear one every day. It's become a good way for people to remember me." He's trying to make a joke, something hidden from the rest of the room but shared between the two of us. He's trying to show me he remembers.

"Very stylish."

"Yeah I try. Can I take that water from you? I'll bring it in to your mom."

Gripping the bottom with one hand and the handle with the other I hand him the heavy container and he walks through the swinging door. I look at my father who simply shrugs.

"It's just one dinner. After everything that happened today I'm sure you can handle it."

A dinner that's set up by your mother with a man you've had anonymous dirty sex with, on the same day that you first see the man who is destroying the secret world you love, though, doesn't go quickly. Shawn keeps looking over at me seductively, trying to peer into my eyes when he has his wine glass tipped over his nose or is sucking the last bit of eggplant off his fork. He seems to expect me to respond in the same manner and develops a look of subtle disappointment every time I don't. My meals are for eating, not sex hints.

My mother tries to get everyone talking. She and Shawn discuss the new laws that are on the table and how the committee is taking such a long time to get them rolling "I don't understand what's taking so long," she says. "The safety of the people is at stake!" He responds equally as emphatically, telling stories of how things were run in his old sector.

"It's been a hard transition," he says, looking at me again. "It would be great to have a stronger support system."

My mother giggles at this comment.

"You can come over anytime you want."

"If you keep cooking like this maybe I will."

The table politely laughs, taking small bites of asparagus to follow.

"How is it being a trash collector?" Shawn asks Gabe, who hasn't spoken for the duration of the meal. "It sounds so exciting and dangerous."

"I don't like to talk about work," he retorts, taking a giant swig of his beer.

"Since when?" My mother asks him. "You've always talked about it before."

"Not anymore." He doesn't speak again until dessert starts.

Ever since Gabe brought me down to the underground he's been aloof. He doesn't want to connect with us anymore, he goes through his day as if we're not there.

My mother abruptly tries to change the subject.

"Shawn, are you as ecstatic as I am to meet Ian Dale?"

My fork clinks loudly against my plate as it misses picking up a chunk of salad.

"Mom, you didn't tell me you were going to meet him."

My mother blushes and gently puts down her spoon.

"Oh, I'm sorry honey. I should've told you! It wasn't official until today. We're holding a Gala for him in about a week. Everyone in my department, including Shawn over here, gets to miss almost a half day of work to celebrate his arrival to the sector."

"Wow, that's... really exciting."

At first, just hearing his name makes my throat tighten. Even more than before, he'll be within reach. My mind starts turning. I lean in a little closer towards my mom and slowly begin to form a plan.

"Mom, is there any way you could get me a ticket or let me come to the office for the day? I would love to meet him. He did form almost my entire education."

"Well, wouldn't that be great. You know what, I'll ask my

supervisor tomorrow, maybe we can work something out."

Shawn taps my mother's arm and leans slightly across the table towards me.

"You might be able to be my guest, you can come with me, as my date. I can ask my supervisor as well."

I tightly smile at him and begin twirling the tomato soup with the tip of my spoon.

"That would be nice," I shortly respond with sly eyes, bringing the spoon towards my mouth and placing the red liquid onto my lips. I'm suddenly rejuvenated.

Shawn asks me whether or not I'm excited to start my career. This time I smile at him through a tilted wine glass.

"Ecstatic." I take a gulp, twisting my finger around the rim of the glass after placing it back on the table.

"I would love to show you around."

"I would love to follow you around."

He's confused, I've changed how I'm treated him and am now exhibiting a wink of compassion. It's amazing how the smallest of smiles can go the longest of ways.

"I'm very excited to show you around at the Gala."

"I'm excited to see everything. Ian Dale is absolutely, without doubt, one of my heroes. You'd be making my dreams come true."

He's pleased. So am I.

"This was a really wonderful meal," he says holding a wrapped piece of strawberry crème cake as he grabs his jacket from the coat hanger near the door. "Thank you so much for inviting me over. This will be delicious tomorrow after lunch."

"Anytime," my mother smiles at him.

"And Micah, I'm looking forward to seeing you in a few days."

"Can't wait," I smile back.

My mother thinks we're soul mates. She can't believe the chemistry she feels, the sparks she saw fly across the room. "It was like you already knew each other," she glows, packing up the leftover food. "I told you that was a good idea." I agree with her and excuse myself to my room.

I lie in bed thinking of tomorrow night when I can go back down to the underground. As I imagine telling them about Dale I drift into a lucid sleep.

I'm standing on top of the skyscraper again. The horn is getting louder, closer. I walk to the ledge of the building and lean into the grey sky. The fog is letting up, I can't see anything yet but know, somehow, that it will clear soon.

Then, the ground starts shaking. I look at my feet and the small rocks around me are chattering, bouncing up and off the edge of the building. I think the buildings around me are getting taller, but then I realize that mine is just getting shorter. I hear glass crack and fall below me. I look around and suddenly everything else is shaking, too. It's crumbling. Everything is crumbling.

I see someone standing on the top of the building closest to me. She's wearing a long red skirt and has a pile of papers in her hands. I'm not close enough to see her eyes, but I can feel them looking at me. The papers fly out of her fingers and into the air, into the oppressing fog, out of the sector. Then, she starts flying away too. One of the papers lands next to me. They have my mother's name on top of them.

I wake up in complete darkness. I open my eyes for a second, take a deep breath, and fall back asleep.

My mom wants me to meet her and Shawn for lunch the next day. I tell her that I need to play hard to get. She thinks I'm being serious and drops the date. I spend the day asleep, waking up completely alert but forcing myself to lie in bed until I dose off again. I want to be as awake as possible when I go down this time.

Silas is waiting in his usual spot. I become unexpectedly nervous when I see him and realize I don't know what my last visit really meant. I don't know if what happened between us is something he's done before or if our actions were just a reaction to the music and air of harmony that circulated across the crowded concert. He smirks when he sees me and hands over the pile of cloth from underneath his chair. He looks away when I begin getting undressed, but I can see him tilt his body to the side and slightly turn his head. He's not looking, but I can see he wants to. When I finish I walk up to him and place a small kiss onto his lips.

"Good week?" I ask.

"Good week." He responds.

"Where are we going tonight?"

"Sonya has requested your help, we're heading over to the warehouse."

I take a deep breath and loosely grip the sides of his arms.

"Silas, I have something extremely important to tell you."

His face suddenly tightens with fear and concern and he grips the sides of my body.

"What is what? What's happened? Are they figuring it out?"

He shoots rounds of questions at me, one after another, each increasing in intensity.

"No, no," I calm him down, rubbing the sides of his arms through his thick grey shirt. "That's not it at all."

"Well, then what the hell is it?"

"Ian Dale is in the sector."

At first I can tell he's still confused, his eyebrows wrinkle even further and he desperately searches my face for an answer. But, then I see the moment that it hits him. First his forehead is smoothed and then his eyes slightly crinkle around the edges as his cheeks rise and lips part into a smile.

He grips my body tightly for a second before turning around.

"We need to tell Sonya right away."

I'm comfortable in the streets now. He doesn't have to hold my hand anymore as we walk through them, but I keep my fingers tightly wrapped around his as he laces me between the moving crowd. It's amazing how different I feel today than when I first arrived just a few months ago. I'm not worried about getting lost within the people anymore, I walk through the winding streets with complete confidence. The roads that used to seemingly appear from nowhere I now expect. I know when to turn down their narrow curves, and even smile at many of the shop owners as they sit promoting their colorful cloths, eccentric kick knacks, and weak produce priced twice as high as what it is above.

"What're rickets?" I ask, as we pass one of the stores I noticed on my first journey.

"When something awful happens to your bones from not getting any sun. They warp, and curve, and there's nothing you can do about it."

"Except for get more vitamin D."

"That's why we have you guys at the hospital," he says. "We're running low on that, too."

"Is there anything you *have* a lot of?" I ask.

"Guns," he laughingly responds. "Now we have lots and lots of guns."

I'm amazed at what he tells me as we walk to Sonya's

warehouse. I've learned that I'm always amazed by what he says. That the Nightcrawlers, he calls them Nightwalkers, first noticed how awful everything was getting when those sent above to do special work stopped coming back down.

"They were promised better jobs up there, they weren't told doing what," he tells me. "But most of them haven't come back."

I know exactly where they went.

We enter a revolving door in the southeast section of the sector. It's amazing, how differently everything is built down here, yet the walls that keep us inside the sector both above and below ground are exactly the same. Long rows of grey cinderblocks encompass the entire city. Unlike the above, though, the walls here have beautiful paintings scattered across them. Before we walk through the doors of the warehouse I squint my eyes to make out what lies on the wall closest to us. It's a painting of a bright purple tree with yellow rays radiating from its branches. I wonder if this is where they think the sun comes from.

We get into an elevator and begin heading downwards. My ears pop with each swallow as we smoothly travel to reach the fifteenth level. Sonya is waiting when the elevators open.

"Micah, great to see you again," she smiles at me with arms behind her back. "Silas tells me you've really been enjoying your time with us."

"Absolutely," I say, reaching out to shake her hand. She grins and shakes back while Silas laughs to himself.

"Sonya, Micah has something important to tell you."

Her face follows in the same reaction as Silas, arms dropping to her sides and body inching closer to us.

"What's wrong? What happened? Silas, I told you when we

started it was a bad idea to bring her…"

"No no no, that's not it, Sonya. That's not it at all," he stops her. "Ian Dale is in the sector."

She can't comprehend this at first, either. But suddenly, more intensely than Silas, she slips into astonishment.

"We have to get to him! We have to get him down here. Can you even imagine, Silas? The man who started it all finally in the place he's destroying. We have to alter the plan."

Silas smiles as he grabs my hand.

"Micah already has one."

Sonya looks at me in suspense.

"What is it?"

"My mom's office is having a Gala for him. There will be a lot of people there and I've already been invited to go with a segregationalist. Silas told me there's an entrance to the underground in the building."

"Well yes, but it hasn't been used in… a while. It's dangerous, not as hidden as we like. It would require you to get him alone."

"We could use some of the others," Silas states. "The other Daycrawlers who have been helping us. They would agree to help her transport him."

Sonya steps closer to me, arm resting on my shoulder and eyes piercing my own.

"Micah, would you take this risk?"

I don't even have to think about my answer. Where I'm standing should be making that clear.

She turns to Silas, arm still on mine.

"You've told her what she'll need to do?"

He nods, I nod as well. It's going to be tough, but it's the only option.

"Well, then. Why you're down here today is much more

relevant than it was five minutes ago. We think it would be good for you to know what weapons we have and how to use them. Especially now."

She turns to walk down the darkened hallway and we follow after, our shoes clinking against the concrete floor.

"Once everyone is assigned a battalion they'll learn how to use their weapons together, but you won't be assigned to one since you'll be above when the revolution begins. It depends on where you'll end up. If you have to come down immediately after we capture Dale, you'll be taking an exit leading you directly to the town meeting hall. There are many entrances, I'll make sure Silas tells you about all of them before you leave here today."

"What's the best way for my family to get down?"

It's the only thing I'm concerned about now. I need to ensure their safety more than my own.

She thinks, running a finger against the left side of her chin.

"Your father should have already decided a way."

She knows my father, too?

"You can't tell him," I suddenly realize. "That I'm going to get Dale. It's too dangerous."

She nods once downward in agreement.

"Your father is as smart as you are, Micah. We can try to keep him ignorant of the plan, but I can't promise he won't find out on his own. Come on, let me show you everything we have."

She brings me around the room, demonstrating everything from a pocketknife to a semi-automatic rifle. "We don't have a lot of these," she explains. "But, if you're lucky enough to find one you'd better know how to use it."

"Will I have any weapons on me when I go to get Dale?"

"If we can sneak one onto you. A pocketknife should be

small enough that no one will notice. We'll make sure to give the others as many weapons as we can, as well."

Great. I was being given a pocketknife to defend myself in a treacherous act and the start of a bloody revolution. Silas could see the fear on my face.

"It's doubtful that anyone from your own group will begin attacking you, even if they do start to understand that you're fighting for the other side. If you follow our plan, you'll be able to get Dale into the underground. By the time your people get past the shock of the ambush you'll be long gone."

I'm glad we're basing whether or not I live off of someone's hopeful disorientation.

"You're doing a very brave thing, Micah." She says. "You'll be protected as much as humanly possible."

God I hope so.

19

When we reach their street level again Silas tells me he has a few friends who he would like me to meet. My hand begins to sweat and I pull it away from his out of embarrassment. Somehow I can handle offering myself up for a covert operation, but can't bring myself to stay calm when meeting Silas's community.

"Do you not want to meet them? It's ok if it's too much, a lot has happened today. I just figured it's another piece of the underground culture you might want to experience."

"I'm fine," I say quickly. I'm going to be living with them soon anyways.

"Good, I'm glad. They all really want to meet you," he says, pulling my body closer to his. "Just... don't say anything about Dale. You never know who could be listening."

We walk near his apartment to the restaurant I noticed before, Jerry's Mushroom Café. I can tell from the outside that this isn't the most up-kept establishment. The windows are murky and riddled with outdated posters and signs.

Babysitter available!
John's Jam Band playing on the 11th!
Down with Dale! a smaller one reads.

He opens the creaking door for me and I step inside. A wall of smoky haze hits me and I instinctually try to push it away. A girl I haven't seen before waves us over.

"Silas! Back table!"

After looking around to follow the voice and locking in where his friends are located he walks in front of me and towards them. I follow, arms crossed tightly across my chest, scanning the room. The room around me has hundreds of pictures of absolutely everything imaginable lining the walls. About half the tables are filled, but none of them match one another and nothing matches the chairs surrounding them. Everything is of some kind of wood, but the stains and designs are completely different. It reminds me of the instruments from last Friday.

There are two chairs available at their six-person table, one on either end. He takes the far seat and I stand awkwardly behind the closer one, not sure if they want me to sit down. When I wrap my fingers around its back I feel small indents of words carved into the frame. BECCA N TONY 4 EVER. LACEY WAZ HERE.

"Micah, hi!" I hear a familiar voice say from across the table. I look over and it's Emily, who has lit a cigarette and is sitting with it resting in her raised hand, elbow on the edge of the table. "Silas didn't tell me he was bringing you today."

"He told me," another girl, sitting next to her but closer to me, says. She reaches out her hand. "Molly." I lean over to shake it. The man sitting next to her, but across from my empty chair, speaks next.

"I'd introduce myself but you'll probably forget my name."

"I don't think so," I respond. The second I open my mouth I'm reminded of our differences. My voice sounds so foreign to theirs, and a little bit foreign to myself.

"If you can remember it's Jason," he says, taking a sip from his beer. "And that's Charlie."

"I'll forgive you if you forget it," Charlie, the man next to my chair, says to me. "Sounds like everyone gives you so much fucking information when you're down here. I would hate to be your brain."

"At least she has a brain," Molly mutters under her breath while scanning the paper menu in front of her. Charlie reaches across to lightly smack her across the head, but she smacks his hand away by darting out her own.

"Your little sister told you to stop hitting me so much!"

"But it's just so much fun."

"You're a dick. Have you had their Portobello burger before? I thought you got it last time we were here."

"Yeah, it's pretty good. Wanna split that with me and I'll get the soup?"

"Yeah, whatever."

"Anyone want another beer?" Charlie asks, standing up.

"Get me one?" Silas responds. "And, Micah, do you want anything?"

I shrug, not wanting to impose but wanting to taste whatever it is they're ordering. I'm sure their beer tastes different than what Gabe spends his days sipping.

"Grab her one too? I'll pay you back."

Charlie nods and crosses the restaurant to the bar.

I can't understand how they're able to talk to one another so easily. There's so much at stake in their lives, but they're talking to each other more freely than any conversation I've had outside of my home aboveground. It's something I've only vaguely experienced within The Red Knob, and every conversation there was sealed with an unsaid promise.

"You look uncomfortable," Jason says to me, folding his hands in front of him.

"Are we intimidating? We must be a little intimidating."

"I'm sorry, I know I shouldn't be but... maybe just a little."

"No need to apologize. I can't even imagine being in your situation. Here, I know a way we can fix this. I'll tell you something ridiculously embarrassing about every person at this table, and then you tell me something embarrassing. I'll tell you about me first," he says, not waiting for whether or not I agree. "I have three nipples."

What!" I laughed.

"Yep, one two three nipples. You want to see them?" He pulls up his shirt and turns to the left.

"You see that bump on my side? That's technically a *nipple*."

"Jason, why do you have to show everyone that?" Emily yells from across the room. "No one wants to see even one of your nipples."

"I'm getting past my awkward stage with Micah! And I'm getting past all of yours, too. Hey Molly, remember when you threw up all over Silas's couch?"

"Do we really have to do this right now?"

"I could tell her about that, or the time that you sucked that lemon off of..."

"I wasn't even sick," Molly interrupted him, speaking towards me. "It literally came out of nowhere. We were, like, ten. Ruined 5th grade for me. Not to mention a piece of Mrs. Durand's garden."

"You guys talking about when Molly licked that lemon out of

my belly button and then kept licking me?" Charlie asks, passing beers on either side of him to Silas and I.

"Dude! It was the dare, I needed to lick everything up or I didn't get the points!"

"You didn't have to swirl your tongue on my abs," he smirked, Adam's apple bobbing as he gulped his beer.

"Yeah, alright. I'll admit. That was a little something extra. Free of charge," she winked at him.

"Emily, you're next."

She and Silas smile at one another before responding.

"But you guys are so great at deciding them for one another. What do you think I'm going to say?"

"When your mom caught you doing shrooms in her room," Charlie yells.

"When your mom caught you skipping school and doing shrooms in her room," Molly states.

"When your mom caught you and Silas doing it in her room," Jason exclaims.

"That was pretty embarrassing," Silas agrees.

Emily just laughs.

"There you go Micah. My whole life laid out in front of you. I'm a sneaky, drug addicted whore."

"I'm sure Silas has already told her his most embarrassing story," Molly says, looking towards her friend. "Right?"

"Probably not as many as you'd think," Silas laughs, putting his beer down in front of him. "Let me think… I'm not really that embarrassing of a person."

"Aside from the sex in Emily's mom's bed."

"And telling your math teacher in 7th grade to… what was it… stick his derisions so far up his ass that they'll come out in 1,000 years as diamonds?"

"Or how about running naked through the street after we went out for your birthday. That's a pretty good one."

"Alright, so I'm a little embarrassing." Silas shrugs, re-grabbing his beer. "But for some stupid reason you fuckers are still friends with me."

"We have to be, you're leading a fucking revolution!" Charlie screams, throwing his hands up in the air. "Being friends with you is the best chance we have of making it out alive." They all laugh at this joke, but I don't understand why. How can they laugh about a death that might be so close in the future?

"Micah, how about you?" Silas asks me after taking a quick sip of his beer.

I hoped that they would forget about me by the time they had made their way around the circle. After hearing about all of them, I have nothing. They've all done something wild, something that's completely against the rules. They laugh about disobeying their laws like it's just a game. I was never given this opportunity, no one around me has ever even mentioned breaking anything, much less a law on something other than smoking in their apartment. The closest I had come was going to The Red Knob, but even that was acceptable in the right circles.

"I used to go to a sex club every week." I say. It's all I have, but I feel like I need to give them something. I prepare myself for their grimaces, immediately regretting this slice of information.

No one laughs at this, or even moves. They all just stare. I look over at Silas, terrified of what he must be thinking of me. Maybe this is a story that takes it too far. I imagine having to get up and leave, or being ignored by them for the rest of the meal. Maybe this detail took it so far that they would make me go back aboveground. Finally, Emily speaks.

"I bet you have some awesome moves."

I smile and pick at the label on my beer bottle.

"Know my way around, I guess."

"You're going to have to teach me sometime."

"Now that's a piece of their society we should keep."

Suddenly we're all laughing, sharing stories about our experiences. They're fascinated by the men I've been with and the things they've asked to do with me.

"There was this one guy that, literally, just wanted to snuggle." I tell them, leaning in closer to the table. "I tried to get him to have sex with me. I even stripped down naked. But he just told me to put my clothes back on and lay with him."

"Was he gay?" Emily asks. "I'm sure he was gay."

"No, no! His girlfriend works with my mom. But, I found out later that she'd been cheating on him the whole time."

"What the hell!" Emily exclaims.

"I know, what the hell."

"Now that I know that's their weakness I'm going to use it in battle," Molly contemplates. "Go up to a guy, tell him I want to snuggle his brains out, and then pop! Whack him straight across the head."

We talk for hours. We talk before we get our food, during, and after, drinking the whole time. They tell me stories about their lives like I was there, like they're just reminding me of "that one time we tried to set up an underground, *underground*, poker game on the bottom floor of the school" or when "we tried to make that special dinner for Emily's brother and his girlfriend and burnt the entire thing." It's nice to feel wholly a part of something and to be surrounded by people who don't seem like they're constantly holding back a string of secrets. I don't notice when the warm grip of the beer begins to take over my body.

Some of his friends are also drinking something else. It's a clear, pungent liquid that's served in small glasses. Halfway through the night Jason comes back with one and takes a large swig, swallowing with a twisted face as if he just ate the sourest lemon.

"What *is* that?" I slur to him over the crowd. "And why does it look so…. intimidating?" That was a lot of syllables to get out.

He laughs and hands over his glass.

"It's something special that every restaurant makes differently."

I put it under my nose and take a giant whiff. The scent is clear, but laced with flavors I've never smelled before. It's alcohol, I can tell that much, but exactly what kind I'm not sure.

"Is it vodka?" I ask. "We have that sometimes in the aboveground."

"Well… kind of. It's a…. stronger vodka. We call it moonshine. I guess you could say it's one of the underground's many claims to fame."

But, I've never heard of it, I think to myself as I raise the glass to my face.

The liquid burns as it goes down my throat. My tongue is on fire as it tries to quickly push the flames into my chest. I can even feel it as it travels down my body, the blaze reducing to residual warmth as it hits my lungs and settles in my stomach. I immediately cough after it's down, as if somehow this will release the taste from my mouth. Jason just continues to laugh.

"You'll get used to it someday."

I'm sitting at the bar with Silas when the question leaks out of my mouth.

"How can you all be like this?" I ask him with large, swirling hand motions and a slurring tongue. "You're all so… calm. You talk about everything so casually. You all know what's coming, but you don't seem to care."

"We care," Silas says, looping his foot around mine underneath the table. "But, you have to understand that we're living with something that isn't going to be stopped. The day when we finally storm the aboveground is going to come. We can't talk about our lives like it's not. But, there's nothing we can do about it. We've all come to terms with it, in our own ways. We've accepted that what's going to happen might be out of our control. We don't know for certain if we're going to win, or if were going to make it out alive. All we can do is enjoy the time we have left. There's no use being angry with one another when there's so much anger to be had towards them."

My drunken mind analyzes and re-analyzes what he has told me. They're living every day as if it's one of their last, and what they choose to do is to simply be with one another. They choose to live as they've always lived, not to coop themselves up in their homes out of fear. They're embracing the time they have left instead of being bitter about the time that's being taken away.

Before bringing me back above, Silas leads me across town and back up the circular stairs to the library. I go straight back to the row from before and pull out my book. I lay in his lap reading as he strokes my hair, his own book suspended in his left hand. "Grundrisse," his text is called. He tells me I should read it someday, and I tell him I will even though it sounds like a painful workout move.

This is how I spend most of my nights for the next few days. Silas and I rotate between the library, his friends, meetings, and his apartment. I begin sleeping through the day and only staying awake at night, seeing my mother only sometimes after I wake up and my father when he picks me up in the mornings. She's counting down the days until the Gala, she can't wait to see me with Shawn again. I'm counting down, too. But for an entirely different reason.

I update my father with what I learn at the meetings.

"They're going to begin the night after Dale gets here," I tell him on the day he drops off a pile of broken defibrillators. "After they take him below."

"Everyone has been assigned to their battalions now," I tell him the next day. "They'll be getting their weapons in two days."

"It's really coming up," he responds. I nod.

"They're calling it Operation Daybreak. Have you told mom or Gabe yet? Do they know that they're coming with us?"

"We'll bring them down when the time comes, don't worry sweetheart."

I am worried, though. I don't see how not to be.

20

On one of the last nights before the Gala, when I'm bringing down a variety of burn creams, Silas brings me to the underground hospital. He thinks it's good for me to know my way around before the revolution starts. I become nervous when he tells me this. He still thinks I'm training to be a doctor.

The entrance to the hospital is just a few hundred feet away from where the dark hallway leads out into the city. It takes up the lower 20 stories of the building.

"I won't be able to help anyone," I remind him when we're in the elevator on our way to the 30th floor. "I'm not really a doctor yet, and I have an actual shift at the hospital tonight so I have to get back pretty soon."

"I know," he replies calmly. "I just want you to see."

When the elevator doors open I'm confused. The floor looks exactly like the inside of the hospital aboveground. To the left of the elevator is a small nurses' station, and in front of me lies a long row of rooms. There are men and women in identical uniforms to ours traveling up and down them, pausing in the hall to talk to one another and pointing to the clipboards in their hands. I step outside the elevator and look closer.

While our walls are a gleaming white, these have been warped by time and have yellow streaks running down the seams of the bricks. The uniforms of the men and women are loose and tattered, the fabric faded and fraying from an abused past life. I look at the faces of those wearing them. They are worn, exhausted, with grey circles illuminating tired eyes.

"Do all the floors look like this?" I ask Silas as we step out of the elevator.

"More or less. Some have fewer doctors in the hallways, but more patients in the rooms. This is the pediatric floor."

We are walking down the hallway, a hallway that looks so much like the one I spent so many afternoons in. Except, in every aspect of this floor there is something a little different from what I'm used to. I know this place, but there's something not quite right. At first glance I'm familiar, almost too familiar, with my surroundings. As I look closer into each detail, I realize I'm not familiar at all. I'm in a foreign territory that looks like a shoddily made copy of my own. Chills rush down my body as we walk. Silas stops in front of a closed room and places his hand on the handle.

"I want you to meet someone. Try not to look alarmed."

I'm confused. If the layout of this floor is the same as our hospital he's about to bring me into a patient's room.

"I don't know if it's possible for me to be alarmed by anything anymore."

He smiles at me and turns the knob.

"We should be quiet at first when we get inside."

He disappears into the room and I slide in after him.

All of our rooms at the aboveground hospital only have one

occupant. Their name is placed onto the outside of the door when they are admitted so that visitors and doctors can easily find their family members and patients. I notice this door has no name, and when I step inside I understand why. Shoved into this room are four narrow metal frames, and on each of them a small, quiet body. There are two large, harsh square lights in the center of the room, directly above the only space that's wide enough to comfortably walk through. Above each bed is a make shift nametag created out of crayon and paper. One, on the far left, reads, "Anna" and has blue ants surrounding the letters. The one next to her, Chase, has a soccer and basketball on the top corners of his page, and to his right is the bed of Cheyenne, whose name is written with a different color for each letter. Silas turns to the bed on the far right and pushes his body into the slender space between two beds, facing the last child. I stand at the end of the bed and look up at the sign above her head. "Alex", it reads, in bubble letters. There is a cartoon sun with oval eyes and a smile too wide in the corner, its rays seeping into her name.

I look below it and see a mass of blonde hair protruding from underneath the yellow sheets. The girl's head is turned to the side so I can't see her face.

Silas places his hand onto her head and quietly begins repeating her name.

"Alleexxxxx….. Alllexxx sweetheart wake up. There are some people here to see you."

Her head stirs, but doesn't rise. I hear a small groan from underneath the cloth.

"Who is it?"

"Come on now, you should recognize my voice."

She turns her head so that she can see him, but I still can't see her.

"Silas," she says, in a voice that I know is intended to be much more excited than it sounds. "Are you bringing me a snack this time?"

"Haha, no. Not this time. Lynn didn't make any treats today. But, I brought you something better."

He reaches into his pocket and pulls out one of the small tubs of burn cream that I had brought down earlier that night. I didn't even see him take one.

"What's that?"

"It's going to make you feel better. Here, sit up so I can put some onto your face."

She stays put, wrapping her covers tightly into her arms.

"You promise?"

"I promise."

"Who did you bring with you?"

"Just a friend, but she's really nice and very excited to meet you."

"Is she going to be scared of me?"

Silas stroked her golden head, his blue eyes tracing his hand as it runs down her locks.

"Of course she won't be scared of you, but you also have to try not to be scared of her. Will you try?"

She nods her head and slowly begins raising her upper body. When her back is against the wall she turns her face towards me.

I don't see the girl's face, I see her scar. She's so light, yet there's a line of raised ghostly skin that unravels from her left temple, across her nose, and to the base of her right cheek. It's a line of craters with a web around the edges that dissipates quickly like crude drawings of blood vessels. Her eyelashes and part of her left eyelid have disappeared and the spot where the line crosses her nose is entirely indented.

When my eyes finally refocus on her entire face all I can see is fear. She's clutching her blankets below her chin with both hands and has sunk as far into the wall as humanly possible. I don't know whether to stand still or walk towards her, to speak or remain silent. Her bottom lip begins to quiver and she turns towards Silas.

"You promised she'd be nice! This isn't someone nice!" She wraps her arms around his waist and burrows her head into his stomach. "Make her leave," I hear in a muffled voice through his body.

"Alex, I didn't lie to you. She is someone nice. She's not like the people who did this to you."

She releases her head from Silas's body and turns it up towards his own.

"But she *looks* like them."

"Not all people that look like her are bad. She's helping us. Emily met her, and she likes her." He bends down, squeezing his body between the beds so that he's at eye level with her. "I would never bring someone here who would want to hurt you. Ever. Will you at least tell her your name?"

Alex thinks this over, playing with the fabric of Silas's sleeve with her fingers.

"You already told her my name."

He smiles.

"I bet she'd like to hear it from you."

Alex takes a deep breath before turning to me again. She stammers as she speaks.

"M-m-m-y name....i-s... Alex."

I don't move, but continue standing stiffly at the foot of her bed, hands wrapped around one another in front of me.

"I'm Micah," I seem to stutter back. I'm nervous. I've never been this nervous around someone so young before. She's still holding Silas's sleeve.

"Did she come from up there?" she turns to ask him.

"Why don't you ask her yourself?"

She looks at him, pleading to answer her question. He simply motions his head towards me. "Go ahead."

"Did you come from.... up there?"

I consider lying. She seems terrified of me just because of the color of my skin, telling her the truth about where I come from may make an awful situation even worse.

"No... I..." I begin, but then stop. I need to take responsibility.

"I grew up... up there, but someday maybe I can live down here. Do you think that would be alright?" She doesn't answer me, but turns again to Silas for approval.

"Well, Alex, do you think she'd be able to live down here with us?"

She looks down at the hand that's clutching his.

"I don't know."

"I told you she's very nice, and she would never hurt you. She even brought down this cream to make your face feel better, see?" He puts the cream onto the bed in front of her. "Would you like her to help you put it on?"

To this suggestion she seems absolutely terrified and again burrows into his body.

"No, no. She can't. Only you."

"Ok, ok. It's alright. She doesn't have to. But, if you let her, I think she would really like it."

"I said no."

"Ok, that's fine. But can I help you?"

She nods against his pale blue shirt.

"Is it ok if she watches?"

She pauses before slightly nodding her head yes and pulling away from his body again.

"I'm going to sit on your bed, is it ok if she sits down too? She'll be on the other side of me. She just wants to watch."

"You promise you won't leave?"

"I promise," he says, untwisting the cap. "I'll always be here to protect you."

She pulls a small purple rabbit out from under her pillow and hugs it close to her body.

"So will Mr. Martin," she says, looking down at the rabbit. "He's here whenever you, or mommy, or daddy, or Emily aren't."

"That's right. He's our soldier." He puts a small dollop of the white cream onto his finger and raises it towards her face. "He's our eyes and ears, good thing he's got some big ones."

She smiles and closes her eyes as he gently wipes across her forehead and cheek. I continue standing at the foot of her bed, watching. I don't know what happened to Alex, or why. All I know is that it happened by the hands of the aboveground. I can't even sit on her bed, I'm frozen.

"There, you're all done." He says, rising from her bed. "I'm going to leave this with you, and when your mom, dad, or sister come to visit you have them put a little onto your scar."

"Will it get rid of it?" She asks hopefully.

"It can't do that, but it will help you feel a lot better."

"When will you come back again?"

"Soon, very soon. I'll be back with cookies before you know it."

She smiles and rests her head back onto her pillow, Mr.

Martin lying underneath her left arm.

"Mr. Martin wants to say goodbye to Micah. Can you bring him to her so he can give her a hug?"

Silas plants a large kiss onto Alex's cheek and re-emerges with the purple rabbit in his hand.

"Of course. Micah, Mr. Martin has something he'd like to say to you."

I smile tightly and shakily reach my arm out towards the stuffed animal. When I come in contact with him it amazes me how much he reminds me of my own, still sitting in my closet.

"It was nice meeting you Mr. Martin," I say to him. "Will I see you again soon?"

"Very soon," Alex peeps from under her covers. "He's glad you came to see him."

I hand the rabbit back to Silas, who places it snuggly into Alex's arms.

"Me too," I say.

"Was that Emily's sister?" I ask after he shuts the door to the children's room. He nods and begins walking down the hallway back towards the elevator. "I try to see her at least once a week."

"What... happened. What did we do?"

"*You* didn't do anything. *Others* did. It's a lot like what happened to Lynn," he says as the elevator door opens. "She got too close to a trash collector near the entrance who just happened to be welding something. He hit her across the face with a hot piece of metal. And then he kept hitting her."

We enter the elevator and begin travelling back up.

"But... why?"

He shrugs.

"The color of her skin I guess. Everyone who was there says that he didn't realize she was just a little kid, that afterwards he looked as terrified as she did."

"Do you think it was an accident?"

"Not quite an accident, but probably not completely intentional. It doesn't really matter, anyways. He's still standing at his post, and she'll continue lying in this hospital bed until she's well enough to go back home. Nothing we can do about either of that right now. We're just happy she wasn't taken above after the incident."

We stand in silence as the elevator rises and pops open at the underground floor. He walks in front of me and towards the door to the street. I follow him, but pause in the center of the lobby.

"Silas, wait."

He turns and walks back towards me.

"What's wrong?"

"Why do you not hate me? Why do you all not hate me? I, my people, did this to her. Did this to everyone. Alex was terrified of me because of the color my skin, and she was right to be. You should have killed me a long time ago."

He stops, and again we are amidst a buzzing crowd. A solemn smile appears on his lips and he brushes back a strand of my hair.

"Micah, our people don't hate one another because of the colors of our skin, we hate one another because of what those colors mean. Our skin shows to the world where and who we come from, and because our skin is different it shows to the world that where and who we come from are different. But, that doesn't mean that within our lives we can't become one in the same. Our origins shouldn't decide our fate.

"Before a few months ago, you used to look at my skin and see only what others told you to see. Your teachers, your books, your parents. You took what members of your own race told you of us as indisputable truth. But, you did that because you didn't know any different. Before a few months ago, you probably thought that my color meant danger. Destruction. Immorality. But I don't blame you for thinking these things. You didn't know any different. You didn't know the difference between a truth and a lie. This has nothing to do with the color itself, but what you thought about it based off of what you were told.

"Think about everything you see now when you look at my skin. I know these thoughts aren't the same as they once were. The meaning of my race has changed for you, but I've stayed exactly the same. I'm still as white as the day I was born, and you are still as dark as the day you came down here. Our colors haven't changed, but the meaning behind them has. Our skin may be stuck as the same color forever, but what we think about that color can always change. We don't hate the darker skinned people, we hate what they are led to believe. We want them to know the truth, and we are going to take down those who have taught them to think these awful thoughts. The members of the government, the trash collectors, Ian Dale- those who know enough to know better but choose to live a life of conspiracy anyways. Everyone, even your people, deserves to be told the truth."

"I'm not really training to be a doctor," I blurt out. "I lied."

"I know, you're a segregationist," he says. "Just like your mom."

"I don't want to be," I quickly add, "they made me be."

"I know, just as they made her be. I don't blame you. I'm proud of you. You chose to ask questions instead of accepting answers. You allowed the meanings behind our races to change.

You allowed yourself to see what others chose to ignore. Even the largest changes start by asking a single question. You were willing to ask questions, without that nothing would have changed."

"But, when do I stop asking questions? When do I really know the truth?"

With the tips of his fingers he pulls my chin towards him and I stand on the tips of my toes as his lips lightly touch mine.

"You don't."

21

Spending every night with Silas expedites our "relationship" faster than I thought possible. I'm with him every night leading up to the Gala. He brings me around the entire sector, introducing me to new members of the group and showing me where each of the secret entrances lead out in case I may need them in the coming few days. At the end of each night, before I go back up, we stop by his apartment and visit his family. Lynn is smiling ear to ear when she opens the door and ushers me inside to an ecstatic Ben and Amanda, already dressed to go to sleep and waiting for dinner. They now jump into my arms when I walk in the door and pull me towards the couch with them.

"Micah, Micah!" Ben yells to me, pouncing from the arm of the seat and soaring into my body. "I need to show you this picture that I drew!" Sometimes it's a drawing of his room, sometimes his family. Once it was even of me.

Lynn always offers me food, or coffee, and gets angry when I refuse.

"What do you not understand about free food," she jokingly yells before running into the kitchen to fix a plate.

On the night before the Gala Silas is quiet. He doesn't want to show me any more of the underground that night but instead leads me straight to his warehouse, stacks of broken electronics still teetering floor to ceiling in long aisles. I sit on the floor and play with some of them, trying to figure out how the pieces go together.

"That's an old toaster," he tells me when I'm holding a square rusting object with slats on the side. He's sitting to my right and gently takes the object from my hands. "It's probably about 75 years old."

I reach over and brush the top of it with my fingers, letting the ancient rust settle on top of them.

"How does it all get here?" I ask him, leaning back to look at the tower of objects above me.

"The trashmen," He says, pressing his lower face against my shoulder. "If an object becomes unusable sometimes they send it down here. We have to make due with what we have."

I'm silent for a moment. He's so calm, I can feel him breathing against my shoulder. In and out, slowly. Deep, and controlled. He kisses my shoulder before raising his face, regaining his posture and once again staring into the toaster.

"What are you going to do when it's all over?" I ask, pulling another item from the bottom shelf. It's a small, rusted silver box.

"I don't know," he replies, not moving his gaze. "If I think about it I'm afraid it won't happen."

"But, you have to think about it. Is there anything you want afterwards, anything you're looking forward to?"

I can tell he has an answer, but he won't move his lips. I try pulling the toaster from his hands, but his grip is impenetrable.

"I want to know what the sun feels like."

He looks up at me, looks straight into my eyes.

"I've read about it so many times but... what does it feel like, Micah?"

I stutter at first, can't find the words to answer him.

"It feels like... I don't know. I can't describe it."

"Please. Try."

I'm silent for a few pregnant seconds, unable to describe something that has always been a part of my life.

It feels like...water." I finally say.

His brow wrinkles.

"Like water?"

"Yeah, like water," I explain, looking away. "When it's out, on a strong day, you feel like you're swimming in it. It takes over your whole body. You can feel it everywhere. It gets in your eyes, in your hair, in your skin, but you don't want it to leave. You lift your face and you're swimming in a warm pool, but... you know you could never drown."

I look back at him. He's still clutching the toaster, but now his body is shaking. I see small drops of liquid fall from his face onto the metal surface.

"Silas, I didn't mean..."

"I hate this," he says, body shaking even more. "I hate that I can only see you at night, that we can't just *be* together. I hate that my family is in pain, that they're about to risk everything because we can't fucking stand it anymore. I just want a normal life, like the ones I read about in all those books. Why does our world have to be this way? What happened? What happened to us?"

"I... I don't know."

I don't. I don't know what to say.

"Everyone that I know might die tomorrow." He chokes at these words, his tears are now coming in sobs. His gaze remains steadfast on the toaster, tears streaming and hitting its hard surface. "I might die tomorrow," he gasps, harshly rubbing the metal with his thumbs. "But I shouldn't have to. Look at us, look at this toaster. This stupid piece of metal. We can both use it. We're not that different."

"Silas," I start, bringing my hand up to the base of his neck. "I don't know. I don't know how this happened. But you can change it."

"Fuck that," he exclaims, looking over to me. "I'm not going to change anything. All I've done is convince innocent people that they can make a difference. They can't. We can't. We're not enough."

"You are." I say. I'm not lying.

"Each of you is worth 10 of them. You're going to win because everyone underground has more passion than anyone above. You'll fight for the same cause, you'll fight for everyone you love, everyone that can't be there. Everyone that we've hurt. You're going to feel the sun, Silas. You're all going to feel the sun."

22

We spend the rest of the afternoon in his back office. There's a tiny red couch on the center back wall, pile of books to either side and a wooden desk with a mismatched metal chair to my left. Other than this the room is empty. Silas has taken a seat on the couch and is rolling a cigarette. I sit next to him and let my head drop onto his shoulder. He offers me one and I accept, letting the haze float above my face.

"I want to stay here forever," I say, watching it tendril and dissipate above me.

I lay on him in silence for a few minutes, feeling his stomach breath in and out, in and out, against the back of my head. I nuzzle into it and he slouches further, flattening and expanding the area that I can lay on. He pulls his legs onto the couch and I become surrounded by his body, head on his chest and left arm draped across his ribs.

"Tell me a bedtime story," I ask him.

"I have one from when I was little," he begins, taking a deep drag and letting the smoke float in a stream right above his face.

"My mom made it up a long time ago. Do you want to hear it?"

I nod against his soft skin.

He laces his hand over my body and pulls me a little closer.

"In a time not so long ago there was a little boy in the underground who loved to dig. For every single birthday, his mother saved up all the money she could to buy him a new shovel. He would spend hours playing in the overflow piles, sorting through them and trying to dig his way to the bottom. He found many, many treasures in his digs and would always bring them back home to his mom to say thank you for all the shovels. He found books, cups, plates, soon everything in their house had come from those piles. After many, many years of digging, and finding hundreds and hundreds of treasures, the boy finally reached the bottom. Underneath all that stuff was dirt. The boy expected concrete or stone. That was all he had ever seen on the ground before. *I wonder if I can dig all the way to the other side of the world?* He thought.

"And so he tried. Night and day he dug and he dug, never giving up. His mom would bring him food, drinks, and even a flashlight when he had finally made a loooong tunnel. She started tying everything onto a rope and lowering supplies down to him, until one day she ran out of rope. Then, she would drop bread. She expected her son to come up, but he never did. She was so worried, she sat on the edge for days, and then months, and then years. She sat on the edge of the tunnel for twenty years. She grew old waiting for him. Everyone thought she was crazy, but she knew someday her son would come back.

"Finally, when she was near her final breath, she heard noises from inside the tunnel and saw a hand emerge from its depths. Her little boy, now a man, popped up.

"Mom! He screamed, leaping out to give her a big hug. You'll never believe what I saw on the other side of the world!

"She couldn't believe her eyes. But then, more and more people started coming out of the tunnel. They were all so happy, with wide grins across their faces.

"No one is sad there, he told her. Everyone gets to live happily together. They're here to take everyone with them!

"The man gathered everyone up from the whole town and brought them into the tunnel with them. Everyone lived happily ever after on the other side of the world."

When he finishes I'm laying on his chest with my eyes open. My fingers have snuck their way in the area between his shirt and pants and are making small circles up and down his stomach.

"We belong on the other side of the world," I say without looking up. "But when I'm with you I feel like I'm already there."

He hugs me tighter and I close my eyes, just for a minute, to soak up his body as it grips mine.

I had never had a sexual relationship with someone where friendship came before the bodily encounter. I lost my virginity at that club, but I had of course lied to Renee when she asked. I pushed through the pain and pretended to enjoy myself as the man thrust into me. The truth is, I was absolutely terrified until I walked back through the curtain and saw my friend looking proudly back at me. She was sitting at the bar by herself and had apparently finished her own conquest of the night a few minutes earlier.

"Wasn't that great," she told me, motioning to the bartender for two more drinks.

"It was… like nothing else I've ever felt." I respond. It was the truth.

"And it only gets better. Once you learn how to take control everything becomes wildly fun."

That's exactly what I learned to do. After my first few timid times at the club I started commanding my partners, telling them what I wanted instead of waiting for them to figure it out incorrectly on their own. The men seemed to like this break from thinking. They wanted someone to tell them the exact steps they needed to take to reach the top. I found power in my sexuality, a power I knew was wrong but was unable to let go of. I didn't want that with Silas, I wanted him to feel exactly what I felt. I want him to know what he means to me.

I open my eyes again and tug at the bottom of Silas's shirt, pushing his body away from the couch to glide the fabric over his shoulders. He immediately leans into me, hands around the back of my neck. They slide down my back until they reach the seam of my dress and snake their way back up, trapping the fabric within them. I pull my body away so he can slip off my dress, my safety net, and fling it behind the couch. I pause in this moment, letting my fingers brush up and down his face, tracing the thin, empty line that lies below his lips. He smiles and twists me under him so that I'm lying on the couch, ancient fabric scratching my bare skin. He grips my leg, sliding my body down so that my neck rests in the curve of the couch's arm. The fingers of my left hand brush down his body while the right ones stay gripped around his neck. I begin winding them around the button of his pants, unleashing their metal hold and pulling them down his lower body. When I can't reach any further I curl my leg up and pull the fabric to his feet with my toes, leaving my leg stretched between his two.

I flip myself on top of him and his arms wrap around my body. He fumbles with the hooks behind my back before being able to release them. Tension is lifted and I pull the straps off my arms, throwing the white underwire support somewhere across the room. There is no pause. He pulls something off of mine, I retaliate with an article of his. We have created a tit for tat rhythm, revealing ourselves to one another in equal stages.

I can feel him through the thin fabric of his boxer shorts and can't control myself. It's been so long since I've been at this point, and never before with someone like this. He wants me for the same reason I want him. I push my chest into him and slide down his body until I reach the one piece of cloth that separates us. I look up at him, plant a tender kiss onto the indented space next to his hip, and pull them off his body.

He grabs the sides of mine next and finally the only fabric near us is the red cotton of the couch.

We tumble and turn, twist angles and run our fingers and mouths across each other's bodies. We warm each other up, grasping the spots we know the other desires and gently working our way in. It's not unexpected when he finds his way into me, it feels completely natural. Like something completely natural that makes you feel like you're on top of the fucking world.

Our bodies move together, like waves rolling onto a beach. I can almost hear them, fierce yet calming, as I push and pull.

I feel myself building, the waves are getting larger, more powerful. They're crashing onto the beach one after each other and I'm trapped within them, somewhere between where they crash and where they hit land. I'm spinning, I can't get any air. I'm caught underneath and have to move with them, it's the only way I'll ever be able to breathe again. My lungs feel like they're going to burst and I'm enjoying the pain, forcing myself to stay under because I know the longer I'm in the water the better my first breath will feel.

There's a large wave coming, a tsunami. I can't see it in the murky water, but I can feel it. It reaches me and I'm tumbling, twisting uncontrollably as the waves push me towards the beach. I open my eyes lying in a mass of seaweed. I'm soaking and gasping for air and I can hear the water retracting around me. It sinks past my ears, my shoulders, and finally my legs until small constant waves are trickling against my toes. I can't move, I don't want to move. I want to be in this feeling forever.

He's still on top of me, face leaning into the space between my head and shoulders. His hands slowly travel down my body and he pulls me so that we are lying next to another. We're silent. I kiss his shoulder and he kisses my hand. He eventually reaches across me onto the floor to grab a cigarette and small wrapped piece of chocolate and I move to lay my head on top of his arm. He lights the cigarette and the smoke travels in a thick blob out of his mouth and towards the ceiling. We share this, one puff after another, watching our releases float high above our faces.

"I want to be here forever," I say.

"This is where you're supposed to be," he says. "Not up there with them. You're better than all of them."

I nuzzle closer to him.

"Some of them are good. They just need to know what good means."

He looks over at me and kisses my dark hair.

"I don't want you to go to the Gala tomorrow. I don't want you to meet him."

"I know, but we both know what I have to do."

He nods against my head, letting his fingers run through my hair.

"I know. But I wish someone else could do it."

"There's no one else," I say. "We both decided that."

He kisses the top of my head, letting his lips linger against my scalp.

"I don't know what I would have done if your father didn't come to me that day."

I'm lethargic, I don't quite comprehend what he says at first. Words and their meanings have separated again.

"What do you mean, came to you?"

He looks back at me quizzically.

"When he came to me at the entrance after finding out where I lived a few months ago. When he asked me to start writing to you."

Waves are crashing again, but this time I'm not prepared to get caught in their wake.

"I don't understand. I was writing to Patrick. My dad has nothing to do with this."

"He didn't tell you?"

He asks this question as if the answer has to be yes, as if I'm just pretending to not know the story he's trying to tell.

"When I was a guard at the elevator your father asked me to start writing to you through my ceiling. He found out where I live and wanted me to start communicating with you. I told him it was too dangerous for me, that if any of my letters were found the entire revolution would be compromised. He asked if there was anyone else in my family that might be willing to help, and I asked my dad if he would write to you. He jumped at the chance. Your father even helped us get rid of the extra layers between our ceiling and your floor. He had everything to do with it. He's the reason you're down here."

I can't think. My thoughts are coming to me in bolts, in

uncontrollable explosions. I always thought I received those letters by chance, that they were a sign from the world that I was meant to be saved. I always thought anyone could be in my position, that anyone could have discovered them in their own room, but that the world had chosen me. Now I'm discovering that it's all planned. Everything. My father decided the whole thing. The whole time. All of the days I snuck out without thinking that he knew, he knew. He's always known. He's the reason I met Silas and his family. He's the reason I was invited to all of those meetings. Without him, I never would have read a book or set foot in the library. I wouldn't be lying here with Silas right now. He's the reason for everything.

"He never said anything... I never..." I'm dumbfounded.

"I thought he would have told you. I thought you knew the whole time."

"He never said a word. I didn't even know you knew each other."

Silas nodded, his fingers moving up and down the top of my arm.

"He was worried you wouldn't come down with him when the time came. He said you were doing so well in school, that they had a grip on you he wasn't sure he could combat. He did it to save your life."

He did it to save my life. He did everything to save my life. I'm shaking, am all of a sudden cold. I curl further into Silas's body.

"Did he tell Patrick what to write to me?"

"No, no. Not a word. Everything my dad told you in those letters came from his own hand. I'm sorry I was... off putting to you when we first met. I thought the letters would be the end of it. My dad's deal with your father was to write to you, it was supposed to stop there. He was never supposed to invite you underground. He just wanted to put a seed of doubt into your mind about what the aboveground was telling you. I thought it was going too far, I thought it was too dangerous to have you down here. But when you told me you knew about the elevator.... I realized there was a safer way. I realized this was something you were meant to be doing. I thought your dad was the one who told you about it."

"No, it wasn't him. It was Tyrone."

I watch his face change in the same way mine did moments before. He's lost for words, doesn't understand anything that is coming out of my mouth.

"But... no. That's imposs...."

"In The Red Knob. Tyrone told me."

His eyes search my face.

"It was you. You were the girl he told me about. This entire time... it was you."

He pulls away from me, sitting up so that my body is still strewn horizontally across his.

"I met him once, just once. After we were finished he told me there was an elevator in the hospital, I didn't know where. I never saw him again."

"You're the girl," Silas keeps saying, over and over. "You're that girl. The one he told. You're..." he looks over at me again as I sit up, naked legs still flooding his body.

"You're the reason they came down for him."

I'm taken aback, I don't know what he's trying to tell me.

"What? That's impossible."

"After he told you about the elevator, the night after, he was taken. We think it's because he told you about us. They came down to punish him."

"But, no. No, it can't be my fault." I'm now sitting naked next to him, hands clenched between my tense parted legs.

"Why didn't they come for me if they knew that I know? Why was he punished and I wasn't?"

"I don't know, I don't know. I..." he gets up and begins pacing across the room before twisting to face me. "You have to be successful at the Gala, Micah. Now I don't know what will happen if you're not."

"What will happen if I'm not? What do you mean? What will happen if we don't get him?"

"I don't know. I don't know. Why didn't they come for you?" He asks again, now moving rapidly in front of the couch. "You're the reason he got taken. Why are you alive? They would have know it was you, they would have known..."

He trails off and his body stops moving, right hand gripping his bottom lip and face staring into the wall across from him.

"You lied to us. You should be dead." He pauses. "You're one of them."

"What? Are you saying... are you saying that I'm a spy?" I stand up in anger and disbelief. "How could you? Look at me!"

I point down to my naked body.

"Look what I did for you? Look..."

I gently grab his arm and turn his body towards me.

"It's just me."

He's still angry, suspicions on the brink of explosion.

"It wouldn't be hard for you," he sneers. " After everything you *have* done."

I throw his arm in front of me and push his body forward.

"How dare you! You know why I did all of that, I thought you understood. I didn't tell anyone about the revolution and I never would. I've risked *everything* for you, for your family. I'm going to risk even more tomorrow. How could you?"

"Why aren't you dead like him then?"

"I don't know, maybe because my family is so high up my parents bought someone off. Who knows? But I didn't, Silas. I couldn't. You have to believe me."

23

Fooled you, didn't I? I hope at least some part of you still thinks that I'm innocent, that I haven't been lying to you this entire time.

Well, guess my father was right.

Once a liar, always a liar.

I mean, do you really think I would've been able to get away with it? Talking to someone about the underground in a government building overflowing with government employees literally on the other side of every curtain? I know you're smarter than that. Or maybe you haven't been paying very close attention.

At first it happened exactly how you think. When I went back into the room with Tyrone I didn't know he was going to talk to me about the underground, I thought he was just another guy. And the sex was actually that good, I definitely didn't lie about that. But, the story doesn't stop after I went to find him on the street. No, it definitely doesn't stop there.

After running out of The Red Knob and seeing Tyrone

wasn't outside I started to walk home. Well, I walked for about ten seconds before five trashmen surrounded me, put a bag over my head, and carried me down the street.

After what felt like hours sitting in that fucking chair they finally took the bag off. My mom's boss was sitting on the other side of a long metal table in a windowless room. Now, it's not the type of thing you might have seen in movies. It was well lighted, her boss was not leaning into me blowing smoke into my face, and he didn't yell once. He said hello, I said hello, and then he told me we needed to talk about something.

Well, obviously.

He motioned with his fingers and Tyrone appeared on the other side of the door painted black to blend in with the rest of the wall. He wasn't handcuffed or beaten. He looked just like he had when I left him.

"Did this man tell you anything about the underground?"

I looked at Tyrone with large eyes, trying to decide if he wanted me to lie through my teeth or tell the truth. He looked calm, and almost happy.

"You can tell them," Tyrone assured. "I already did."

"He did," I stuttered.

"Hm, hmmm. Well, this is very troublesome Micah. You see, now you know a secret about the underground that most people shouldn't. There's a lot you can do with that information."

I nodded and promised him that I wouldn't tell anyone.

"No no, that's not what we want." He smiled, patting my hand frozen on the cold metal table. "We want you to *use* the information."

"You see," Tyrone took over. "We need to make sure you use what I told you about the underground for the good of our people. We need you to help us."

My eyes danced between them.

"What will happen if I don't want to?"

Tyrone dropped his head and laughed, as if he had answered that question many, many times.

"We'll kill you."

And then he looked up again and repeated.

"We'll kill you. Right here. In three minutes."

"What do I need to do?" I immediately asked.

I'd like to say I was a strong person, that I offered up my body to the gods of morality right then and there. But, I didn't and I wasn't. I was ignorant, stupid, and weak. They told me I was going to be a spy and that I was going to find a way into the underground. They needed me to do it. They wanted me to get in with the female underground youth and report back the gossip. They thought my eyes would help. I couldn't tell anyone, not even my family. I had until after graduation, when my career began, to find a way to get to the elevator in the hospital and to keep going down.

The letters were completely coincidental. I'd been wracking my brain for months trying to create a plan that would fool everyone except for a few members of the government and get me to that elevator. I kept going to The Red Knob thinking I would see Tyrone there, but after the meeting with him in that office he never showed up again. I didn't know what he was doing until Silas told me about their connection during the meeting.

Brother Tyrone my ass.

When I started going down it was a secret. I didn't tell the government because I didn't know how long it would last.

I took my time.

And I was rewarded. They invited me down again.

I was spying, I'm not pretending that I wasn't. But I didn't tell the government about the letters and I didn't tell them how I tricked my way into a nightshift at the hospital.

I was going to tell them, I really was. I took my job seriously, at first. At the very, very beginning. But then I really started thinking about everything the Nightcrawlers stood for. I started believing what they were telling me. The government warned me about this, said the hardest part of it all would be to see through their lies. But I couldn't. What I saw through their lies was truth. My historytexts proved that better than anything else.

And then I saw my father on the other side of that fucking elevator. I didn't know he was helping them. And the sad part is he wasn't even a government agent like I was. He was actually helping them. It turns out that I was supposed to find a different elevator in the hospital, that this one was a secret even to them.

And then I went to those meetings. God, were they beautiful. Everything I told you about the dancing was true. Everything I told you about seeing those books was true. Everything I told you about Silas was true.

I didn't have sex with him because the government wanted me to. I did it because I wanted to. Because I love him. Because I want to be a part of something, to be a part of them. It's why I'm risking so much.

I'm getting Dale for them, I swear.

Guess my mother was right.

Sometimes the darkness is the only place where your mind can truly be free.

So finish my story. Make your own conclusions. But this is me telling you the truth. This is really what happened.

I open my eyes at exactly 7:10, three minutes before my wrist starts to ring. The sun is dripping through the closed blinds, making diagonal patterns across my pink comforter. I lie in bed, but I don't fall back asleep. I soak in the sun as it gently heats my face, closing my eyes to let it drape across my eyelids. When my wrist begins to vibrate I simply pull my blanket away and walk towards the mirror.

The formal dress of the segregationalists is hanging on the corner where my red pants and white shirt used to balance. I pull my pajamas off my body and stand in front of the mirror with the dress pressed against my front. It's long and red, with a V neckline and thick white satin belt that ties around my waist into a bow in the back. All women going to the Gala were given the same one.

"GOOOOOOOODDDD MORNING SECTOR 15! It is a glorious 62 degrees outside, a perfect start to a perfect day! As always, I hope you've had a restful night in preparation for a restless day!"

I begin to pull the dress off the hanger and over my arms as the morning announcements continue.

"AAANNNDDDDD now for last night's report. Wow, this one is a doozey. 20 Nightcrawlers were arrested last night for leaving the underground. They were heavily armed and planning to attack an apartment building in the southwest sector. Thank God for our trashmen, working both day and night to protect us. The hangings will take place immediately after the Segregationalist's Gala held in honor of historytext writer Ian Dale. We would love to see everyone come out and support the trashmen by attending these hangings. Hope to see you all there!"

I press into my INSAV to end the message and bring my face back to the mirror in front of me. The dress fits my body snuggly, accentuating the curves that I hadn't really noticed before today. I pull my hair back into a tight ponytail, dab the smallest amount of lipstick onto my lips, and quickly brush eyeliner under my eyes. When I'm finished, I take a step back and look at myself in the full-length mirror.

I look older than when everything started. My eyes have small bags underneath them and the rolls that used to grace my body when I leaned a little to the left or right have disappeared, moving to my breasts. Four months ago I never would have thought that I'd be standing here today getting ready to do what I'm about to do. I never would have thought it was even possible.

When I get to the kitchen my entire family has already started their breakfast. My mother drops her fork when she sees me and brings her hand up to her mouth.

"Micah, oh my Micah, you look wonderful. You're just, wow. You're all grown up! Denzel, doesn't she look so grown up?"

I force a tight smile onto my lips and sit down across from her.

My father pulls down his wrist projection and smiles over at me, the same smile that I'd given my mother.

"You do, sweetheart. I'm so proud of you."

I think I see his eyes begin to water, but can't tell through the lens of his glasses. He pulls up his projection again and continues reading.

"You look great too, mom. They picked out really nice dresses."

"They really did. I don't think I even remember last time I wore anything but my uniform. It must have been, gosh, maybe 15 years ago? When the head of Sector 30 came to visit? I think you were about... 3 years old. My goodness, to look at you now."

She pauses to once again look me over as I grab a piece of toast and some eggs.

"Gabe, dear, are you excited to work the event as well? You might get to meet Ian Dale, too."

My brother sits quietly across from my father, pushing a triple stacked sandwich into his mouth. He shrugs, more concerned with his food than the question.

"Honey, I told you not to eat that fast. Shawn is going to be here soon, we have to at least seem polite."

"He doesn't care," Gabe proclaims with a fresh bite of food in his mouth. "All he cares about is getting some."

I smile into my plate, pushing a broken yolk around with the corner of my toast.

"Who ever said I wanted to give him any?"

"It's implied." Gabe states, picking up his glass.

"You two need to stop before he gets here," our mother

demands.

We laugh and lock eyes, for just a second. I pray that this won't be the last time.

There's a knock on the door and my mother rises to greet Shawn. He's been given a white suit and red shirt, but he's still wearing one of those bowties. Red and white polka dots today.

"Shawn! We're so excited that you're here!" My mother says, giving him a quick hug and leading him to the breakfast table.

"Here, sit next to Micah."

She pulls him a chair from the wall and places it directly to my left, between my father and me. I continue looking at my food, refusing to make eye contact with our visitor.

"I hope you're hungry."

"Oh, no Mrs. Davis. Thank you. I ate before I got here. You and Micah look wonderful."

My mother glows and takes a last sip of her coffee.

"Well, then, if you're ready we can get everything prepared to leave."

"I'm not done yet." I say, looking down to my plate. "A few more minutes?"

I'm not ready to leave yet, not ready to confront everything that must be done.

"Sure, sweetheart. I'll pour myself a little more coffee. Shawn?"

"Sure, why not."

Before he reaches across the table to grab the cup from her his hand tightly grabs mine underneath it. I'm confused, I don't understand why he even needs to do this or why he's already making such advancements. But then I feel something. He's placed something into my hand, something flat and coarse. I rub it between my fingers and, as he puts a little sugar into his cup, realize what it is. My eyes dart to his, I'm trying to hide the alarm on my face but know I'm not doing too great at it.

Does he know about my plan, is he going to arrest me? Or is he part of the aboveground railroad, one of the men Silas told me would help? He looks at me, into me, for a split second.

"It's ok." He says, staring at my nervous face.

I search his quickly.

"Pardon?" My mother interrupts, milk in hand.

He looks at her and smiles.

"It's ok. I don't need any milk."

He reaches under the table, into my hand, and takes back the small slip of paper.

"Well, I'm off," my father says, grabbing his briefcase. He circles around the room, giving my mother and I a kiss on the forehead and patting Gabe and Shawn on the shoulder.

"I'll see you after the Gala," he says when he comes over to me.

I nod, hands beginning to shake under the table. Shawn grabs my left hand once again, squeezing it and releasing quickly.

*　　*　　*　　*　　*　　*　　*　　*　　*

I hold his arm tightly at we walk to the event. Everyone is looking at us, they know who we are and where we're going. I look straight ahead, at none of them, as we make our way to the government house. The projections running across each building are all advertising the Gala or Ian Dale.

"He's here!" Some of them say, with an image of Dale posing with the text projected from his INSAV.

"A Day to Honor the Segregationalists for All their Hard

329

Work," others read, with groups of people in red and white smiling at everyone walking to work and school.

I can't focus on them. I can't focus on anything. I just have to get there.

The entrance to the government house is right behind the gallows. I grip Shawn's arm even tighter when we pass it, and he presses his loose hand against my own. My mother looks over and smiles.

"I'm going to grab a few mimosas," Shawn whispers to me after we get inside, pulling away and walking across the room.

There are already hundreds of people there. The lobby of the government house is covered in red and white decorations, tables and people interspersed throughout the room creating conversational clusters. I go and stand next to an empty table in the center, staring at my bright red nails as they rest on top of a white cloth. In the middle of each table is a small centerpiece with red and white artificial flowers and a collection of bright red apples, the bowl of each reading "Protecting from Within." I laugh when I see it.

"Micah, I didn't expect you to be here today." A voice is coming from behind me and I whip around to see who it belongs to. Renee stands proudly a few feet away, clutching the hand of a man I vaguely remember.

"Oh Renee. I, yes. Well... I was invited by one of my mother's co-workers."

"Hm, interesting." She responds with slanted eyes. "You remember Travis, don't you?"

I suddenly remember everything about him.

"Travis, yes. Hello." I'm not sure what else to say or do.

He nods in greeting and takes a sip of his mimosa.

"It's nice seeing you again."

"I thought we wouldn't see each other until our positions started at the office, and even then I wasn't really sure. We haven't seen you around much over the past few months." Renee stands completely still as she speaks, as if moving would elongate the conversation we're both forcing ourselves to have.

"Yes, I didn't know I'd be coming either. Actually…"

"Travis! My man, so glad I found you!"

Shawn walks back over with the drinks and quickly kisses my cheek before handing me one. Astonishment drips from Renee's face.

"Shawn, you didn't tell me you'd be bringing such a beautiful date."

"Got approval last minute, but I don't even know if I would have come if Micah had refused to join me."

The men laugh. Renee and I stand silent.

"Well, I made sure to ask for an extra ticket on the spot. I knew this was something my baby couldn't miss out on. Right, sweetheart?"

Renee hasn't taken her gaze off of me since Shawn came back over.

"Right." She responds, a look of complete perplexity still plaguing her face.

We stand silently for a moment before Shawn grabs my hand once more.

"Micah, come over here with me. I want to show you a painting of the old sector. It was great seeing you, Renee."

Drinks in hand he leads me across the room, across the crowd, to a large image in the far corner.

"Look at that little park here," he says, pointing to a small green spot on the painting. That was the last one, it was taken out about 50 years ago."

"Shawn, why did you give me that... thing?"

"And this, do you know what that building is? It's the old hospital."

"Shawn, I know what that is. But... what do you want with me?" I'm whispering as quietly as possible against the enlarging crowd.

He wraps his arm over my shoulder and pulls me close to him, pressing his scruff face against my ear.

"Your mother's office. 20 minutes. I put the code on your INSAV. Dale will be there. Do what you did at The Red Knob. Then get him in the closet."

He keeps his head against my own, pressing his lips into my cheeks and tightening his body against mine before pulling away and refocusing on the painting.

"Now this dot here, do you know what it used to be? Did your parents ever tell you about the old apple orchard?"

15 minutes go by. He doesn't answer any of my questions. Three minutes later he taps me on the arm and points his head towards the hallway.

"Why don't you go freshen up? The bathroom is down there."

I don't know what else to do. I nod and walk away, passing women and men all dressed exactly the same as us. Everyone exactly the same, including my mom's boss who now stands just a few feet away from Shawn. He's leaning into a portrait of the old prime minister. I see Shawn turn and point to the prime minister's sunken eyes. The two men laugh. I disappear down the hall.

My mother's office is at the end of the second hallway. I'd been there a few times before. She's the only person with the code to get in, though. I don't understand how this is going to work. After looking around to make sure no one else is in the hallway I press my INSAV against her scanner. I hear it click, unlock, and, although confused, I slide inside.

Ian Dale isn't there. It's a small office, large enough to fit a desk and cabinets. I would have seen him immediately if he was. One of the cabinets against the closest wall is long with two doors that open vertically and a lower longer drawer that spans across the entire bottom. I open one of the vertical doors and peek inside. There's a jacket and nothing else. I still don't understand.

The office has changed since I was last here. I think the chairs are a different color but I can't be sure. When I was little I used to hide underneath my mother's desk as she worked, projecting movies and games from my INSAV onto the top. I'd lie at her feet and giggle to myself for hours, emerging only when it was time to eat and time to leave. She'd even conduct meetings with me secretly underneath, kicking me a little when I'd try to distract her by playing with her shoes.

I stand behind the desk and imagine myself as her, sitting in the same spot every day, every year, from the day she graduated school until today. And she doesn't even know that it's the last. I carefully pull the chair out and sit myself in it, placing my arms onto the desk on either side of me.

I don't know if it's how I'm sitting, or because of how similar I am to her, but suddenly a projection appears in the center of the desk.

It's a map of a sector. I know it's not my own, everything is similar but not quite the same. My eyes follow the map as the projection rotates in front of me. There's a town hall, a hospital, and long, narrow roads that twist and turn.

It's of the underground. I push my fingers up and away to

enlarge the image. This acts sets something else off, the entire projection is blinking red. Over most of the buildings there are two words.

MASS TERMINATION.

I quickly jump up and the projection disappears.

Silas was right. The underground was right. The revolution was their only option. Without it, they were all going to die. I'd thought it all along, but only at that moment I finally knew. I'd chosen the good guys.

The door to my mother's office pops open and a man slips through. I know who it is. He doesn't speak at first, just looks at me. It takes everything within me to not wrap my hands around his throat. I told Silas I would bring him beneath, and that's what I'm going to do.

I take a deep breath. This is it.

25

"Mr. Dale."

I'm rigid when I speak, I can't control the inflections in my voice.

"Miss Davis," he calmly responds. "Thank you for meeting me here today."

Do what you do in The Red Knob.

"The pleasure is all mine." I push my chest out and slowly walk around the desk to him, brushing my fingers across the surface as I move.

He nervously walks towards me, already sweating from anticipation.

"I'm sorry to meet you here, like this. I'm leaving the sector immediately after the Gala. But, Shawn told me that your... skills... are not something to be missed."

So that's how they want me to do it.

"Hm, I think I might agree," I say in a low tone, inching forward and taking a calming breath. "I'm sorry you couldn't make it to the club while you were here."

"Oh no, no. It's ok. I have a family at home, it probably wouldn't have looked good for me to be at that public of a place."

"But this works?" I ask. There are still a few feet between us, we have yet to touch.

"Well this is, a little more hidden," he stutters, tugging at the bottom of his red shirt. He's wearing an inverted uniform to the other men at the rest of the event, white shirt and red pants. "I've done things like this before, don't get me wrong. But, you understand why this needs to remain a secret, don't you?"

I nod and take a single step forward. My hand reaches out to him. It's still at first, but the closer it gets the more it shakes. My red fingernails get closer, closer to his ghostly white shirt. I pause before they make contact, close my eyes, and wrap them around the center of his chest. He brings his body into mine and pushes me against the back of the desk. With eyes still closed I let him kiss me.

My eyes try to flood. I can't do this.

I can't do this.

I think of the underground, of Silas and his family.

Silas.

I hold back the tears and open my mouth, letting his tongue enter it. His hands run up and down my body, gripping at my waist. My arms are pushing against the desk, I'm fighting his force and trying to keep myself standing. I can't do anything else with them. I don't want to touch his body, to feel the man that destroyed those I love. I feel a hand pull at the bottom of my dress, bringing it up to my calves, my knees, my waist. He tries to grab at my underwear, to pull it off my body.

"Wait," I gasp, pushing his chest away from mine and opening my eyes. His wet mouth pulls away and he looks at me, concerned.

"What's wrong? Isn't this what we both came here for?"

This isn't what I came here for. I came here to destroy him.

"Just..." I don't know what to say. But I have to say something.

Get him in the closet.

"Let me trap you."

I bring my mouth to his again and push his body across the room. He slams into the closed side of the closet and I push him even further. His hands race again across my body, gripping anything they can get a hold of. I open my eyes quickly and look to the open side of the cabinet. With a free hand I push the door so that it opens all the way.

It takes everything within me to pretend passion in this moment. I need to get him there, just a few inches further. I think of Silas, I see his face. His blue eyes. The scar beneath his chin.

Dale lets me bring him to the left. He mustn't have noticed the door was open and falls into the cabinet, landing in a sitting position. He thinks it's part of the game.

"Hop on up here," he says, patting his lap with a thick hand. I look behind him.

There's nothing. No one to get him, no one to save me.

I can't stall any longer, he'll know something is wrong. But I can't do it. I can't push myself any further. Tears begin to swell in my eyes again, but I can't stop them. I bring my right hand up to my mouth, over my nose, to try and cover my sobs.

His goofy, sex-fueled smile transforms in disbelief.

"What's wrong?" He asks, unmoved from his position in the cabinet.

I try to keep it in, but can't.

"Why did you do it?" I cry.

"What? Micah, what?"

"Everything," I sob. "Why did you lie about everything? They're people, they're fucking people."

His body slightly lifts off the cabinet and arm outstretches towards me.

But, all of a sudden he's scared. He pulls it back. He knows why he's here.

"Who have you been speaking to? Who told you...."

A pair of white arms reaches out behind him, wrapping around his neck and pulling him back into the cabinet. He fights, kicks his legs, and I have to step back to avoid getting hit. He tries to scream, but the arms are chocking him. I know those arms.

Silas's face appears behind Dale.

I can't describe what it looks like. He smiles at me, but it's not a smile I know. It's too big, too angry. He laughs, a single chuckle, and pulls Dale's entire body in with him.

I drop to the floor. I can't think, can't breathe. My body starts to hyperventilate and I press my hand against my chest to try and steady myself. I hear the door open, but I'm too terrified to get up. What if they found out, what if they already know and are here to kill me? I knew it was a possibility, but until I was sitting on this floor with the shadow of a man in front of me I didn't think it would ever happen.

The intruder drops to the floor next to me and puts his hand onto my back.

"Micah, it's me. It's Shawn."

I don't look up but burrow myself into him, face soaking his red shirt. My contacts blur and move from my pupils in this interaction and I tear them out of my eyes, throwing them to the floor of my mother's office. It doesn't matter anymore.

"It's ok Micah. He's gone."

"I'm done." I tell him between tears. "We need to get away."

With a thumb and middle finger he brings my face up to meet his.

"We have one more thing to do."

My tears well in frustration. We can't. We don't have time.

"Micah, I need you to take a deep breath."

I stare at him but say and do nothing. What the hell could he be telling me now?

"Do it." He repeats. And I do. It doesn't do much to calm me down.

"There's been a change of plans. You're not going to like them, but you're the only one who can save him. Do you understand?"

"What is it? What could it even be?"

"Look at me, don't stop looking at me," Shawn says, fingers still on my chin. He takes a deep breath.

"On the way to work this morning your father was arrested."

I go blank. I can't hear. I can't see. I can't breathe but I don't care. There's ringing, everything is ringing. He's the reason for everything. He's everything and he's gone.

"Don't stop looking at me."

My eyes refocus, but not as they were before.

"You have to go to the jail and save him. Do you remember what Sonya told you? About the entrance?"

"I... it's too dangerous. She said no one's ever used it."

He pulls his hand behind my ear.

"They haven't but it's there. You're the only one that can go in. No one knows about Dale yet, I have to stay here and stall until they do. You tell them that you're visiting your father. You get to that entrance. However you can."

He pulls a small knife out from under his pants and places it in my hand.

"However you can."

I let the weapon sit between my fingers.

"You... you want me to kill someone?"

He wraps my fingers tightly around the warm metal.

"You need to get to that portal."

I don't know why, I don't know how, but all of a sudden I become calm. I tighten my grip on the knife and stand up, above him as he remains on the floor.

I push it into my bra, making sure the blade points downward. I wait for the rest of his instructions.

I cut through the crowd, out of the building, and walk across the town center. No one knows what's happened yet.

I'm not nervous anymore. I'm not scared. I'm prepared for something to happen to me, and if it does I'll go down fighting. My father fought for me with all he had and I'm prepared to do the same for him.

I ascend the marble stairs and notice the sunlight glittering off of their shining finish. I pull open the heavy metal doors to the building and walk straight to the end of the hallway until I reach a wooden door that reads, "Office of Corrections."

They never really corrected anything, I think to myself as it opens.

There's an older man behind a glass wall reading paperwork. He must be one of the trash collectors who've been taken off of active duty. I walk up to him.

"I'm Jane Davis's daughter," I proclaim. I try to break any positive association with my other parent. "I'm here to see my father."

He looks up at me, compassionately. He knows exactly who I

am.

"We don't normally let anyone do that," he says. "Your father has done an awful thing, do you understand?"

I nod.

"But I just need to see him one last time, I need to tell him…" tears well up in my eyes. Somehow there's still some left. "That I'll never forgive him for what he's done. What he's doing to my family." Tears stream down my face in heavy sobs.

I'm pulling on the man's heartstrings, I can tell. But, he doesn't know the real reason I'm crying.

"I'm really not supposed to."

"Please," I say with a loud wail. "He has to know! I need to see him." My hands are pushing against the glass, leaving sweat stained marks in their path.

"Well… it's really against our policy."

"He needs to know how much I hate him! He needs to know where he's going," I say, pretending to break down. "Please, I'm Gabe Davis's sister. You have to let me see my father."

The man thinks about this, all while I continue to cry. I lock eyes with him and break down again, practically falling against the protective glass. Men are so awful at knowing what to do when a woman is sobbing. Well, most men.

"Alright, alright. But just for a few minutes." He says. "I'll bring you down the hall to his cell."

"Thank you," I say, wiping my eyes. "I just need to see him."

"I know, sweetheart, I know."

The hallway is lit by a few stationary lights scattered too many feet apart. This is going to be the hardest part. This is what they've been trying to prepare me for. The man is walking in front of me, not looking back. I pull the small knife that Shawn has given me out of the space in my shirt.

I've never hurt anything before. Never anyone. I remind myself of the faces that need to be avenged.

The boy on the street.

The woman in the noose.

Alex.

My father.

Thousands of hangings, thousands of deaths.

I reach around the man with both hands, push one over his mouth, and with the other push the knife into his throat. Warm liquid pours into my fingers. He drops. I catch his weight and slowly bring him to the floor.

He's not a life, he's a body. I haven't killed a man, I've killed a piece of an idea. The idea that we can oppress an entire population with false beliefs. If I separate him from the idea he becomes human. He becomes a man with children, with a past. To me, in this moment, this man has no past. He had no future. He is only a part of the idea that must be killed.

I remember Shawn's instructions.

The portal is at the end of the hall, past all the cells. It will come to a dead end. The wall will be made of cinder blocks. One of them will be loose, use your knife to help you get it out of the wall. Reach as far as you can inside and there will be a button. Press it. You'll hear loud clicking, then run away. There will be an explosion. They'll be waiting on the other side.

I run but can't feel my feet touching the ground. I swing open the door that leads to the prisoners' hallway and am immediately confronted with a swarm of boos. They think I'm a guard. I continue running. I can see the wall, it's a few paces away when I hear his voice.

"Micah, Micah!" I look to my left and my father is standing behind bars. He has cuts across his face, hands and arms. I immediately run to him, grabbing his hands as they grip his cell.

Real tears begin flowing down my face.

"Dad, I'm getting you out of here," I cry. "I'm going to save you."

He stares at me, searching his mind for how.

"You know about the portal," he says with a raised voice. "They told you."

An alarm rings throughout the jail. Someone must have found the body.

I nod, grip his fingers one last time, and run towards the wall. My eyes frantically run over it in a race against the clock to find the loose brick. Suddenly, in the lower right corner, I see it. I flip open my knife and run the blade around the edges before pulling it out with all my weight. My arm reaches into the void and disappears. I feel the button, press it with the tip of my fingers, and run back down the hall. The explosion erupts, sending hard chunks of brick flying across the chamber.

A swarm of light skin and tattered cloth bursts forth. They run to each cell and cut through the locks. Sonya emerges last and runs towards me.

"See you on the other side."

They unlock my father and throw him a handgun. He grabs me and we're running.

"We need to leave," he screams. "We need to get your mother. I told her to go home after the Gala, that it's the only way she'd be safe."

"Wait," I say, as he grabs me to move forward. "Gabe is probably somewhere in the government house."

From the look in his eyes I know.

"He's not coming with us," he tells me. "He's chosen his path."

I don't have time to ask my father any more questions, or

really comprehend what he's just told me. We're running with the warriors down through the hall to the street.

When we get out of the building most in the sector hasn't realized what's happened yet. The streets are empty and we fly down them, running into our building as gunshots echo behind. We run down the dark cream-colored hallway and my father raises his hand to swipe into our home.

"Wait, how are we getting back down after we get mom?" I ask.

"I have tools in the house," he says hurriedly. "We're going to rip through the floorboard in your room. It's the only place that we can safely access the underground without anyone noticing or compromising their own passages. Patrick and I created a space thin enough to fit through." He swipes his card, throws it to the side, and pushes open the door.

My mother is sitting at the kitchen table smoking a cigarette. She stares straight in front of her and lifts the stick up to her mouth.

"Jane, we have to go," my father yells to her, grabbing her arm to pull her up.

"Don't touch me," she calmly replies. "Don't ever touch me."

Horror leaches onto my father's face.

"Jane, they're coming. If you don't come with us they're going to kill you."

Her hand shakes as she lifts it towards her mouth. She lets out the smoke with a tattered breath.

"I can't come with you."

"You have to."

"Denzel. I can't."

He bends down onto his knee and grabs my mother's face.

"Jane. They're going to kill you." His lips begin to quiver.

He's searching her face for a glimmer of hope.

"I know." She says. Her body doesn't move. There's a line of smoke swirling to her left.

"You don't love me? You don't love your family?"

He's trying to use guilt. He's still gripping her face, his fingers curl tightly around her ears. She's turned away from me, but I can feel her shaking. She's holding back tears.

"I love you, I love our family. But I love this world. It's everything I've ever known. It's everything I've ever worked for." She's crying, her words are broken by sobs. "I can't help you destroy it."

The cigarette goes out in her hand.

There are gunshots outside our window. They're coming. My father holds onto my mother and sinks his head into her shoulder. He absorbs her, taking deep breaths as his head rests below hers. He slowly rises, kisses the top of her forehead, and places his gun next to her on the table.

"Micah, it's time to go."

I walk past my mother, who blindly stares at the wall across from her, both arms resting on the table. Cigarette butt in one hand, gun lying next to the other.

I try to look at her, try to get her to look at me. She just keeps staring forward, eyes fixated on a blank spot on the white wall. I plant a small kiss onto her forehead and can feel her body shaking beneath me. My lips are salty from our tears.

"I love you, Mom."

I walk into my room, he pulls a crowbar and saw out from under my bed, and we begin to pry open the carpet and pull up the floorboards.

A single gunshot is fired.

ABOUT THE AUTHOR

Kaylee McHugh grew up in St. Louis, Missouri. She is a graduate of American University.